"Where... girl?" Hannah asked on a sob.

"We'll find her," Quinn answered softly. Any lingering doubts that he'd been a fool to involve himself in Hannah's search disappeared. All doubts that he would survive this unscathed skyrocketed. He was not objective. Somewhere along the way his emotions had become entangled with Hannah's. Somewhere along the way he had begun to fall in love with this woman.

There was nothing he could say to ease her pain. He had uttered all the platitudes, but they both knew that was all they were. They might find Hannah's little girl, but every day that passed made it more unlikely. They could search forever and have nothing but missing posters and receipts from shabby motels to show for their efforts.

He held her instead, simply held her, and felt her breasts pressing against his chest, her hair caressing his collarbone. She moved away at last, spent and heartbroken. He let her go, although he knew that he wanted to hold her forever.

Dear Reader,

You'll be glad the kids are going back to school, leaving you time to read every one of this month's fabulous Silhouette Intimate Moments novels. And you'll want to start with *One Moment Past Midnight,* by multiaward-winning Emilie Richards. You'll be on the edge of your seat as Hannah Blackstone and her gorgeous neighbor, Quinn McDermott, go in search of Hannah's kidnapped daughter.

Elizabeth August makes a welcome return with *Logan's Bride,* a cop-meets-cop romance to make your heart beat just a little faster. With *The Marriage Protection Program,* Margaret Watson completes her CAMERON, UTAH miniseries, and a memorable finale it is. Historical author Lyn Stone has written her first contemporary romance, *Beauty and the Badge,* and you'll be glad to know she intends to keep setting stories in the present day. *Remembering Jake* is a twisty story of secrets and hidden identities from talented Cheryl Biggs. And finally, welcome Bonnie K. Winn, with *The Hijacked Wife,* a FAMILIES ARE FOREVER title.

And once you've finished these terrific novels, mark October on your calendar, because next month Rachel Lee is back, with the next installment of her top-selling CONARD COUNTY miniseries.

Enjoy!

Leslie Wainger
Executive Senior Editor

Please address questions and book requests to:
Silhouette Reader Service
U.S.: 3010 Walden Ave., P.O. Box 1325, Buffalo, NY 14269
Canadian: P.O. Box 609, Fort Erie, Ont. L2A 5X3

EMILIE RICHARDS

ONE MOMENT PAST MIDNIGHT

Silhouette®
INTIMATE™ MOMENTS®

Published by Silhouette Books
America's Publisher of Contemporary Romance

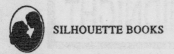

SILHOUETTE BOOKS

ISBN 0-373-07949-4

ONE MOMENT PAST MIDNIGHT

Copyright © 1999 by Emilie Richards McGee

Visit us at www.romance.net

Printed in U.S.A.

Books by Emilie Richards

EMILIE RICHARDS

Award-winning author Emilie Richards believes that opposites attract, and her marriage is vivid proof. "When we met," the author says, "the only thing my husband and I could agree on was that we were very much in love. Fortunately, we haven't changed our minds about that in all the years we've been together."

Though her first book was written in snatches with an infant on her lap, Emilie now writes full-time. She loves writing about complex characters who make significant, positive changes in their lives. And she's a sucker for happy endings.

For Connie, Mary, Leigh, Cheryl,
Claire and Bonnie,
a writers' group to treasure

Chapter 1

Jolie Blackstone was three years old, blond, like her mother, left-handed, like her father…and missing.

No matter how badly she wanted to, Hannah Blackstone resisted resting her face in her hands. Trying to compose herself, she stared instead at a wooden wagon filled with colorful blocks and carved farm animals.

Of course Jolie's toys were the last thing she ought to be looking at.

A man's voice boomed from the other side of the room. "You know, Hannah, we're just trying to find out where your little girl is."

Hannah struggled to keep her voice level. "I've told you and told you. I don't know where she is. If I knew, don't you think I'd be there with her?"

This time chair legs scraping polished maple floors preceded the voice. "Would you? I don't know. We're getting reports that last night you weren't that happy to be with little Jolie. I hear you hauled her out of Tasty Burger like a fifty-pound sack of fertilizer."

Hannah lifted her eyes and gazed at Detective Tony Chandler. All pretense of objectivity had fled from the brown-haired policeman's expression. His lips were twisted into something wider than a smirk and grimmer than a leer. She supposed that Tony, who had once been her ex-husband's closest friend on the Port Franklin police department, was concerned about her daughter. Somewhere behind his posturing, his innuendo, his glee that Hannah was under his control, was a sliver of genuine worry. But Tony wasn't the kind of man to give his best instincts free rein.

"She's three." Hannah cleared her throat. "If you spent any time with your own children, Tony, you'd know how badly a three-year-old can try your patience."

Tony had dragged a spindle-legged dining room chair into Hannah's living room and reversed it, straddling it like a cowboy on his favorite mount. He leaned forward, his eyes glittering.

"Jolie tried your patience, Hannah? You admit that, then?"

Hannah twisted her long, blond braid in her hand until her scalp shrieked in protest. "Of course she tried my patience. I'm sure I tried hers. It was late. She was hungry because my last job took longer than I'd expected. On top of everything I think she's getting a cold. I decided it would be better to take her to Tasty Burger than to make her wait for dinner. It's her favorite treat."

The young woman standing behind Tony stepped forward, moving into Hannah's line of vision. "But?"

Hannah nodded at Faye Wagner, Tony's sidekick. Faye was probably thirty to Hannah's twenty-seven, a chic, petite brunette, while Hannah was an athletic blonde, but the two women shared a glance that told Hannah Faye was fully aware what kind of man Tony Chandler was.

"It wasn't a treat last night," Hannah continued, taking

heart from Faye's sympathetic expression. "Jolie wanted a soft drink. I wanted her to have milk. We compromised on a milk shake, but she dumped it on her tray when she saw it was pink." Tears sprang to her eyes. "It was strawberry. She didn't realize it would be...pink."

"And that's when you dragged her out?" Tony said, cutting off whatever Faye planned to say.

"I *carried* her out when she threw her hamburger on the floor. It had mustard on it. She hates mustard."

She remembered the scene as clearly as if she were reliving it. The stunned silence of the other patrons as Jolie threw her sturdy little body to the floor, too. Jolie's screams of outrage as a too-long day turned into a nightmare. Hannah's momentary feeling of helplessness, followed by a quick return of her common sense.

"Look, I don't want you to think she acts that way most of the time," Hannah said. "But she'd just had it last night. For a minute I didn't know what to do." She looked to Faye for support. "Then I realized there wasn't a thing to be accomplished by staying. So I cleaned up the mess and told her we were leaving. When she refused, I carried her out."

"You spanked her?" Tony said.

Hannah's breath froze in her chest. Her answer emerged like the low rumble of a freight train. "I never, *never* hit my daughter."

"Oh, come on now. You're human. She threw a real honest-to-God temper tantrum. If she was my kid, I'd have slapped her cute little butt a couple of times, just to let her know who was boss."

"I don't doubt you would have!" Hannah narrowed her eyes. "Did you learn that from Marsh, Tony?"

Tony leaned closer. "What, Hannah? Are you trying to say that Marsh hit Jolie? Back in the good-old-days when he was still allowed to see her?"

"No. He never spent enough time with her to hit her. But he would have. As soon as she was old enough to talk back to him."

Tony Chandler liked to throw his weight around, and in his years in the department he had gained enough, both physically and professionally, to make that a considerable weapon. He hadn't been good-looking during high school, when he and Hannah's ex-husband Marshall Blackstone had been stars on the Port Franklin football team, and he hadn't improved with age. His eyes were too close together and his nostrils too far apart, but he had refined a storm trooper demeanor that served him well. For one moment he looked as if he, like Marsh, would like to take his ham-shaped fists to Hannah's body.

He sat back, instead. "Tell you what, Hannah, just once let's not make this about Marsh, okay? Let's make this about *you*. You're the last one who saw Jolie."

"It might help," Faye said, moving to block Hannah's view of Tony, "if you would go through the whole story again. Can you do that, Hannah? It might help us pick up something. Some clue, some lead—"

"Please, you just have to find Marsh, and you have to do it right away! I know he has Jolie. He's taken her to get back at me." Hannah aimed the words at Faye. "Please…" Her voice nearly broke, despite a superhuman effort to control it.

"One more time," Faye said. "That's all, Hannah. We need all the information you can give us. Do this for me?"

What else could she do? Hannah drew a ragged breath. "Where should I start?"

"Tell us everything that happened after you left Tasty Burger."

Hannah closed her eyes. She pictured the asphalt parking lot, lit by the glow of streetlights and the six-foot neon sign that featured Tasty Burger's grinning guernsey. She could almost feel her daughter's tiny bottom squirming against her hip, the impotent thud of red sneakers against her wrist as she struggled to lift Jolie into her car seat.

"I managed to get her in the car, but it wasn't easy," she began.

"Nothing is with kids." Faye's tone was encouraging.

"I went around to the driver's seat and got inside. It was just after seven o'clock, by then. I know because I looked at the dashboard clock...."

"Jolie, you can scream all you want, but we're still going home." Hannah glanced at the dashboard clock, surprised it was still only a few minutes past seven. She could have sworn an hour had passed since Jolie had astounded a sizable portion of Port Franklin with her tantrum.

Just another of life's little lessons in humility.

She thrust her key in the ignition, delighted to see that her hands weren't shaking. She was upset and embarrassed, but she was also philosophical. Both she and her daughter would survive this minor bump on the road to Jolie's adulthood.

She switched on the radio to drown out the backseat shrieks. If music didn't soothe the savage beast, it might make the zookeeper's job more tolerable. She turned to the local oldies station and sang "Wake Up Little Suzie" with the Everly Brothers as she pulled onto State Street, the town's main thoroughfare.

Port Franklin was small by city standards but growing steadily. It embraced Lake Erie to the north, and spread ever-widening fingers into rich farmland to the south, making it an idyllic spot for developers hoping to cash in on a boom economy. Nowadays condos dotted the lakeside, and communities of pricey, look-alike town houses were taking root where sweet corn and sour cherries had grown. A third of the faces Hannah saw each day were unfamiliar, and when the telephone rang at Lakeside Landscapes, the company she owned and operated, the voices requesting her services were often those of strangers.

"I...don't wanna go home!"

Hannah drove slowly through town, knowing full well that she couldn't afford to go even a mile over the speed limit. Her ex-husband still had friends on the police force who believed she was responsible for his dismissal, and they liked nothing better than to show their displeasure, particularly Marsh's former partner, Tony Chandler.

In the two and a half years since Hannah's divorce from Marshall Blackstone, she had been fined for having one foot out of a pedestrian crosswalk, for going twenty-one in a school zone, for not coming to a full stop at a deserted crossroads. She had fought the tickets, winning each time when the officers didn't show up in court, but the emotional turmoil was taking its toll.

There were days when moving away from Port Franklin seemed like the only intelligent thing to do. But Hannah Blackstone was *never* going to let anyone control her again.

"I...wanna hamburger!"

Hannah flipped off the radio as a car dealer began to scream bargains across the airwaves. "You had a hamburger," she said, without turning around. "You threw it on the floor. Remember?"

"Another hamburger..." Jolie's voice shook.

Hannah glanced at her daughter in the rearview mirror. A tumbled mop of golden curls and two streaming brown eyes testified to Jolie's misery. Hannah's heart squeezed in sympathy. "We'll be home in a few minutes."

A fresh set of wails greeted that announcement, but the energy had gone out of them.

Hannah swung into the right lane and slowed as the traffic light turned yellow. A car pulled up beside her, and she glanced over to be sure it wasn't one of Port Franklin's finest.

Howdy, Hannah, I'm going to have to give you a ticket for violating the noise ordinance.

The car to her left was a low-slung coupe, and she saw with a mixture of relief and dismay that the man in the driver's seat had never been on the force. Quinn McDermott, a sleek shock of black hair falling over his forehead, leaned across an empty passenger seat.

"Everything okay, Hannah? It sounds like you've got your hands full."

She flicked on her turn signal and waited for the traffic to clear, firmly ignoring the rustling inside her chest. "Thanks, but we're fine."

"Not too fine, judging by the noise level." His voice was low, a pleasant bass rumble with just the right note of concern. It was a resonant voice, tuned, in some annoying but elemental way, to a traitorous symphony inside her, one that burst defiantly into song whenever Quinn plucked the strings.

Hannah ignored her own reaction. She had been studiously practicing indifference since Quinn McDermott arrived in Port Franklin some months before.

"Jolie's tired, and so am I. That's all."

Quinn had a lazy, easy grin. He used it now, and she was reminded why she made it her business to stay away from this man.

"Hannah…" He caressed her name like sacred scripture. "You work too hard. All work and no play…"

"Right now 'Jill' doesn't even have the energy to be a dull girl," she snapped.

By Port Franklin standards Quinn was a curiosity—a black-haired, black-eyed newcomer who kept to himself and didn't seem to have a job. Lakeside Landscapes had taken out the dead trees and overgrown shrubs on the lakeshore property he had inherited from an eccentric aunt. In return, Quinn had tried repeatedly to take out Lakeside's owner, but Hannah had known better than to let that happen.

"Anything I can do?" Quinn asked now. "Will she succumb to bribery?"

"Not if I have anything to say about it."

"You don't believe in pouring oil on troubled waters?"

She looked him straight in the eyes, long-lashed, languid eyes that were wholly masculine. "And teach my daughter it takes a man to make her happy?"

His grin widened appreciably. "I was talking candy bars or Cracker Jack. What are you talking about?"

"I'm talking men. Period."

"Did we just move from Cracker Jack to something more important?"

She was too tired to smile, too irritated to be polite. "*We* aren't moving anywhere. *I'm* moving out of this lane."

She turned the steering wheel and stomped on the accelerator, risking a ticket to leave Quinn in the dust. In her years with Marsh Blackstone, Hannah had developed a fine sense of impending danger, and in her judgment, Quinn McDermott, with his shadowy past, his intelligent face and indolently assessing eyes was more of a threat than the local police.

In a minute she was out of Port Franklin and into the country. In another five she turned down the lane that led to Lakeside Landscapes.

Lakeside Landscapes sat on three acres spreading back from the shore of Lake Erie, like a fan opening to catch the lake breezes.

The old farmhouse where she and Jolie lived was a century old and two stories, with a wide front porch facing the lake and a narrower one facing the road.

An overcrowded cottage fifty yards away housed her

business, with a reception area for clients, a private office for Hannah and a kitchen and lounge where Lakeside's staff came to relax during breaks. There was also a medium-size greenhouse for annuals and perennials, and a good-size nursery of shrubs and trees, as well as a large holding area where plant material shipped in from other growers could be easily loaded on trucks.

Hannah's grandfather had started Lakeside Landscapes just after the war. Hannah's father had joined him, and Hannah had joined them both after graduating from college with a degree in landscape architecture. Her grandfather had died soon after, and her father had developed such severe allergies that a move to the Southwest had been mandated. Hannah had been married at the time, and even though Marsh had demanded she sell her share of the business, she had resisted. Her father and mother had sold several lots to finance the move to Arizona and deeded the remaining acres to Hannah.

Now, at summer's peak, Lakeside Landscapes was as idyllic and picturesque as the glossy brochures that advertised its services. Hedges lined the drive and hid the tidy rows of the nursery, and sturdy-limbed trees swayed above them. Closer to the house and office, flower beds and shrubs added bright notes of color, and in the distance the glass walls of the greenhouse glistened in the setting sun. The farmhouse with its white siding and green shutters sat at the end of the drive, a three-dimensional welcome mat.

"We're home, Jolie," Hannah said, her voice louder than the backseat whimpers. "Fagan and Oliver will wonder why you're crying."

"Will not!"

For a moment Hannah regretted rejecting Quinn's offer of help. What would it be like to have a man to share these trying moments with? She parked and rolled up her windows, then she opened the back door of the sedan and reached for the buckle on Jolie's car seat. Jolie, in one final act of defiance, slammed her sneakered toes against Hannah's elbow with a resounding crack.

For a moment Hannah saw red. Her arm went numb, and so did her mind. The urge to spank her daughter was so swift and strong she was surprised it had time to register. She jumped back, recoiling from the realization she had come within millimeters of striking Jolie. She took a moment to collect herself, then another to phrase her response.

"Jolie, if you kick me, I won't be able to get you out of the car seat. Is that what you want? To stay in there all night?"

"Don't wanna!"

Hannah wondered what had happened to the beatific child with the smiling rosebud mouth, the golden-haired angel other children's grandmothers fussed over when they passed her on the street. "You have to promise you won't kick me, or I'm not getting you out of that seat."

Jolie sniffed. Her bottom lip drooped toward her chin.

"Jolie? Do you promise?"

Curls bounced as Jolie finally nodded.

"Kicking people is bad," Hannah said.

The lip drooped another inch and Jolie hung her head.

Hannah reached for her daughter again, and this time Jolie allowed her to unbuckle the car seat. Hannah lifted the little girl to the ground, then she straightened. "Fagan and Oliver have been cooped up for hours, so they'll want to play."

"I'm hungry."

"Would you like some cinnamon toast and an egg?"

Jolie's face screwed up in a grimace "I wann—"

"Jolie, don't start this again," Hannah said sharply.

Jolie fell silent.

Hannah started toward the house, knowing her daughter would follow. Fireflies speckled the twilight, and no matter how often Hannah had reassured her, Jolie was not convinced fireflies were harmless. She climbed the back porch with Jolie close behind her, then scooped up the little girl and braced herself as she unlocked and opened the door. Two large dogs barreled through the doorway, rumbling ecstatic greetings.

"Hey, guys." Hannah reached down and scratched Oliver's ears, then did the same to the thick ruff around Fagan's neck. "Boring day, huh?"

Both dogs rubbed against her in frenzied hellos. Fagan, a black-and-gray collie-shepherd mix, tired first, heading down the steps to see what he could find. Shiny black Oliver, half rottweiler, half bluetick hound, leaped off the porch into the center of a Persian lilac. In a moment they had rounded the house and disappeared.

Hannah set Jolie back on her feet. "Let's feed you, then we can feed them."

"I wanna lot of cinnamon."

"You got it."

Half an hour later Jolie sat in the old blue and yellow kitchen, staring morosely at a plate of scrambled eggs that had long since gone cold. Hannah stood at the sink washing her own dishes. "I think you're getting sick, sweetie. Does your throat hurt?"

"No!"

Hannah knew there was no winning with Jolie tonight. "I'm going to run your bath, then it's time for bed." She nudged Oliver from her path and went into the bathroom, half filling the old claw-footed tub before she returned for her daughter. She discovered Jolie feeding Fagan bits of egg.

Hannah ignored the challenge. "Do you want toys in the water?"

Jolie shook her head.

"Dinosaur soap?"

"No!"

Hannah lifted Jolie's plate and took it to the sink. "Go ahead and take off your clothes. I'll be in to check on you in a minute."

Surprisingly, Jolie headed for the bathroom without argument, Fagan right behind her. Hannah finished cleaning the kitchen, then she followed her daughter's path. Jolie stood in the middle of the tile floor, shampooing Fagan, who sat proudly in an inch-deep puddle.

"That's not exactly the kind of thing we need to hear about," Tony Chandler told Hannah. "I don't much care what the kid was doing. I'm a lot more interested in what *you* did."

Hannah looked up at him with a measured gaze. At the moment she would give anything to have Jolie right there defying her. Her heart, her soul, all the years of her life.

"I cleaned up the bathroom and the dog, then I made her take a bath. I dried her off and helped her put on her nightgown—"

"Pink, with yellow flowers?" Faye said, checked her notes.

"That's right. It goes down to her ankles. No sleeves." Hannah tried to think of anything else. "My mother bought it for her."

"Well, that's real helpful," Tony said sarcastically. "Just the kind of stuff we need, huh, Faye?"

"Hannah's trying to think of everything, aren't you, Hannah?" Faye said. "I'd do exactly the same thing in your shoes."

Hannah continued. "She wanted a story, but by then I thought she needed to go right to sleep. I turned off the lamp and checked her night-light. Then I shut the door and left her."

"And what time was that?"

Hannah recalculated, but the answer was the same. "Almost eight-thirty. I stayed up for a couple of hours, straightening the house. Then I watched the news and a little bit of one of the late shows. Just before midnight I went into my bedroom and got ready for bed. I heard Jolie coughing...."

"And you didn't check on her?"

"I was afraid she would wake up. She's a light sleeper, and I thought it would be better to leave her alone. She didn't have a temperature, just a runny nose."

"So you just let her cough?" Tony said.

She took a deep breath. "She stopped after a minute. I wanted her to sleep."

Tony leaned forward again. "How badly, Hannah? And for how long?"

For a moment she couldn't believe what he'd said. "What do you mean?"

"You say she sorely tried your patience. You say you nearly spanked her. You *say* you wanted her to sleep—so badly, in fact, that you refused to check on her when she began to cough. But maybe that last part's not true. Maybe you did go back to her room, and Jolie sassed you again. This time you couldn't control yourself, and you hit her hard, too hard. So hard, in fact, that her neck snapped or her heart stopped beating."

"No!" She leaped to her feet. "How can you say that? I told you, I was afraid if I went back in, I'd wake her and she would never get back to sleep. Even later, after I went outside to check on the sprinklers—"

"You went outside? You left her alone?"

"I was gone for five minutes, and I locked both doors and left the dogs in the house with her!"

"But you said you were dressed for bed," Faye reminded her gently.

Hannah pushed her long braid over her shoulder. "I put

on my nightgown, then I remembered that one of the sprinklers had been spraying erratically. I needed to check on
it, so I slipped on my robe and went outside. And I'm sure
I locked the doors because I'm always worried Jolie might
go down to the lake.''

"No one else was there?"

"No one I saw."

"Do you make a habit of parading around outside in
your nightgown?" Tony asked.

"I was wearing a robe! As far as I could tell there was
no one out there but me. It was midnight."

"What did you do then?" Faye asked.

"I walked down the path to the nursery. After a minute
I saw that the sprinkler was fine. I stayed long enough to
turn a couple of plants. A few pots had fallen over, and I
righted them. That's about it. I crossed the lawn to the
greenhouse and checked the lock. If you remember last
summer a couple of high school kids broke inside for a
party. I just wanted to be sure it was secure."

"And then?" Faye asked.

But Hannah wasn't listening. A flash of blue caught her
eye. Outside the window a sandy-haired policeman—someone she didn't recognize—was hunched over, his back to
her. He straightened, then bent again. She hadn't noticed
him before. "Faye, what's going on out there?"

Faye stood and peered over Hannah's shoulder. "I'll
have a look. They're probably searching for footprints. I'll
let you know if they've found anything." She left the room.

Hannah started toward the window, but Tony stopped
her. "You don't have to worry about anything going on
out there."

She faced him. "I've told you everything. After I
checked the greenhouse I went back to the house and let
the dogs out for the night. They didn't bark then or later,
not that I heard. I locked the doors and went to bed. And

when I woke up this morning and went to check on Jolie, she wasn't there."

"Just like that. The dogs don't bark. You don't hear a thing. And Jolie just disappears?"

"Tony, there's only one person who could have done this, and that's Marshall Blackstone. For all I know he still has a key. The dogs know him. They wouldn't bark at Marsh if he dropped bricks on their heads. He doesn't want Jolie. He's hardly visited her since the divorce, but he hates me, and he knows this is the only way he can get even. I divorced him. I got custody of his child and I let the world know he was a vicious, abusive drunk. Now he's punishing me."

"*You* say he was abusive."

She couldn't believe that with all the evidence, Tony still refused to accept that his boyhood friend had beaten her. "The court agreed. He nearly killed me the last time he took his fists to me, remember? I was in the hospital nearly a week."

Tony pulled a toothpick from his shirt pocket and stuck it in the corner of his mouth. "You know, Marsh claimed it wasn't him that beat you, that you had a boyfriend. He lost his job because of you—"

"He lost his job because the evidence was overwhelming, and he didn't want to risk an official hearing. So he resigned."

"He lost his daughter—"

"He gave up his daughter! You want to know why? Because I promised if he did, I'd get them to reduce the charges against him. He got probation, I got Jolie."

Tony chewed his toothpick, rearing back in the chair so he could look up at her. "It's a good story, but here's a different one. You get tired of living with a cop. You don't like his hours, his salary. So you find yourself another man, maybe one who's richer and better looking. But he turns out to be a nutcase, and when you try to break things off, he beats you silly. You don't want anyone else to know, so you blame old Marsh. That way you can get a divorce and custody of your kid, and Marsh has to leave Port Frank. He can't even ask for his rightful share of this place—''

''His share?'' Hannah was still standing, and she bent over him. ''*His* share? Lakeside Landscapes was never Marsh's. It's been in my family for three generations.''

''But maybe not for four, huh, Hannah? Because maybe you lost your temper last night and took care of that fourth generation for good.''

She was shaking from rage. She had to turn away to control herself. She focused on the window again. She saw Faye pass, then stop beside the policeman Hannah had seen before.

''What are they doing out there?'' She skirted Jolie's wagon, ignoring Tony's order to stay where she was. ''He's digging for something.'' Now she understood why the sandy-haired cop had been bending and straightening. He had a shovel in his hands. ''What's he looking for?''

She watched Faye motioning the policeman away from the house. Faye glanced up at the window, then bent her head to his in whispered consultation. For the first time Hannah realized that the window was shut. She hadn't shut it. Why had Tony or Faye done it? To keep outside noise to a minimum as they questioned her?

Or to hide something?

''Why is this window closed?'' she demanded.

Tony answered from directly behind her. ''You really want to know what they're doing, Hannah? I'll tell you. They're looking for something, all right. Just like Faye said. Only the clue they're looking for is Marsh's little girl…''

Hannah's eyes widened in horror as she realized what he meant. She whirled to face him. ''You think I killed Jolie and buried her out there?''

His smile was as cold as steel. "That's exactly what I think."

"You're insane!"

"Not *me*, Hannah. That's freshly dug dirt. Did you think we wouldn't notice?"

"This is a landscaping business and that's a flower bed! I had Buck and Lou turn over the soil day before yesterday. They took out spring pansies so I could put in lobelia and petunias."

"Maybe you decided to plant something different."

"You bastard!"

Tony lunged forward and gripped her arms. "Maybe you could cow poor Marsh, Hannah, but that crap doesn't work with me. I know what you did, and I'm going to prove it, if we have to dig up every single inch of this property with a teaspoon!"

She tried to shake off his hands, but she couldn't. His fingers were digging into her arms, and terror rose inside her. She had been held captive like this before, by a man as strong as this one. She had nearly died at his hands.

"Let me go!"

"You killed your little girl, and I'm going to prove it! So admit it right now, why don't you? Tell me you did it and where you buried her. Make this easier on Marsh. Let me be the one to break the news to him."

His fingers dug deeper. She gasped for air, but there was none. Her lungs refused to inflate. "Get your hands off me."

He laughed without humor. "You can even say you didn't mean to do it, that sometime after midnight last night you killed your daughter, but it was an accident. We'll do the rest."

She didn't know where she found the strength to break out of his grasp. Perhaps from the place deep inside where she had vowed she would never again let a man hurt her.

She wrenched free, and when Tony grabbed for her, she slammed her palms against his chest and shoved with all her considerable strength.

Hannah hadn't expected to catch Tony off balance, but his feet were still placed side by side. In the second he teetered backward he slid a foot behind him for balance and stumbled against Jolie's wagon. He looked stunned, his arms flailing as if he might find something to grip. She dodged as he made a desperate grab for her, then he fell, his head slamming against the corner of a side table on his way to the maple floor.

Hannah covered her mouth with her hands. "Tony?"

He lay perfectly still.

She squatted beside him and shook his shoulder. "Tony?"

He didn't respond.

She heard voices from outside. She knew she had only minutes at most before Faye returned.

And what would she say? *Tony tripped, and it's true—the bigger they are, the harder they fall....*

She had just destroyed whatever shred of credibility she had with the Port Franklin police. No one would believe anything she had said about last night. No one would believe she hadn't murdered her daughter. No one would look for Marshall Blackstone until he was impossible to find. Because Hannah was sure that by the time the authorities admitted that Jolie *might* have been kidnapped, Marsh would be in another state or country, living under a new identity and caring indifferently for their daughter.

Someone had to find Marsh and Jolie. Faye would find Tony, but it was up to Hannah to find her own daughter.

She grabbed her purse as she left the room, but it was the only thing she took as she slipped away.

Chapter 2

Quinn McDermott liked the slow rhythm of Port Franklin life. He liked the fact that there was only one newspaper stand in front of the town pharmacy, one service station with a car wash, one traffic light on the busiest street. He preferred Tasty Burger's guernsey over the more famous golden arches, and high school football over season tickets to Yankee Stadium. The local diner might not serve cappuccino, but the meat-loaf special was food for the gods.

Quinn had never worn rose-colored glasses. He knew exactly what he'd left behind when he'd moved to Tina's house. A life lived at full speed, in full view of the world. A job other men would kill for. A woman they would die for.

But Quinn didn't regret any of it. One morning he'd peered at himself in the bathroom mirror, face pale with shaving cream and razor in hand, and he had wondered if the blade was sharp enough to slit his throat. He had carefully set down the razor and picked up the telephone to dial the Realtor he'd hired to list Tina's house. In three weeks' time he had closed one chapter of his life and opened another.

Now, after eight months in rural Ohio, he was a different man. The black pit that had nearly sucked him under had been safely filled again, and he was ready for the next challenge.

"You looking for a job, Mr. McDermott? Because I hear they're looking for somebody to write ads over at the Franklin Press. Just part-time, but you being a writer and all…"

Quinn glanced up from the morning paper. After eight months he was still surprised when Millie, the head waitress at Guy's Diner, interrupted his reading. She was middle-aged and frowsy, and her idea of dressing up was changing the color of the socks she wore with her blue uniform. But she was a kind woman, and eternally interested in everything and everyone around her. Despite himself, he had grown fond of her.

He folded back the front section. "How do you know I'm a writer?"

"Somebody told me. Is it true?"

"I used to work on a newspaper."

"Then you'd be a natural for this job. My cousin Hank works in circulation. I could tell him to put in a good word for you."

Either Millie was worried about his finances or unbearably nosy. "I'm not interested in a job just now, but I appreciate your thinking of me."

Millie plopped her ample rear on the bench in front of him. "I always wanted to be a reporter, but I can't write to save my life. It's too bad, too, because I sure know a story worth reporting."

He knew he had no chance of getting rid of her—or of

getting a refill on his coffee—if he didn't play along. "What's that?"

"You know Hannah Blackstone?"

Quinn wondered if his ears had curled noticeably forward. "She did some work at my place before the weather warmed up."

"She's the best landscaper in Port Frank. Even after everything that happened with her husband and all, nobody would hire anyone else."

"Her husband?"

Millie settled in for the long haul. "Hannah and Marshall Blackstone were high school sweethearts. She married Marsh after she got out of college and he started at the police academy. Things seemed all right for a while, then Marsh started drinking. Some guys just don't do well in a uniform. You know what I mean? Marsh was one of them."

Quinn knew that Hannah was divorced, but he had studiously avoided searching for more information. Now he couldn't resist. "Were they married long?"

"They had Jolie sometime after he joined the force. I think Hannah tried to tough things out, even after he took his fists to her the first few times. She hoped things would get better. Maybe she still loved him. I don't know. Then one day he just about killed her. Broke her arm, dislocated a hip." Millie shook her head. "She had surgery on her jaw. Maybe other places, too. I never heard."

Quinn couldn't imagine the independent woman he'd admired living with a man who beat her. "I hope they locked him in jail and threw away the key."

"Nope. Hannah traded Marsh's freedom for Jolie. He stayed out of jail, and she got custody. He left town and I don't think he comes back very often. He was the star linebacker at Port Frank High, but now nobody looks him in the eye. Nobody but his buddies on the force."

"The cops thought it was okay for this guy to beat his wife?"

"Some of them don't believe he ever did. That was his story, you know, that somebody else beat Hannah, and she was too ashamed to admit it."

"But you don't believe it?"

"I saw Marsh Blackstone drunk one time. He's meaner than a snake when he's liquored up. I think it was him that beat her, just like Hannah said."

Quinn didn't like imagining Hannah at the hands of a bully. "A husband beating his wife isn't exactly news, Millie. Especially if it happened a while ago. Unfortunately it goes on all the time."

"No, that's old news, all right. But my cousin is the dispatch over at the police station. And she tells me there's something going on at Hannah's right this minute." Millie lowered her voice. "Something to do with Jolie."

Quinn's stomach knotted around the stack of pancakes he'd consumed. Hannah was a tall, willowy blonde who thought sunscreen passed for makeup, and faded jeans for high fashion, but she was still the sexiest woman he had met since leaving New York. She was a corn-fed Midwestern beauty, as natural as Mother Earth and every bit as ornery. Her young daughter was a Renaissance cherub.

"When you say something's going on," he said carefully, "exactly what do you mean? Has Jolie been hurt?"

"I couldn't get anything else out of Latrelle, but she sounded upset. Everybody loves Jolie." She paused, as if she had just thought of something. "You live over by Hannah, don't you? You didn't see anything odd when you were on your way into town?"

Now he understood why Millie had befriended him. Not only did she want to gossip, she was hoping he had something to add.

He searched his memory. What had he seen? He remembered last evening, a frazzled Hannah at the traffic light, a shrieking Jolie in the seat behind her.

"I didn't notice anything unusual when I passed the turn-off to Hannah's," he said. "But her house and business are set back from the road."

"You didn't hear sirens?"

He shook his head.

Millie's disappointment was palpable. "If the cops are mixed up in this, it could be bad for Hannah. They aren't crooked like some, you understand, but they hold Marsh's leaving against her. Latrelle says they keep after Hannah. Last summer a bunch of high school kids broke into her greenhouse, and when she called for help, Tony Chandler took the long way there. She had the glass all cleaned up by the time he arrived."

Quinn scowled. "Tony Chandler?"

"Detective Tony Chandler now, but back then he was just a patrolman, and before that he and Marsh trained together at the academy. He's the one who's really out to get her."

Quinn was liking the sound of this less and less. "If people in town know what *you* know, why haven't they done anything to help?"

"Hannah doesn't complain, and the cops don't talk. And if I say much about it in public, Latrelle could lose her job. I've talked to Hannah, and she says to let it go, that things will settle down. But I'm worried, you know? They're out there with her. And something's wrong. I just know it is."

So now Quinn knew that they had come to Millie's third reason for talking to him. "You want me to check on things?"

Millie's eyes lit up. "You'd do that?"

"Why me?"

"You live nearby. And you're not from here. Nobody knows much about you, so there's no history."

"Uh-huh." Quinn checked his watch. "I've been meaning to go by Hannah's and talk to her about trimming a tree. Maybe I'll do it on the way home."

"Now that'd be swell." Millie slid from the booth. "I'll get you some more coffee. And one of those cinnamon rolls you like."

"When I ordered, you said they were all gone."

Millie grinned. "Not for special customers."

Quinn McDermott had made a list of commandments for his new life. Millie was gone before he realized that he had just broken number one.

Don't get involved.

A man who broke commandments was either a sinner or a fool. Quinn knew exactly which category he fell into.

Hannah knew every tree, every shrub, every grain of dirt at Lakeside Landscapes. But it was dumb luck that helped her escape. She made the dash from the roadside porch to a cluster of tall trees, then on to a shed where equipment was stored. She hid in the shadows as, frantically, she tried to think what to do next.

Jolie was gone, and Hannah herself had just laid out a detective. She could explain that Tony had grabbed her, show the finger marks on her arms, repeat a hundred times that she only pushed him to make him stop hurting her. By the time she made bail, Jolie would be a thousand miles away.

Marsh had Jolie. Hannah was absolutely certain. Stealing their child to get even was exactly the kind of thing Marsh would do. Tony could dig for days, delaying a real search, because she was sure he knew full well that Jolie was safe.

Safe was a relative term, of course. Hannah wasn't worried that Marsh would hurt Jolie right away. He might even attempt to be a good father, just to show the world that Hannah had been lying about him all along. But someday, when the fun wore off, when he'd had too much to drink, when the moon was full... Tears sprang to her eyes. She had to find Jolie, and she had to find her now.

Hannah knew she had to get away from Lakeside and find a car. Hers was parked in plain sight of anyone rounding the house. Two of Lakeside's pickups were with employees who had gone directly to jobs. The third was at the garage getting a new transmission.

Her best friend, Amanda Taylor, would lend Hannah her car. But she and Amanda had been friends since elementary school; it wouldn't take long for the police to figure out Amanda had helped her. Mentally she ticked off others who might do her a favor, but the problem was the same. Anyone who helped her would suffer the consequences.

She had to *steal* a car. Then, if she was caught, she would be the only one in trouble.

At lightning speed she sorted through the possibilities. Her target couldn't be far. She considered her neighbors, but some were too old to recover from a theft. Another drove hundreds of miles a week as a pharmaceutical salesman, still another made twice-daily visits to a mother in a nursing home.

It was a good thing she didn't steal cars for a living.

Hannah moved toward the hedge that ran along the driveway, then she darted between hedges and outbuildings toward the road. There was only one car she could steal, even under desperate circumstances, only one man who would bounce back easily from the theft. Ironically, from the moment he'd met her, Quinn McDermott had tried—at least figuratively—to get her into the back seat of his car. She wondered how he would feel when he discovered that she had preferred the driver's seat instead.

"Police business. Move along now."

For fifteen years Quinn had worked around cops, frequented their bars, listened closely to their tips and gossip. Instinct told him that the sandy-haired young man staring at him through narrowed eyes was new at his job. He was pretending to be tough, but some part of him wanted to run home to mama.

"I'm here to see Hannah Blackstone," Quinn said, with a friendly grin. He was parked in Hannah's driveway, but he was still behind the wheel, and his engine was idling. "We have an appointment," he added.

"You'll have to move along, sir. Nobody's allowed inside."

"Sorry, but unless she's dead or under arrest, I have a right to see her. That's the law." Quinn kept all antagonism out of his voice. This was buddy to buddy, the veteran instructing the rookie.

"Are you her attorney?"

Quinn had a law degree, but he had never bothered with the bar exam. Law school had simply helped him understand the finer points of the cases he covered. "More or less," he lied, "but I'm just here as her friend. Can you tell me what's going on? Does she need an attorney?"

"There's nothing I can tell you, sir."

"Well, who could, do you think?"

"You can call the station and speak to the chief."

"I'd rather speak to Hannah." Quinn settled back, as if he was preparing for the long haul. "Why don't you go inside and ask her if she wants to see me?"

"Sir, if you don't move your car right now, I'll arrest you for interfering in an investigation."

"What investigation?"

The young man was beginning to look confused. He rested a hand on the open window. "I can't tell you that."

Quinn glanced down and frowned. The rookie's nails were embedded with dirt. His fingers were clean enough, but either he had been digging or making mud pies. "Does

Hannah have you putting in trees?" he asked, looking pointedly this time at the young man's hand.

The cop flushed and his hand fell to his side. "I told you, I can't—"

"Or maybe you've been digging for something else? I can think of a lot of things a cop might want to find. The worst being a body..."

"Either you move along, like I told you—"

"Whose body, son?" Quinn leaned out the window, his expression paternal, though at thirty-two he wasn't nearly old enough to be this man's father. "Like I said, I'm a friend of Hannah's, and if you're keeping a secret that I should know about as an attorney and a friend, you could get yourself in some real trouble."

Quinn could almost see the young man replaying police academy lectures in his increasingly foggy mind. Quinn didn't give him time to get to the one that said the police had the right to do almost anything to secure a crime scene. He glanced down at the cop's brass nameplate. "Officer Mullins, I need to know what's happening, then I'll move along, nice and quiet."

"You'll leave?" The deflated Mullins sounded more and more like an insecure teenager.

Quinn nodded gravely.

"The little girl's missing."

Quinn's heart dropped to his stomach. He had expected a break-in. All talk of digging for bodies had been to scare Mullins. He had guessed the young man's hands were dirty because he'd been scratching around in flower beds, looking for clues or measuring footprints. Even Millie's contention that this might have something to do with Jolie hadn't really penetrated.

This was Port Franklin. This was Ohio. People took care of their children. Mothers and fathers coached soccer and led Girl Scout hikes. Children didn't disappear.

"Sir, are you okay?"

Quinn nodded. He felt as if all his blood had drained to his feet. "I saw her last night." He tried to remember details. "About seven. She seemed fine."

"Well, she's not fine now."

Quinn thought of the lake, lying forty yards from Hannah's door. "Do they think she wandered outside? That she might have…"

Now that the secret was out, Officer Mullins seemed in no hurry. "We're looking into everything."

"How's Hannah taking it?"

The warmth went out of the young man's eyes. "You won't be able to ask her, that's for sure."

Warning bells sounded in Quinn's head. "No? How come?"

"She's gone."

"Gone? Is she looking for Jolie?"

"Nobody knows where, but now we're searching for her, too."

Quinn remembered what Millie had said about the cops harassing Hannah. "Was she here earlier?"

"I can't tell you anything else."

Quinn leaned out the window. "You'd better tell me that much, because if you don't, I'm going to assume the worst. And you don't want me to assume something happened to Hannah while you boys were questioning her. That's the kind of assumption that does a lot of damage to a department."

Officer Mullins looked chagrined. "She took off. That's what happened.…" He paused, as if sifting through information. "She just took off. But it makes sense, doesn't it? If she was the one…"

Quinn's blood went cold. "It doesn't make sense. Hannah loves that little girl."

"A good mother would stay around to see if her kid was found, don't you think?"

The conversation had ended. Not because Quinn thought that Officer Mullins had run out of information, but because Quinn knew if he stayed a moment longer, he would step out of his car and choke the life out of him. Without another word he made a U-turn and sped away.

As a child Hannah had spent long, lazy summers wandering Port Franklin's roads and fields and playing elaborate games of hide-and-seek, with rules that changed as often as the children who wandered in and out. In later years she had cut down trees, planted shrubs, dug borders and fanciful fish ponds. She knew everyone along the lake, but even better, she knew their property.

By the time she got to Quinn's house, she was perspiring from the late-morning sun, her legs scratched by brambles but her mind made up. She had no choice but to steal Quinn's car. It was unfortunate that he drove such a distinctive model. She wasn't much on cars, but she knew it was an odd color, a red so dark it was nearly black, with shiny chrome and a low-slung, sculpted body. She supposed the car was expensive. Quinn didn't seem to work, but he did have money. He hadn't even blinked when she'd told him what she would charge to clean up his lot.

Now she stood under the shelter of sycamores and gazed at Tina McDermott's cottage. Quinn's aunt had been Hannah's first-grade teacher, but Tina had been a lesson in herself. Never married, Tina hadn't lacked for men in her life, but for long-term companionship she had preferred the birds she hosted at feeders and the chipmunks she tamed to eat from her hands. Port Franklin had thought Tina McDermott was a little crazy, more suited to a state like California than to the Midwest. But Hannah thought Tina was the smartest woman she'd ever known.

The cottage was as interesting as the woman. Tina had liked porches, so there were porches circling the house. Tina liked tin roofs and gables, gingerbread trim and widow's walks. She built the latter herself and claimed she spent the nights up there in the summers, staring out at the lake her own generation had nearly destroyed. Tina claimed to be the night watchman, making sure that no one tampered with the lake's health while Port Franklin slept. After Tina's death Hannah had lain awake at night sometimes, wondering who would take up the job.

To Quinn's credit, he hadn't made any significant changes in the cottage. Perhaps the quirks suited the man, because like his aunt, he seemed to have a few of his own. He lived alone with no visible means of support. He drove an expensive car, but he ate his meals at the local greasy spoon. He lived on the lake, but he didn't fish or sail. He kept no pets, had no noticeable visitors and, most of all, he showed no interest in any of Port Franklin's eligible women.

Except for her.

Soon, of course, he would find that his interest in Hannah had been sadly misplaced.

The garage was a windowless addition at the side of the house because Tina had reasoned that cars didn't need lake views and sunshine. Hannah couldn't tell if Quinn's car was inside until she circled the garage and peered through the door. She prayed that he had left the garage open and that his car was there. Another prayer that he wasn't peering out his lakeside windows was a hasty addendum.

She inched her way around the garage to discover that prayers one and three had been answered, but number two, the most important, hadn't. The door was open, but the car was gone.

Disappointment was scalding, like the tears that slid uncontrollably down her cheeks. She could wait, would have to wait in fact, until Quinn returned. But every minute she wasted was one Marsh would use. Even now he might be buying Jolie's airplane ticket or driving toward some isolated town where he would change their daughter's name and tell her that Mommy didn't love her anymore.

Hannah looked around for a place to hide. The garage was her best bet, but it was also the most dangerous, since Quinn might spot her when he drove in. She instantly rejected a workbench and a precarious pile of firewood. The only possibility was a corner piled haphazardly with gardening tools and flanked by a canvas-draped riding mower. She could crouch under the canvas without disturbing it, and unless Quinn was in the mood to mow his lawn, she would probably go undetected.

The decision was made for her when she heard a car slowing in front of the house, then the crunch of gravel. Quinn or someone was coming up the drive. For a moment she stood paralyzed, wondering if it might be the police. Were they searching for her already? They, unlike Quinn, would know immediately that the canvas was worth a check.

She didn't have time to invent another plan. She scurried across the floor and ducked under the canvas, crouching beside the mower so that the canvas wouldn't bulge suspiciously. Then she said her final prayer.

Chapter 3

Jolie Blackstone was missing and so was her mother. For the first time in months Quinn was sorry he had retired his press card. Once he would have known exactly who to call for more information, who to bribe with a couple of beers—and knock out with a couple more. By now he would know exactly what the police suspected and what they were doing about it.

But most of all, he would know why Hannah had fled.

On the short drive from Hannah's house, Quinn had come up with a list of possibilities, but none made sense. If Jolie was missing, there were only two reasons Hannah might be missing, too. Either she was fleeing prosecution, or she was searching for her daughter.

Since he couldn't believe that Hannah had harmed Jolie, the second was more probable. But why had Hannah disappeared? No matter how tattered her relationship with the local cops, they had resources she wouldn't have on her own. No matter how childishly they behaved, they could help find her daughter.

Unless they had refused to help. Unless they had proved by word or deed that they were even more corrupt than Millie had hinted.

Kidnapped. When the reality had finally penetrated Quinn's fog of denial, he'd wanted to run. But he had run away once before, and that flight had brought him here to Port Franklin, where parents protected their children, and madmen stood so far outside the crowd they couldn't harm anyone.

Of course there was no place on earth like the one he'd imagined. Quinn had known that, even as the fantasy propelled him forward. But he'd made the sanest choice, a land of milk and honey, over a wasteland where children disappeared and nobody cared.

He had come here to rest and recover, and now, without his permission, he was on the front lines once more.

Quinn parked inside his garage and turned off the engine, removing the keys. He was slowly sinking into the patterns of rural life. He *had* trained himself to leave the garage open during daylight hours and the car unlocked. He still didn't leave his keys in the ignition, as did most of his neighbors.

He stayed at the wheel painfully pondering Hannah's situation. He knew a reporter at the *Cleveland Plain Dealer*, a hungry young man who reminded him of himself at the beginning of his career. He wondered if Jake Whattley had information on the Port Franklin Police Department. Port Franklin was seventy miles from the city, but they did share the same lake. Jake might be able to tell him something. If nothing else, it was a place to start.

He got out and slammed the car door. As he unlocked the door into the house he realized that something was nagging at him. Something he ought to notice. Something that wasn't right.

He turned and swung his gaze over the garage. Nothing

looked out of place, and nothing seemed to be missing. His eyes settled on the tarp covering the lawnmower.

"Damn grass." The nagging voice was silent now. He had planned to cut the grass today. There was more grass on the property than anyone deserved. When Hannah cleaned up the lot, she'd suggested shrub borders and a brick patio to cut down on maintenance. She'd suggested easy-care perennial beds, too, and flowering trees near the house. He had declined. At the time he hadn't been sure he would stay in Ohio very long. He hadn't been sure of anything.

Now, whether he wanted to or not, he *was* sure he had to discover what was happening to Hannah and Jolie Blackstone. For the first time since leaving New York, his life had a purpose. Something familiar joined the sadness inside him. He felt the prickling of adrenaline as he opened the door and went inside.

Hannah didn't know how long she should wait before she drove away. She couldn't wait until dark, and she couldn't risk Quinn emerging, either to apprehend her or take off in his car again. She slid out from under the canvas and crept around the car, noting, as she did, that the keys were not inside. When she reached the door into the house, she put her ear against it and listened carefully, trying to visualize the interior layout.

She remembered that the door led into a narrow laundry room, which led into an L-shaped hallway. Her best chance to steal the car would come if Quinn went upstairs to his bedroom. The master bedroom faced the lake, and it was farther from the garage than any part of the house. Not only would Quinn have less chance of hearing her, he wouldn't have a view of her driving away.

If she escaped undetected, she could drive to a Sandusky shopping mall, park the car and go on from there. She wasn't sure what she would do at that point. Take a bus, rent a car, buy a clunker at a used car lot. But until she got away from Port Franklin, it was foolish to worry.

She heard a toilet flush and footsteps. She prepared herself to hide again, but the footsteps grew dimmer. Then the house fell silent once more.

She was sure she would have heard Quinn climbing the stairs. He was young and athletically built. He would take them at a run, as men usually did. Just as she was about to give up hope of knowing his whereabouts, she heard a voice. At first she thought it was a television, but the peculiar silences and brief snatches of conversation weren't accompanied by a sound track.

Quinn was on the telephone.

Hannah had only been inside the house once after Tina's death to present Quinn with her invoice. She hadn't paid attention to much except this rare man she'd had to look up to, a man whose warm gaze had stirred feelings she hadn't welcomed. But she thought she remembered a wall phone in the kitchen.

Marsh had learned a lot during the brief golden days of his academy training. He had been a different man then, funny, and for the most part, amicable enough. One night he had come home after classes and summoned her to the driveway. "Look what I learned today," he told her. Then he proceeded to hotwire their '92 Chevy.

She teased him, because those had been the days when she still could. "You're supposed to be the good guy," she said.

He grinned, because those had been the days when he still did. "Can't be a good guy unless you know how the bad guys do things."

Now, standing in Quinn's garage, Hannah wasn't sure which category she fell into, but it didn't really matter. She backed to the car and quietly opened the driver's door.

* * *

There were birds making a racket in the tree outside Quinn's kitchen window, big black birds with lousy manners. Tina had been a champion of birds, feeding them at multiple feeders and housing them in hollow gourds and multiperch condos. He continued to feed the birds in her memory, but he had never counted on the mess and the noise. He put one hand over his ear and hoped that Jake Whattley hadn't already gotten on and off the line.

"Hello?" He realized elevator music was coming over the line. He was still on hold.

He tapped on the glass to scare away a squirrel who was causing the commotion. His life had come to this, baby-sitter of birds, connoisseur of Barry Manilow. When he left New York he had wondered how it would feel to be nobody again, and now he remembered.

"Jake here."

"Jake, it's Quinn McDermott."

There was a heartbeat pause, then an oath that nearly blew out Quinn's eardrum. "Quinn McDermott, and nobody told me? Heads are gonna roll."

Quinn grinned, mollified. "How're you doing, Jake?"

Jake told him, in great detail. Quinn listened until he couldn't stand it any longer. "Great. I knew you'd work your way up fast." Jake had been his intern at the *Times*, a promising young man with no intention of settling for anything but the biggest stories.

"You didn't call to chat, did you?" Jake said, confirming that Quinn had been right about him all those years ago.

"I'm living in Port Franklin. Had you heard?"

"Rumors. I knew you'd left New York. I tried to get your job, but I guess I haven't paid my dues yet."

Quinn laughed. "Pay some more right now, would you? What can you tell me about the Port Franklin Police Department?"

There was a silence on the line while Jake accessed his

memory banks. Quinn watched the squirrel dart from the feeder with two blackbirds dive-bombing in pursuit. The squawking stopped. The only audible sound was somebody struggling to start a car.

"Port Franklin's just not big news," Jake said at last. He sounded chagrined. "Damn, I just failed the test."

"Maybe there's nothing to know." Quinn repeated what Millie had told him that morning. "I just wondered if there was a history of abuse or corruption here."

"You must have reason to worry if you called me...."

Quinn wished that his neighbor, whoever it was, would start the damned car and drive away. The engine's scraping was grating on his nerves. He had lost a New Yorker's ability to screen out noises.

He covered his ear again. "Look, something's going on with a woman down the road. I'm not sure what, but if I find—"

He stopped midsentence, his body tense as an iron rod. He dropped the receiver, vaguely aware that it was banging against the wall as he sprinted toward his garage.

He flung open the door just in time to see his Lexus backing into the driveway.

And not by itself.

He sprinted after it, arms pumping like an Olympic medalist. The blond-haired woman behind the wheel stepped on the gas the moment she straightened the tires, but she was a second too late. Quinn grabbed the handle and jerked open the door. Then he made a grab for the steering wheel.

His running shoes scraped along the gravel as the car sped up, but his grip didn't slacken. "Stop, Hannah! You'll get us both killed."

She pounded his hands with one fist. "Let go!"

"Not on your life! This is my car!"

For a second he wasn't sure what she would do. His feet banged against the driveway, and the car door slammed repeatedly against the backs of his legs. Finally, with something that sounded like a sob, she stomped her foot on the brake.

"Get out!" Quinn let go of the steering wheel and grabbed Hannah's shoulders, lying half on top of her to do it. Her breasts were soft against his chest, her breath warm against his cheek.

She was sobbing. "It's not what you think. It's not—"

"You mean you aren't stealing my car? I'm imagining those wires dangling from my dashboard?"

"Quinn, please…"

He placed his feet firmly on the ground. "Get out."

"Let go of me."

"Why? So you can drive away?"

She slapped his hands out of the way, then she slid out from under the steering wheel and faced him.

He took a deep breath, then another, but he didn't touch her again. "So, you're not missing."

"You knew I was gone?"

"I stopped by your house."

She swiped her cheeks with one hand, a disturbingly childish gesture that lowered his fury to mere rage. "They're telling people about me already."

"Not people. Me. I know how to get information." He peered over her shoulder into the car. "Where's Jolie? Tell me she's with you."

"She's not."

"Why not?"

"Because *she's* missing! And they think I killed her. Or that's what they're pretending."

The sun was beating down on his head, but his blood chilled. He heard a sound out on the road, a car slowing to a near stop. Someone looking for a lake view…or for a casual blonde with the longest legs on God's green earth.

"That will be them." Hannah squared her shoulders. "Let me leave. Please don't tell them you saw me."

"I'm supposed to forget you were stealing my car?"

"I was going to leave it in plain view somewhere. I had to get away. I have to find my daughter, because they won't look for her. They'll let Marsh get away until the trail's so cold a thousand bloodhounds wouldn't catch it."

"Marsh?"

"Jolie's father." Hannah faced the road. The car was idling. Whoever was out there was probably going to turn into the driveway. "I'm leaving now. Don't try to stop me."

He did try, noting with surprise that she winced when he grabbed her arm. "Have they charged you with anything?"

"No!"

"Then why did you run?"

"I have to find her. Nobody else will."

"But you didn't have to run away to do that, Hannah. What else is going on?"

She tried to pull away. "You're hurting me!"

"I'm barely touching you." He looked down and saw thin marks encircling her arms. "Who did that?"

"Tony Chandler." She pulled away successfully this time.

"He grabbed you that hard?"

She looked up at him. "And you want to know what else? I shoved him when he did. He toppled like a statue and cracked his head." She began to edge around him. "And now they're going to throw me in jail for assault. Then no one will look for my daughter. Pretend you didn't see me or tell the truth, I don't care. But I'm leaving."

Quinn's reporter instincts, one notch sharper than a prosecutor's, buzzed for attention. He wasn't always right about people, but he'd built a career on his record. He knew Hannah, had watched her with her daughter, had heard Millie's story about what Hannah had suffered. But most of all, when he looked in her eyes he saw the fierce defensive gleam of a lioness protecting her cub. Hannah Blackstone hadn't harmed Jolie. She was going to find her daughter, if she had to swim the length of Lake Erie to do it.

"Go inside," he said curtly. "They can't search without a warrant. I'll stay out here. Don't leave until I tell you it's safe."

The crunch of gravel punctuated his last sentence. As he feared, the car was turning into his drive. He reached inside the car and grabbed her purse, glad he'd seen it. He thrust it at her. "Go on!"

Indecision filled her eyes, then she turned and fled up the driveway, through the garage and into the house. He pulled out his keys and jammed them in the ignition, then he shoved the wires she'd displaced up under the dashboard.

He was cursing under his breath when the patrol car rolled up the drive. He got out and went around the front of his car to open the hood.

A lone policeman got out and approached him. "Having problems?"

Quinn summoned a grin. "Is it against the law to have dirty spark plugs?"

The gray-haired cop, who looked to have twenty more years on the force than Quinn's rookie, gave a thin smile, but his eyes didn't warm. "You haven't seen anybody prowling around your property, have you?"

"I'd have called you if I did." Quinn knew better than to assume this cop hadn't heard about his conversation with Officer Mullins. "Are you talking about Hannah Blackstone?"

"What do you know about her?"

"Well, I was just over at her place, and one of your pals

said both she and her daughter are gone. I figure you're out looking for them."

"You haven't seen Hannah?"

He edged around the truth. "That's why I went to her house. But she wasn't there."

"Is she a friend of yours?"

"I have a tree that's not looking too healthy, and I wanted her opinion. You don't know anything about trees, do you?"

"Then she's not a friend?"

Quinn cocked an eyebrow. "Not because I didn't give it a try."

"Do you mind if I have a look around?"

"Be my guest. I hope you straighten this out. Hannah's a good woman."

"Not everyone thinks so." The cop started around the house. Quinn, whose knowledge of cars was limited to where to put the gas and oil, poked around under the hood just long enough to look as if he knew what he was doing. By the time the cop returned, he was inside the garage, wiping his hands on a rag.

The cop stopped just outside the door. "You been inside your house since you came home from Hannah's?"

"Uh-huh. Besides, I always lock my doors. It would be a hard house to break into."

"Most people here don't."

"Don't lock up, or don't break in?"

"You're a funny guy." The cop set off down the driveway. Quinn made a point of not watching him go.

The sounds of the patrol car had completely died away before he tossed the rag on the workbench and went inside. He roamed the downstairs searching for Hannah. He found her in the kitchen rummaging through his refrigerator.

He slouched in the doorway watching her. "First my car, now my lunch."

"Leftover pizza, half a cantaloupe, three bottles of tea. No wonder you eat all your meals at Guy's." She slammed the door and faced him. "He's gone?"

"You know he is, or you wouldn't be going through my refrigerator."

"I'm giving him a few minutes, then I'm out of here." She crossed her arms over her chest defiantly, but her voice softened. "Thanks for not giving me away. I owe you one, Quinn."

"Why don't I collect right now?" He watched her eyes narrow. He went on, as if he didn't know exactly what she was thinking. "All I want is the truth, Hannah. If I've obstructed justice, I'd like to know the facts."

She sighed, and the sound caught and lingered. She cleared her throat. "Jolie was gone when I woke up this morning. I know she was still there at midnight. It happened sometime afterward."

"What time did you discover she was missing?"

"She's usually up by seven. I peeked in her room at seven-thirty. I was going to take her with me on a job this morning."

"And she was gone?"

Hannah nodded.

"You didn't hear anything in the night?"

"I have two big dogs, and they don't like strangers, especially men. They didn't even bark."

"Are you a sound sleeper?"

"When I'm exhausted."

"And last night?"

"I was."

"So it's possible someone came inside?"

"Someone did. Jolie's gone, and I'm damned sure that someone was Jolie's father. The dogs know him. He probably still has a key."

"You didn't change the locks after everything the man did to you?"

Her eyes narrowed again. "How do you know what he did to me?"

Quinn knew this was no time for damage control. "Millie told me. And she asked me to look in on you this morning. She heard the cops were at your house."

"No, I didn't change the locks. What would have been the point? There's not a lock in the county Marsh can't pick. He was the cop the department sent to help people get back into their cars or houses if they locked themselves out."

"Interesting sideline."

"A man of many talents. He taught me how to pick a lock and hotwire a car. But yours was a real challenge." Her purse was on the counter, and she tucked it under her arm. "Now you know as much as I do."

"What are the chances someone else took her? Or that something else happened to Jolie? She wandered outside, she ran away...."

"I live right on the lake!" She shook her braid over her shoulder then back again, as if she was taking a moment to calm herself. "I take every precaution. The locks are so high she couldn't possibly undo them by herself."

"Could a stranger have taken her?"

"It was my ex-husband." She paused, as if considering whether to tell him something. Then she shrugged. "On the day of our divorce Marsh promised he would get even. He told me he didn't know how and he didn't know when, but one morning I would wake up and my life would change forever."

His stomach clenched. "The bastard..."

"Actually his parents are married. Decent people on the surface. But his mother thinks Marsh walks on water."

"Where are you going to start your search?"

"I can't tell you that."

"Hannah, don't you think I missed my chance to turn you in?"

"Why do you care where I go?"

"Simple," he said, moving toward the cupboard and getting down a bowl and a box of Cheerios. "Because I'm going, too."

"Like hell you are!"

He cocked a brow. "We can be emotional, or we can be rational."

"You're not coming. I can move faster on my own."

"Right into the arms of the law. How are you going to get wherever you're going? I'm sure as hell not going to let you take my car. And in case you haven't noticed, you stand out in a crowd. You're young, beautiful, and so jumpy you'll make everybody suspicious." He reached over and lifted the braid off her shoulder. "This alone will give you away."

"Then I'll cut it off."

He winced.

"Do you think I care? Hand me a knife."

"That's not exactly a look people would ignore."

"Then do it for me."

"Hannah, first we have to get out of here, then we'll worry about disguises."

"There is no 'we.'"

He ignored her. "How are you with enclosed spaces? Since I don't have a real back seat my trunk's big enough for you. Think you can stand it until we're out in the country?"

"You're not coming with me!"

"Then tell me your plan. Are you going to hitchhike? Botch another car theft? Saunter down State Street to a pay phone and call Avis or Hertz?"

She was sizzling. The next sentences hurtled to completion. "Why do you want to come, anyway? I'm nothing to you. Jolie's nothing to you."

For a moment he couldn't breathe.

He's nothing to you, Quinn. Just somebody else's little kid. You've got to get hold of yourself. You're losing your perspective.

"Is this some kind of recreation?" Hannah demanded. "Maybe running from the law sounds like a good way to spend the summer. Or maybe this is your idea of seduction...."

He knew this was anger speaking, not at him, but at a world that had exploded around her. Hannah was frantic, frightened, furious....

But he wasn't going to let her get away with it.

He took a step, then another, until he towered over her. This wasn't easy to do. She was five foot ten to his six feet, and she wasn't a woman who backed away.

"Listen to me, Hannah," he said softly, just inches from her face. "I have my own reasons for coming along, but trust me, it's not the need for excitement, and it's not a way to get you in my bed. For the record, I used to work for a newspaper. There's nobody like a reporter to find a man who doesn't want to be found. If you want a reunion with your daughter, then you'll let me help. But if you think your independence is more important, go ahead and walk out the door. I sure as hell won't stop you."

Her expression didn't change. She didn't shrink back even a fraction of an inch. But when she spoke, her voice was softer. "You're really doing this because you want to help?"

"I'm a regular bleeding heart."

"How cramped is your trunk?"

"I wouldn't bring a book." He grimaced. "I'll drive like a bat out of hell, Hannah. I'll get you out of there as fast as I can."

then..." "Why do you want to come, anyway?"

He nodded. "I'll close up the house. I don't know how long we'll be gone. Then I'll pull into the garage so you can get in without being seen. In the meantime eat some cereal. You probably haven't had anything all day."

Her expression chilled. "I'll come with you, but I won't take orders. This is my child and my search."

"Fine, just think of a story I can tell the cops when I pull an unconscious woman from my trunk."

"I'll eat because I know I have to."

"We'll find her."

"I'll find her. I won't stop looking, as long as I live."

Quinn wasn't sure he liked the sound of that.

Chapter 4

Quinn turned on his car radio and rolled down his windows. He was painfully aware he had a woman in his trunk, a long-legged blonde who had been forced to coil her elegant limbs like a sideshow star.

The Amazing Snake Woman. Hear her hiss. See her strike. Feel her venom, ladies and gentlemen....

He unbuttoned the top two buttons of his sport shirt, then he started the engine. He forced himself to take the driveway slowly, planning silently all the way. He was a man with too much money and too much time on his hands. He was off to visit a friend. He didn't know when he'd be back—or so the story went—just whenever the mood struck him. Quinn knew better than to leave town without a story. Even if no one stopped him to hear it—and he didn't expect to be stopped—preparation was cheap insurance.

"I'll get you out of there as soon as I can, Hannah," he muttered under his breath, even though he knew she couldn't hear him.

Every road had two directions. It made sense to go west, since Hannah's house and the search lay directly east. Unfortunately the western road would be twisting and narrow, winding miles through cornfields and housing tracts before it reached an interstate. He didn't want to chance an encounter with the police, but neither did he want to go even a mile out of his way. He was heading east to Cleveland, and the woman in his trunk would not appreciate a detour.

At the end of the driveway he turned toward Hannah's house. He was not under suspicion. He wasn't even interesting. He would breeze by her house, driving under the speed limit, and soon enough he and the little surprise wrapped around his spare tire would be beyond Port Franklin and immediate danger.

He was surprised to see it was a beautiful day. The sun was gilding treetops and the calm surface of the lake. A light breeze cooled the air and ruffled newly green lilacs and forsythia. It was a perfect summer morning, except that Jolie Blackstone was missing and the woman in his trunk was accused of her murder.

Quinn's hands tightened on the steering wheel as he neared the turnoff to Lakeside Landscapes. He slowed imperceptibly as he drew closer. From this distance there seemed to be no excitement and no traffic. He was fifty yards from the turnoff when he spotted the same patrol car and police officer who had stopped at his house. The man was parked across the entrance to Hannah's drive, clearly to prohibit traffic from coming as close to the crime scene as Quinn had that morning.

Quinn lifted a hand in salute when he was almost opposite the patrol car, but his heart sank when the policeman motioned for him to stop. He knew better than to ignore the summons. He pulled over to the shoulder and waited, his engine idling.

The policeman was in no hurry to get out of his car.

When he did he ambled toward Quinn's window. "See you got your car running again."

Quinn forced a lazy smile. "Spark plugs, like I thought. Thought I'd take her for a little spin."

The cop's gaze flicked to the suitcase in the rear. "Looks like more than a little one."

"I'm heading for the big city for a couple of days. If I have more problems there's a Lexus mechanic in Cleveland who can take a good look at her."

"My brother works down at the station on State and Ordway Road. Give him a try if you need a good mechanic."

"Thanks for the tip."

The cop stepped backward, then changed his mind and leaned forward again. His expression was neither friendly nor suspicious. "You mind if we check around your property while you're gone?"

"I'd welcome it," Quinn said. "Still looking for Hannah?"

"We'll find her."

Quinn nodded, as if he thought that was perfectly possible. "I just hope she and the little one are okay."

"You'd better move along now."

Quinn waited until the cop had crossed to his car, then he pulled carefully to the road and continued on his way.

How long would it take the cops to question his sudden absence? How long before they realized that Hannah had left the area and someone had helped her? Quinn was driving a Lexus, a car that stood out, even in rush hour traffic. He was an easy target, and any cop in the state who was looking would find him quickly.

He was pondering this as the road curved away from Hannah's property, but suddenly the problem paled in comparison to a more immediate one.

Hannah's dogs.

Quinn didn't like dogs particularly. He had grown up in a tiny apartment over a barber shop where even goldfish had been forbidden. As a successful journalist he had maintained a Manhattan walkup with a bed and a television, but he'd traveled so much that sometimes he'd struggled to remember where he lived. Pets were for people who came home every night, people like Hannah. And the proof was running beside his car, yelping like bloodhounds hot on the trail.

Quinn sped up, and the dogs—he'd never seen mutts that were uglier than these—sped up, too. He'd been chased by dogs before, and he knew that usually, at some invisible boundary, the dogs gave up. Something told him that this time, it would be different.

He sped up again, cursing, but the dogs had seemingly boundless energy. Not only did they stay beside him, the pitch of their yelping grew higher. Between them they sounded like a pack of foxhounds.

He had seconds to make a decision.

"Hannah," he said loudly. "Your dogs are chasing us. I'm pulling over."

He thought he heard something from the trunk, a thump and a murmur, but he couldn't be sure. By now the dogs were barking like the hounds of hell.

He pulled over to the shoulder once more. He got out, praying that the dogs wouldn't attack, and opened the back door of his car. One dog, the furriest, snapped menacingly at him, but when the other jumped inside, the second one followed. Quinn slammed the door, got back in and started down the road again.

A drooling canine snout poked between seats, tongue lolling and teeth bared.

"Great. Just great." Quinn slammed his palm against the steering wheel. And now what would he say if he was stopped?

The answer came lightning swift. He would say that he was taking the dogs to a friend, Millie, perhaps, who could look out for them while Hannah was away. Or he could just open his trunk and be done with the whole thing.

The dog sniffed suspiciously in his direction, then it turned and replaced its dripping muzzle with a scrappy looking tail. He heard scratching on the seat behind him and knew exactly what was happening. The dogs were trying to free their mistress.

He drove faster and regretted that months ago as he had climbed out of the black hole of depression, he had thought that a Lexus with an expensive leather interior would bring him happiness.

Even through the walls of the trunk, Hannah had heard the baying of her dogs. She didn't know why their distress made her want to cry when there was already so much to cry about. Surely someone would take care of Fagan and Oliver. Even Tony Chandler wouldn't be cruel enough to consign them to the pound. The moment she was out of here, she would call Amanda and ask her to find them and care for them at her house.

Surely Amanda would take care of her dogs. But who was taking care of her daughter?

The trunk was so cramped that the best she could do was wiggle her toes and fingers. Heat was building, and she was already drenched with perspiration. There were terrible stories about people who died in car trunks, and she tried to put them out of her mind and concentrate on what was happening around her. They had stopped once already. She wasn't sure why, but before the car began to move again she had heard men's voices. Now the car was slowing for a second time. The dogs' barking grew louder, Quinn shouted something, then the noise stopped suddenly and the car was moving once more.

She tried to turn over a little, but she was so tightly wedged there was no place to go, and she bumped her head. Had Quinn hit one of the dogs? Scared them away with rocks or sticks? She tried to breathe deeply to calm herself, but even though she knew there was still plenty of air in the trunk she couldn't catch her breath. Fear pricked at nerve endings and pumped up her heartbeat. Quinn was a stranger to her, yet she had taken his offer of help and climbed into this trunk like a volunteer at a magic show. Presto-chango and who could predict what might happen? Maybe Quinn would stop up the road as promised and let her out.

And maybe he wouldn't.

For the first time it occurred to Hannah that Quinn lived just down the road and had seen Jolie any number of times in the past months. His background was murky, and even though he had inherited his aunt's house, he had never visited Tina, and she had never talked about him. For all Hannah knew the house had become Quinn's, simply because he was Tina's only living relative.

Quinn had appeared in town, then just a few months later Jolie had disappeared. And this morning, when Quinn confronted her in his driveway, he had known more about Jolie's disappearance than he'd had any right or reason to.

Fear spiraled to her stomach, and nausea followed on its heels. "No," she whispered. She couldn't have been that stupid. She couldn't have put her own life in the hands of the man who might have taken her daughter. Everything Quinn had told her made perfect sense.

Except that there were things he *hadn't* told her, too. Like why he cared so much about what happened to Jolie. Like why he cared so much about *her* that he was willing to risk going to jail to help her.

She was no judge of men. She had proved it by marrying one who had used her body for batting practice. In the hospital she had vowed that she would never trust any man again. *No* man, no matter how kind or gentle he appeared on the surface. Because she had realized in those agonizing days of recovery that she could never again count on her own instincts. Then, today, she had climbed into the car trunk of a stranger.

She might never climb out.

"Get hold of yourself." The words emerged as if someone had forced a fist down her throat. Her body felt bruised and inert, and each bump on the road rattled the trunk lid above her. She pushed against it tentatively, hoping it rattled because it wasn't shut tight, but it was closed as securely as a coffin.

One moan escaped before she clamped her lips together. She had to hold on to the hope that she hadn't made another mistake, that somehow, in the years since her divorce, she had learned to judge men. She had to believe this was not a mistake. Or in the next minutes she might very well go crazy.

The heat built, her heart beat faster, and the air grew so stifling it would not fill her lungs. Just when she was sure that she couldn't stand it anymore, the car slowed for the third time, then stopped.

She lay perfectly still, afraid even to breathe. Her fingers wrapped around the handle of the jack which had been shoved into a corner. She heard what she thought were footsteps, then the click of a key.

And the trunk filled with fresh, clean air.

"Hannah?" Quinn leaned over her. "Are you all right?"

"How in the hell do you think I am?" Her voice sounded as rusty as her joints.

He grimaced and reached for her. "Are you too stiff to sit up?"

She shoved his hand away and managed on her own, still gripping the jack.

He took a good look at her face and grimaced again. "I'm so sorry."

For a moment she couldn't breathe, but not because the air was scorching or fear compressed her chest. She could not breathe because Quinn had apologized to her. For caring about her daughter? For risking jail time to rescue a fugitive?

Or for something else...

"Why?" She hadn't wanted to ask the question. It emerged anyway. "What are you sorry for?"

He looked surprised. "For putting you through this. Obviously it was hell in there."

She slung her aching legs over the bumper and tentatively stood, holding on as she did, just in case. "I made it, didn't I?"

"We made it. All four of us."

She lifted her eyes to the back window and saw the ecstatic, panting faces of Oliver and Fagan. "You didn't—"

"I didn't have any choice. They were making so much noise I knew somebody would get suspicious. They weren't going to stop."

"They knew I was in there." For the first time she looked around. It took only seconds to figure out where they were. Quinn had turned on to a side road about seven miles from town. She recognized the grove of trees where he had parked.

"I don't know if it's safe for you to ride up front now, but we can't leave you in there any longer. We have to leave the dogs here and hope they find their way back—"

"No!" She faced him, one hand on her hips, the other gripping the jack. "I'm not leaving them. That's a busy road. They'll get hit, even if they're smart enough to find their way back."

"So what do you suggest?"

"They have to come with us."

He looked incredulous, as if she had just suggested they hitch the dogs to the front bumper to save gas. "We can't go back, and we can't leave them," she pointed out.

"If we tie them to a tree, can you send a friend to pick them up?"

"Do you have anything to tie them with?"

He had the fine-boned features of an aristocrat and a wide, sensual—and surprisingly expressive—mouth. His grimace said everything.

Hannah straightened her Lakeside Landscapes T-shirt, which clung to her small breasts. When she saw the effect, she held it away from her chest. It was wet enough to gain her admission to a certain Friday-night contest at Port Franklin's Moosehaven Bar. "Then they're coming."

"Hannah, every cop in Port Franklin is looking for you. The state troopers are probably looking, too. Don't you think you, me in a sporty red Lexus is enough of a give-away without two drooling dangerous-looking dogs?"

"I'm not leaving my dogs to die on the road!" Her breath was coming in short puffs now, and her head was whirling. The events of the morning were taking their toll. She had never fainted, but she guessed that if she had, it would have felt something like this.

Quinn was watching her closely and seemed to realize what was about to happen. He grabbed her around the waist just as the jack slipped from her fingers. He eased her to the ground. "Put your head between your knees."

"I don't take...orders." The last word came from between her legs.

"I'll remember that." The voice came from above her. She was floating, and there *were* spots in front of her eyes, just the way there were supposed to be.

The world receded a moment, then she felt someone fanning her. The spots merged and disappeared. She lifted her head slowly and saw that the woods were no longer revolving. "The dogs...are coming," she said. Her voice caught. She couldn't tell Quinn what she was feeling. Everything she loved was being taken from her.

Everything.

As the world came back into focus she realized he was squatting in front of her. He rested his fingertips on her shoulder. "We'll take them. Okay? But we've got to put some miles behind us and quickly. Can you make it?"

She shoved his hand away. "Of course."

He stood and opened the back door, reaching inside for the suitcase on the back seat and somehow avoiding nipping canine teeth. He retrieved two items. "Put on the shirt and the cap."

She gazed at a men's sport shirt and a Yankee baseball cap. "You expect me to wear *this?*" She batted the cap away. "In Northeast Ohio? You thought the *dogs* would draw attention?"

"I'll buy you an Indian cap. Okay? But stuff your hair under this one for now."

"Turn around."

He nearly smiled. His mouth didn't move, but his eyes crinkled. "Sure you don't need my help?"

Hannah had scooted down in the front passenger seat after an ecstatic welcome from Oliver and Fagan—Quinn still didn't know which was which—and closed her eyes. The events of the morning and the encounter with his trunk had left her worse for wear. Her cheeks were as white as the cumulus clouds gathering overhead. Almost anyone else would have fainted dead away, but Hannah was in such fierce control of her emotions that she had somehow managed to control an involuntary physical reaction. Now she was so drained she appeared to be sleeping.

But he knew better.

They hadn't talked for thirty miles. He had told her that

they were going to Cleveland where he had a friend who might be able to help find her ex-husband. Then he had called Jake from his car phone. At the very least he needed to switch cars with Jake, and she needed to buy clothes.

She hadn't opened her eyes. "I think Marsh is living just south of the city somewhere."

He'd understood for the first time why she hadn't protested their destination. "You don't know for sure?"

"He doesn't pay child support. So far he's figured I won't pursue it, and he's right. He's kept his whereabouts a secret, though, just in case."

"But you have some idea?"

"Lolly, his mother, blames me for the divorce, so she would never consider telling me where he's living. But once last year, while she was criticizing me for working, she said that Marsh's sister, Ginger, had never worked and that now, Marsh gets to see up close what a good wife and mother is like."

"Let me get this straight. She criticized you for working, but she wouldn't tell you where her son was living so that he could pay child support?"

"It makes sense to Lolly."

He marveled at her lack of emotion. "And the sister lives in Cleveland?"

"Not far away. In Brunswick. I think Marsh probably went there after the divorce while he was figuring out what to do with his life."

"And you think he might be there still?"

"It's a place to start."

That time he had heard emotion flood her voice, and he'd heard what she didn't say. But even if Marsh was there once, he's probably not there anymore.

Now as he traveled east into Cleveland, the dogs panting on the seat behind him, he wondered what he could really do to help. He had unusually thorough connections all over the country, including a number of FBI field officers who specialized in kidnappings.

But what exactly could he tell that network of professionals who remembered a sane and objective Quinn McDermott? That the Port Franklin police suspected the woman at his side of murder, but that he, on impulse, had decided the police had to be wrong? That he had helped her escape, and now he was helping her search for her daughter?

Without the cooperation of the authorities, their search for Jolie was a needle in the proverbial haystack. And with Hannah hiding from the authorities, the job was doubly difficult. Until there was a full-fledged search for Marshall Blackstone himself, the possibilities of finding Jolie were slim.

The worst part was that even with the full cooperation of the police, this was, by their standards, small potatoes. Noncustodial parents snatched children all the time. And the number of them who got away with it testified to the underwhelming support of law enforcement. Understaffed police departments all over the country were smothering under red tape, petty crime and cutbacks in funding.

As if she had heard his thoughts, Hannah spoke. "What can you do to help me, Quinn?"

With a mental sigh he wrote off his best resources and settled for the second tier. "My friend at the newspaper has connections. We'll see if he can find someone at the state police who'll run your husband's name. Then we'll try the motor vehicle folks, maybe social security..."

"He can do all that?"

No, Quinn himself could have done it in New York, with his connections. But he didn't know exactly what Jake could do. "Let's just see, okay? Do you have the sister's address?"

"No. I'm lucky I have a pack of tissues and my wallet. But I'm betting she's in the phone book."

"Your husband was a cop. Did he have any other training he might put to use? He had to get a job, didn't he?"

She was silent so long he wondered if she'd heard him. When she spoke, her voice was bitter. "Believe it or not, he studied art."

He gave a low whistle, and his picture of Marshall Blackstone changed.

"He was good, too," she continued. "But his parents finally convinced him that art wasn't a real man's career. So he quit school and went into the police academy. And that was the end of that."

"He wouldn't be working as an artist? Doing commercial work of some sort?"

"I doubt that his hands are steady enough."

"Then what? A security guard?"

"Maybe. If they didn't check his record too carefully. He loved wearing a uniform."

"We can look into that."

"Whatever he was doing, he's not doing it now. He's running. With my daughter."

"We can start where he was and follow him, or start where we think he's going. Does he have strong connections somewhere? Old buddies on the force who might take him in? High school friends? Distant family?"

"In an odd sort of way Marsh is a loner. He didn't even have that many friends on the force. Just Tony and a couple of others. But, of course, the moment his job was in jeopardy, everyone circled around him. He was a cop, and that's all they needed to know."

"How about family?"

"Right after we got married, his parents moved about two hours south of Port Franklin. Except for Ginger, the sister in Brunswick, the rest of the family lives close to them. I don't know of anyone who lives out of state. Our high school friends were my friends, too, and wouldn't help him steal my daughter."

He wasn't so sure about the last, but he didn't want to make her feel worse. "Keep thinking about it. In the meantime maybe we can find out where he's been living and go from there."

"Why are you doing this, Quinn?"

He glanced at her and saw that her eyes were grave. She wasn't asking because she was warmed by his generosity. She was asking because, quite simply, she didn't trust him. And why should she?

In the seconds that she waited for his answer, he considered telling her the truth. But the truth gave him nightmares he couldn't share. Certainly not until her daughter was safely back at home, and perhaps not even then. Because dwelling on the past might very well plunge him back into the void.

"I've never been married, and I don't have any kids," he said when the silence had stretched far enough. "But I like kids, Hannah. I was in the right place at the right time to help you. That's about all there is to it."

"Why didn't you visit Tina? Why did she leave you her house?"

The rapid change of subject mystified him. He glanced at her again and this time he saw suspicion in her eyes.

I was in the right place at the right time.

He clamped his lips shut a moment, letting the impulse to curse or worse pass over him. He remembered the car jack gripped in Hannah's hand. He had assumed she had simply prepared herself in case somebody else opened the trunk.

He hadn't even realized that she'd been protecting herself from him.

When he was calmer he spoke again. "You think I had something to do with Jolie's disappearance?"

"I didn't say that."

"I'm a quick study. I saw it in your eyes."

"Then *did* you have something to do with it?"

He forced his fingers apart on the steering wheel. "No."

"You're a stranger, the only stranger living in the vicinity of my house. You never visited Tina. She never mentioned that she had a nephew. Maybe she had reason not to?"

"This is none of your business, Hannah."

"Anything that might affect my daughter is my business."

"Tina left me her house because I'm her closest relative and she wanted me to have it. That should tell you everything you need to know."

"You're just full of secrets, Quinn."

"I'm not going to blurt out my life story right here on the interstate. But I can tell you what *isn't* a part of my past. I'm not a kidnapper or a child molester. I live in Tina's house because I'm taking a long sabbatical trying to decide what I want to do with the rest of my life. And stealing children for fun and profit is not one of the options I'm considering."

"My daughter is missing! I can't trust you, I can't trust anybody!"

He didn't look at her. He wondered how he had gotten into this, what perverse desire for more pain had propelled him forward.

"If you can't trust me, then I can't help you," he said at last. "You'll have to decide, Hannah. But don't decide until we've seen what Jake can do for you. Don't cut off your options. Just stay with me long enough to see what we can do together."

Chapter 5

"You're absolutely sure about the car?" Jake Whattley twirled Quinn's keychain around his index finger with the enthusiasm of a teenager about to take his first solo drive.

Quinn looked distinctly pained. "Just park it out of sight whenever you can."

Jake, an appealing young man with cinnamon-colored hair and a choirboy smile, nodded as if he'd heard every word. But Hannah guessed he was planning exactly which woman he was going to impress with Quinn's Lexus. "Just remember when you shift from third to fourth in my van, you have to ease off on the gas. And throw that old quilt over the seat in the back if somebody has to sit there. The springs poke."

Hannah might have found the whole exchange funny if her daughter had been cuddled in her arms. As it was she wanted to scream at the two men to hurry. They had arrived in Cleveland an hour ago, and Quinn had called Jake again, who had driven to a fast-food restaurant to meet them. Now over French fries and hamburgers in the parking lot, Quinn was trading his Lexus for Jake's battered panel van.

"Can you help me find my daughter?" she demanded, when Jake had gone on another sentence or two about the van. "Is there anything you can do besides trade cars with Quinn?"

"I can try to get an address for your ex." Jake's clear blue eyes assessed her, as they had since his introduction. "But I still don't understand why you're not working with the police."

She answered Jake. "Because I laid out a cop who grabbed me."

"She has bruises ringing her arms," Quinn said. "The cop is a close friend of Hannah's ex-husband. Does that tell you something?"

Jake didn't look convinced. A carload of shouting adolescents pulled into the parking lot. He waited until the lot had quieted before he replied. "Laid him out isn't descriptive enough."

"I don't know how he is, if that's what you're asking," Hannah said, coming straight to the point. "I pushed him, he cracked his head on a table on the way to the floor. I knew if I stayed around..." She cleared her throat and glared at both men, daring them to pity her. "If I stayed, nobody would be looking for my daughter. They're going to use their energy digging up my lawn, and with every shovelful of dirt, Marsh will be that much farther from Port Franklin with Jolie."

"Quinn?" Jake's shrug left everything up to Quinn.

"Hannah's a good mother, and her history with the local cops seems real enough. I'm going to see this thing through with her."

"You're sure you're in it for the long haul?" Jake said.

"Yes."

"I don't understand where this is going." Hannah faced Quinn. "Would you put that last part in plain English?"

"It's simple. I'm going to see this through to the end."

"I never asked for your help, and I haven't asked you to see anything through."

"I can make it plainer, Hannah," Jake said. "Your daughter is missing, and you brained a cop. Just by sneaking you out of town Quinn's an accessory. If something did happen to Jolie at your hands, then Quinn made a bad decision, didn't he? And *I* don't want to make one, too."

She was stunned into silence.

"I don't have any choice but to stay with you," Quinn finished. "If I've been wrong about you, I'll have to turn you in."

"You don't trust me?"

He smiled humorlessly. "Weren't you the woman who was clutching my car jack?"

"I'd trust Quinn with my life," Jake said. "And that's the only reason I'm going to be part of this. That and an exclusive on any story that comes out of it. Unless you're planning to freelance this one yourself?" he asked Quinn.

Something Hannah didn't understand passed between the two men. But she was still turning over the fact that Quinn didn't completely trust her. He would be watching everything she did until he was sure Jolie was safe.

"So, to answer your first question," Jake said. "I'll get whatever leads I can on your ex. I'll need his full name, birth date, social security number and anything else you have on him. But you and Quinn will have to do the footwork."

"When we find Marshall, we'll find Jolie. Then this will be over."

"We'll need a place to stay tonight," Quinn told Jake. "Any suggestions?"

"My apartment's tiny, but I have keys to a colleague's

house. He and his wife are in Europe for a couple of months, and I'm supposed to stay there once in a while to make it look like somebody's home. The neighbors are used to my van, so no one will ask questions.''

"You're sure there won't be any trouble?"

"No, the house is off by itself on a cul de sac. And there's parkland behind it.'' He scrutinized Hannah. ''Diane's tall, too. About your size. Borrow some of her clothes. She's a good sport. She'll understand.''

She nodded, unsmiling. ''Thanks.''

''I just hope you know what you're doing....''

''I'm looking for my daughter, Jake. What would any mother do?''

Marshall's sister, Ginger Anspath, lived in a suburban clutter of houses, a family neighborhood of swing sets and tricycles and tree trunks as narrow as porch posts. The Anspaths hadn't been listed in the telephone book, but Quinn took the interstate to Brunswick, anyway, where Hannah narrowed the search to an area behind a sprawling shopping mall. They drove up and down the residential streets for almost two hours before Hannah recognized the house.

''That's it. The one with the painted mailbox. Ginger paints them to sell.''

The mailbox in question was shiny black with stenciled ivy and morning glories trailing over the door and down the wooden post. The house was ranch-style, and the yard geometrically neat. ''Your mother-in-law doesn't consider that work?'' Quinn said.

''Lolly's children can do no wrong. That's why she protects Marshall.''

Quinn parked down the street from the house. As odious as the van was, it made sitting at the curbside a breeze since the windows were tinted and the dogs were sleeping in the back. ''What's your plan now?''

"Ginger's the best of the Blackstone bunch, but I don't think she'll tell me where Marsh is."

Quinn watched as Hannah considered her next move. She was still too pale, and almost painfully pensive. "The moment somebody in your ex's family sees you, they could alert the police," he pointed out. "And we can't keep trading cars. We need to keep some anonymity."

"What's your suggestion?"

"What I'm about to tell you is confidential."

She faced him. Her brown eyes were shadowed, and the skin surrounding them seemed thin and bruised. His heart ached for her. "Go ahead," she said without expression.

He smiled. "Reporters are not always honest. You're about to see a demonstration." He opened his door and slipped out, slamming it before the dogs could signal their disapproval. "Stay here."

"Wait a minute, Quinn."

He ignored her, strolling up the sidewalk until he'd almost reached the Anspath house. Up close he saw that the sidewalk was decorated with colored chalk drawings. Obviously Ginger was not the only artist on the premises.

Quinn put Hannah out of his mind and concentrated on what he would say. He wanted to get this right, had to, in fact, if she was going to trust him to be any help along the way. He rang the doorbell and waited, looking around as if he had all the time in the world.

Someone threw open the door, and Quinn's gaze traveled down until it met bright green eyes staring up at him through the screen door. "My mommy isn't home."

He judged the little boy to be about six. He had bright red hair and an aquiline nose that was too long for his face. "That's okay," Quinn said with a cheerful grin. "I'm here to see your uncle Marsh. Is he at home?"

The little boy frowned. "Uncle Marsh?"

"That's right. Is he home?"

"Sandra!"

The boy's bellow brought an older girl of maybe ten to the door to hover beside him. From the color of her eyes and the length of her nose, Quinn judged that she was the boy's sister. If they were the only two at home, he guessed they wouldn't be home alone long.

"He wants to know if Uncle Marsh is here," the boy told her.

"He's not," the girl said shortly.

"I can't believe I missed him," Quinn said. "Will he be back later?"

"He doesn't live here anymore."

Quinn didn't blink. "You're kidding. Since when?"

"A long time ago."

Quinn managed to look surprised. "I worked with your uncle, and the last I heard, he was living here. You don't have his new address, do you?"

"My mommy's mad at him," the boy supplied.

"We're not allowed to talk about Uncle Marsh," Sandra told Quinn. "My grandma says so." She started to close the door.

"Lolly?" Quinn asked. "How is Lolly? I haven't seen *her* for a while, either."

"She smells funny," the boy said. He made a face.

"Brian!" Sandra shoved her brother. "We have to go now," she told Quinn.

"Look, kids, can you tell me anything at all? I owe your uncle some money, and I'd like to pay him back. I hate to miss seeing him."

"Give me the money!" Brian giggled.

"Wait a minute." Sandra left, then returned in a few seconds. "My mom keeps this letter on her desk." She held it up proudly. "That's his address in the corner."

Quinn squinted to read the envelope through the screen, memorizing it as he did. The postmark was blurred and he would have given a lot to see the date. He wished he could snatch it, but he drew the line at terrifying children for any cause. "That should help. Thanks. You don't have to tell anybody that you told me. I don't want you to get in trouble."

"Bye!" Brian screeched.

Sandra hauled Brian backward and shut the door. He heard the lock turn and knew he'd been lucky that Brian had been the one to answer the doorbell.

Back inside the van he turned to Hannah. "I talked to a little boy named Brian and his sister. They say he hasn't lived there in a long time, although who can say what that means to children. It sounds like Ginger and Marshall may have had a fight, and Lolly told the children not to talk about their uncle. But I did get an address from a letter he wrote Ginger. He was living in a place called Millersburg when he wrote it."

She was like a sponge, absorbing the news completely and hoarding it once she did. Her expression was guarded. "That's south of here by maybe a couple of hours. It's an unlikely choice for Marsh. Quiet and conservative. Not a good place for a man who drinks and beats women." She pushed her cap back on her head. He was sure her neck was tired from the weight of her hair jammed under the cap. "Let's go."

He put his hand on hers. "Hannah, it's almost dinnertime."

"So? We can do fast food again."

"Look..." She had jerked her hand out from under his so fast that his palm hovered in the air with no place to go. "It's doubtful he's still at that address. You said so yourself. And we can't knock on doors and ask questions tonight. In the kind of town you're describing, we'll stand out like Bonnie and Clyde. We've got to get some food and sleep, and we've got to do something about getting you different clothes. Let's take Jake up on his offer.''

"My daughter is missing. I'm not worried about food or sleep!"

"Jake may have discovered something by now, too. Do you want to drive all the way to Millersburg just to find out your ex-husband got a parking ticket in Toledo?"

She clamped her lips together. He watched her struggle. Maternal instincts were a powerful force. He coaxed her gently. "This may take a few days. We've got to be rested and alert, and we can't do anything to draw suspicion."

"The only time Jolie ever spent the night away from me was when I was in the hospital."

He wanted to comfort her, but he knew better than to touch her again. "Are you afraid your ex will hurt her? Is that what you're most worried about?"

She went completely still, then she shook her head. "For a while, at least, Marsh will play the good daddy. She's safe enough with him for now."

He hoped her prediction was right. Because he knew from experience that people weren't always good to children, even when they claimed to love them.

Rick and Diane Everest's house was on a street so pastoral it was possible to forget that the heart of a bustling city was only a few miles away. The house was a contemporary, split-level with an interior heavy on stainless steel and abstract art in bold sweeps of color. It was as different from Hannah's homey farmhouse as Diane's wardrobe was from the jeans and T-shirts Hannah always wore.

In the doorway of the master bedroom closet Hannah swept a hand over the earth-tone skirts and vibrantly colored silk blouses, the butter-soft leather belts and woven vests. "I can't just take this woman's clothes."

"You can clean or replace everything. Jake says she'll

understand. But it's a different look for you, Hannah, and that's what you need.''

Since discovering that Jolie was missing, Hannah had felt like a stranger to herself. It had taken her so long to build a new life, and in one more stunning act of betrayal, Marshall had swept it away. She was awash in emotion, confused about where to go and what to do. She had even allowed a stranger to help her, a man she barely knew and certainly didn't understand.

She turned her back on Diane Everest's personal style. "I have to call my friend Amanda Taylor. I have to let someone in Port Frank know I'm okay. Will it be safe to call her from here?"

"How close are the two of you?"

"She's been my best friend since I was five."

"I can't imagine that."

"Why not?"

"Because the moment I was able to leave my childhood behind, I did."

"You missed something special."

He looked skeptical but didn't reply to that. "I doubt that the police have gotten around to tapping telephones. Even if they wanted to, there's a lot of red tape they would have to go through first. And it sounds like Amanda wouldn't volunteer to let them do it."

"Then I'll call her from here."

"I'll see if there's anything in the cupboards for dinner." He held up a hand when she started to protest. "Look, Hannah, you hardly ate a bite of lunch. You have to have something for dinner. Force yourself. You can't look for your daughter if you're sick." He left the room.

Her stomach was tied in so many knots she couldn't believe food would pass through it. But Quinn's concern warmed her. No man had fussed over her in a very long time. She had made herself forget how nice it could be.

She sat on a black satin comforter splashed with scarlet Chinese characters and picked up the receiver, glad that the Everests had not had their number disconnected during their absence, since Quinn's car phone was now in Jake's possession. She dialed Amanda's home as she had nearly every day of her life and waited for her friend to answer.

Amanda answered on the first ring. "Hannah?"

Hannah swallowed, her throat suddenly thick with tears. Amanda had been sitting beside the telephone waiting for her to call. It was a testament to their friendship. "Mandy, is it safe to talk?"

"Nobody's here. Even Daniel is out searching for Jolie. Are you all right? My God, what's going on?"

"Daniel's searching for Jolie?" Daniel, a quiet, steadfast CPA, was Amanda's husband of seven years. So far the Taylors hadn't been blessed with a child of their own, so Jolie was particularly special to them.

"The police organized search parties. They're combing your property and all of the neighbors', too. Why aren't you here? What's going on?"

Hannah pictured her best friend, sitting on the big over-stuffed navy blue chair beside the fireplace, where she did needlepoint in the evenings. Hannah could see Amanda bent over the receiver, her short dark curls tumbling against her cheeks, her wide, mobile mouth pursed in concentration.

Hannah quickly filled her in on the basics, including Quinn's help. "We've already got a lead on an address for Marsh," she finished. "We're going there first thing in the morning."

"Oh, Hannah, this is the most awful thing I've ever heard."

"Exactly what have you heard?"

"Just that Jolie's missing, and you vanished after you gave your report to the police. They're trying to find you for further questioning. That's all I know, but they seem to think Jolie's—" Amanda's voice caught. "Hannah, what if it wasn't Marshall? What if—"

"It *was* Marsh. After the divorce he told me I'd wake up one morning and my life would be changed forever. Don't you remember?"

"But that was a long time ago, and he'd been drinking. He doesn't want Jolie. He doesn't even visit her."

It was just like Amanda to be overly fair. "Of course he doesn't want *her*. He wants me to suffer. Don't you see?" Hannah exhaled in frustration. "Look, Amanda, have you heard anything about Tony Chandler? Do you know how he is?"

"He came by this afternoon to question me. He's a jerk, that's how he is. You didn't push him hard enough."

For a moment Hannah could only swallow. Amanda rarely criticized anyone. To call Tony a jerk was the equivalent of someone else's vilest profanity. "He questioned you? Did he say anything about arresting me for assault?"

"Not a thing. I didn't know what had happened at your house until you told me just now. He seemed perfectly fine."

Hannah mulled this over. "And Faye didn't say anything?"

"No, but I'm sure Faye's upset about the way Tony's handling the investigation. I've known her since we were kids, remember? And she miscarried a few years back, so I'm sure she knows what it's like to grieve for a child. She has to be on your side."

Unlike Amanda, Hannah didn't know Faye well. Although Faye had grown up in Cleveland, Amanda's and Faye's families had owned property on Kelley's Island in Lake Erie, and the two girls had spent weeks each summer at their cottages. Hannah had only gotten to know Faye when she had moved to Port Franklin several years ago and joined the police force. But when Marsh's colleagues had gathered at the Blackstone house, Hannah had always found her both friendly and intelligent, with the human touch some of her male colleagues lacked.

From the moment Faye had arrived at Hannah's door that morning, Hannah had prayed that Faye would be her ace in the hole. "Then you think Faye might be an ally? Could I trust her to go behind Tony's back and help me?"

"I don't know, but I could feel her out...."

"I need to know what's going on there. I can only do so much on my own."

"You're not exactly on your own, are you?"

Hannah began to deny it, but she stopped herself. "I didn't want to involve anyone else," she said at last. "But I didn't have much of a choice."

"Hannah, why would Quinn McDermott risk anything to help you? You're practically a stranger."

Since the same thing had occurred repeatedly to Hannah, she couldn't protest. "I'm watching him closely. Look, Mandy, I have to go. I'll call you again as soon as I can. Can you look after things while I'm gone? Ask Buck and Lou to handle what they can of the business. If the police will let him, maybe Buck can sleep there at nights."

"Hannah, oh, my Lord, what about the dogs?"

"We have them. It's a long story. If anyone asks, can you say that you found them wandering on the road and took them somewhere to stay with a friend? That way if the cops start searching for me, they won't add the dogs to the equation."

They said their goodbyes, then Amanda added. "God bless you and Jolie, Hannah. Find her and bring her home."

Hannah hung up. For a moment she could only sit there, in a strange bedroom immersed in this horrifying new turn in her life. "Jolie, where are you?" she whispered.

She pictured her daughter confused and frightened, alone

with the father she hardly knew. Marsh had never changed a diaper, never soothed their daughter to sleep. On the rare occasions he had visited since the divorce, he had been annoyed at Jolie's childish patter and demands.

"Hannah?"

Quinn's voice from the doorway startled her back to the present. She wondered if he had listened to her conversation. Had he stood in the hallway, waiting for her to incriminate herself?

At some point during her conversation he had changed his clothes, exchanging a sport shirt for a more casual polo. "The local news is about to come on," he said. "I think we'd better watch it to see what they've got."

"Amanda says they've organized search parties in Port Franklin."

"At some point they'll have to justify all that expense. They should have tracked Marshall first."

She got to her feet. "How helpful will Jake's databases be?"

"Truthfully?"

"We don't have time to spare feelings, Quinn. I can take anything you have to say to me."

"Fifty-fifty. It gets easier and easier to track people these days. Computers can pick up any paper trail. If your ex had a car registered in Ohio, a traffic ticket, a court appearance, we can probably nail him fast. But he may have dropped completely out of sight. If he's still driving, maybe he won't be licensed, and the car will be registered to a friend. If he's working, he'll be sure he's paid under the table. He'll be moving around, probably to medium or large cities where he can stay anonymous. He won't join unions, register to vote, get a credit card...." He turned up his hands. "He was a cop, Hannah, and he knows how the system works."

Disappointment stabbed at her, but she didn't let it show. "Then we have to do this on our own."

"We've made a start. Now we just continue to follow his path, one address to the next. Along the way we think like Marshall Blackstone. After dinner you're going to tell me everything you remember about his likes and dislikes, his hobbies and places he liked to hang out."

Her voice was bitter. "That part's easy. He drank. He hung out in bars."

"Then we'll narrow it down to what kind. Working class? Upscale? Cop bars? Did he drink whiskey or beer? Designer microbrews or Budweiser? Did he sit at the bar, beside the jukebox? Play pool? Talk to strangers, keep to himself?"

For the first time she felt something like a ray of hope. "You know what you're doing, don't you?"

He smiled. She liked the way Quinn's smile warmed his austerely handsome face and transformed him into someone more approachable. "I didn't come along for the thrill of it."

For the first time since it had occurred, she thought of the exchange between Quinn and Jake. Jake had claimed to want an exclusive, unless Quinn was planning to freelance the story.

She questioned him. "You did this sort of thing as a reporter?"

"Uh-huh."

"At a large paper?"

"Large enough." He tilted his head toward the living room. "It's almost six. We'd better turn on the television."

"Are you writing for the paper now? Are you going to freelance this?"

He had already turned away. Now he turned back. "Helping you has nothing to do with a story. I left my job—"

"Where?"

He paused, then grimaced. "New York."

"And the paper?"

"The *Times*."

"I'd say that's large enough. We've even heard of the *Times* in Port Franklin." Her voice was icy, even to her own ears.

"I was burned out. It happens more frequently than it should, and I don't like to talk about it."

"Can you promise me that when this is over, everything I tell you, everything I do to find my daughter isn't going to be sold to a newspaper under your byline?"

"I don't write for a newspaper now, and I don't intend to start again with this story. Any other questions?"

He had told her all he would. She could see it in his eyes. She didn't know what Quinn was hiding or why, but despite his disclaimers, she felt increasingly uneasy. If she stayed with Quinn would she find her daughter faster? Now she had only to decide if he'd chosen the possibility of monetary gain over his personal risk.

Chapter 6

"I don't cook very often," Quinn said. "But I can boil water."

From the kitchen doorway Hannah watched Quinn put the finishing touches on their meal. He had boiled rotini pasta and warmed a jar of sauce to serve over it. The cupboard had also yielded Parmesan cheese and a can of green beans.

She crossed to a set of cupboards and searched for china, removing black octagonal plates she found behind one of the doors. "Don't you like to cook? Or is it just too much trouble?"

"I was always on the run. Home cooking tastes odd to me now." He looked up from stirring the sauce. "I imagine you cook most of the time?"

She knew he was trying to distract her for a few minutes. Reluctantly, she was touched. "Eating out with a child isn't fun." She thought of last night and wished with all her heart that she was facing Jolie's tantrum at Tasty Burger again.

"Don't you yearn for grown-up food sometimes?"

Grown-up company, too, but she wasn't going to admit it. The decision not to let another man into her life had taken its toll, but never as great a one as her marriage.

"I cook just for myself sometimes, after I put Jolie to bed at night," she admitted.

"What do you make?"

"Quinn, I appreciate what you're trying to do, but it's not working. I can't put her out of my head. I don't even want to."

He didn't deny his strategy; he changed the subject. "I found a bottle of cheap Cabernet. We can send them a case of something better when this is over."

She was so tense that her mind was moving in multiple directions. He seemed to sense it, because he added, "You're going to need to tell me everything you can about Marsh. You'll do better if you mellow a little."

"Mellow? My daughter was kidnapped today."

"I'm talking about taking the worst edge off the anxiety."

She could see the value, even though it felt like a betrayal. "I'll have one glass."

He seemed satisfied. "You pour." He nodded toward the counter beside the sink.

The Everests' kitchen was blinding white with chrome wall splashes. Although it looked as if no one had ever cooked here, Hannah found a high-tech corkscrew in a drawer filled with garlic presses and fancy cheese slicers. She worked at opening the wine, glad for something to do. "You said the news was coming on?"

"In about five minutes. We can watch television while we eat."

"Do they have a family, do you suppose?"

"I'm guessing young upwardly mobile professionals. I didn't see anything to indicate kids."

"That description sounds like your niche." She flipped the catch on the corkscrew and began to turn it. "From the bits and pieces I've dragged out of you."

"Not upwardly mobile. I got where I wanted to go." Quinn set the plates, piled with food now, on the white tile island.

He sounded as if he were sharing something important, but she realized not a bit of it was new. He was good at that. He might sound as if he were baring his soul, but in the end, he remained a stranger.

He came to stand beside her, reaching high into a cupboard above her head to retrieve two wineglasses. His hip brushed hers, and his arm grazed her hair. She had the most absurd desire to throw herself into his arms and sob against his shoulder. Crying wouldn't bring back Jolie, but it might help her mother go on.

Instead, she bolted backward, as if he'd singed her. "I'll take the plates while you pour the wine."

"Hannah..." He rested his hand on her shoulder, and it tightened when she tried to shrug it away. "Look, please don't get me wrong. I'm not making a pass at you."

"Had your fill of rejection, Quinn?"

"You're an attractive woman, and you interest me. I'm not going to deny it. But maybe you interested me most because I knew you didn't want a man in your life."

She was caught off guard. "You went after me because I wasn't available?"

He dropped his hand. "I showed an interest in you. I didn't go after you. I'd like to think that if I had, you might have taken me seriously."

"What an ego."

"Look, all I'm saying is that both of us had reasons not to have a relationship. But I was attracted to you, and maybe you were attracted back...."

"There's that ego thing again."

"All this is to say that I know things have changed. I know what you're feeling—"

"You have no idea in the world!"

"I know what you're feeling," he repeated. "And I'm trying to help. I'm not here to take you to bed. You don't have to defend yourself every time I get within a foot of you. Am I making myself clear? Shall I be clearer?"

"How much clearer could you be?"

His voice hardened. "A damn sight more, if I'm challenged. I could spell out exactly what you're afraid of and deny it step by step, act by act."

She was vaguely ashamed. She didn't trust him on several fronts, but she had no reason whatsoever to assume that his decision to help her had been based on a hope of sexual favors.

"The last man who showed an interest in me broke my arm and jaw," she said at last. "If I'm edgy around you, I guess that's the reason."

"Tell me what frightens you, and I'll be careful."

"Nothing frightens me. I didn't say frightened, I said edgy."

"What can I do to make you more comfortable?"

Find my daughter and get the hell out of my life. But she didn't, couldn't say it. Because despite all the rules she'd made for her own peace of mind, she was beginning to like Quinn McDermott.

"Just don't touch me," she said at last. "That's a good start."

"You need touching, Hannah. You need somebody to hold you and help you through this. You're a prisoner of your own resolve."

She wondered if her longing had showed, even momentarily, on her face. She shook her head. "The news will be coming on."

"I'll remember what you've said." He turned away to

pour the wine. She watched him a moment, torn between apology and thanks. Then she picked up their plates and left him standing alone.

Late in the broadcast the local news had a brief account of Jolie's disappearance, newsworthy primarily because the Port Franklin police hinted that they suspected foul play.

"The FBI isn't involved yet, or they would say so," Quinn said tersely. "The Port Franklin cops are stonewalling."

A recent photo of Jolie flashed on the screen, then one of Hannah playing with her daughter. Hannah assessed her own image, the denim shorts and Lakeside Landscapes T-shirt, the long braid hanging over her shoulder. She thought her face was unremarkable, oval and plain featured, but the way she presented herself was less so. When the news anchor moved on to other stories, the picture that was left in Hannah's mind was of a tall, outdoorsy woman who could not be bothered with feminine wiles or cutting her hair.

Quinn used the remote to switch off the set. "If the station thought this was just another parental kidnapping, they probably wouldn't bother to cover the story."

Anger rose inside her. "It's not newsworthy enough when a mother loses a daughter?"

"It happens more than you think. The numbers on abductions vary wildly, depending on which agency's doing the reporting. But the biggest percentage is committed by parents. Estranged fathers and mothers try to settle old scores and get even for past hurts, or sometimes they're genuinely worried about their kids. It's common enough that it's not news. But the station *did* report this one. Jolie's picture was shown. Someone might spot her with Marshall, and if they're showing the photo on television, it will be in the local papers, too."

"Somebody might spot me, too. And if Marshall sees the publicity, he might try harder to hide Jolie."

"Or he might see the story and call somebody to let them know Jolie is all right."

"He won't. This is Marsh's dream come true. He has Jolie and I'm suspected of—" She couldn't even say it.

"How likely is it that Tony Chandler is in on the whole thing? Could he have helped Marshall? Could he be stalling so that Marshall can get away?"

She'd been agonizing over the same question. Now she told him her conclusion. "I don't think Tony knows anything for sure, except maybe where Marsh has been living. If it ever came out that the two of them were in on this together, he'd lose his job, and Tony's bucking to be police chief someday."

"So, at the worst he knows where Marsh has been living, and suspects Marsh kidnapped her?"

"He probably *knows* that's what happened, just because he knows how Marsh operates. I think he's digging up my lawn because he wants Marsh to get away. And if he's trying to keep the FBI at arm's length, it's because of that. Or because he wants to make a name for himself in Port Franklin without their help."

"We have one vindictive cop heading the investigation, one ex-husband seeking revenge, a newsworthy kidnapping and a mother on the run—"

"With a stranger," she added.

"On the run with a stranger, although hopefully no one has figured that out. This is real tabloid stuff. Somebody's going to get hold of it and take it national."

"And then Jolie's picture will be all over the country." She fell silent, wishing as she had so many times since that morning that she could just go back one day into the past. She would not leave the house to check the sprinklers. She would insist Jolie sleep with her, in her room, in her bed, with the dogs on the floor beside them.

As if he knew she was thinking about him, Oliver got up from his place beside the family room hearth and came over to rest his head in her lap. She stroked his shiny black fur as she struggled for equilibrium.

Quinn rose and gathered their plates and wineglasses, even though Oliver growled when Quinn got too close. Hannah had barely made a dent in her pasta, but at least what she'd eaten was still cuddling up to the knot in her stomach.

"How about if I get a notepad and we start putting together a profile on your ex?" Quinn gazed down at her. "Can you handle that?"

"How much of a difference will wearing Diane Everest's clothes make in my appearance?"

Quinn didn't seem surprised at the change of subject. "It's better than nothing."

"By tomorrow my photo will be in the papers, too, won't it?"

"Most likely."

"That's what I thought." She stood, pushing Oliver away. "You get the notepad, I'll find some scissors. I'm going to get rid of this braid."

He looked pained. "You're sure?"

"I don't have a choice. I can't look like me or we'll get caught."

"Then let me do it. At least I can see what I'm doing."

"Can you do a credible job?"

"My grandfather was a barber. I worked in the shop with him."

"I don't need a crew cut."

He grimaced. "You're in luck. I'd need clippers."

While Quinn was searching for paper Hannah tried the downstairs bathroom, then progressed to the one off the

master bedroom. She found scissors, along with a comb
and brush and some hairpins. She spared a moment to look
at herself and saw a pale woman with a sprinkling of freck-
les that stood out in sharp relief. Even braided, her wheat-
blond hair fell past the center of her back. She had let it
grow because she simply hadn't had the time to do anything
else with it. But secretly, she had enjoyed the weight and
feel of it, the feminine luxury.

Everything was changing, even this.

She found Quinn in the kitchen. He had pulled a stool
from the island and set it in the middle of the floor. "We
could just buy more hats," he said. He sounded hopeful.

"I'd be conspicuous." She perched on the stool and
wrapped the towel she'd brought from the bathroom around
her shoulders. "Let's just do it, okay?"

"How short?"

"I don't care. Just make me look as different as you
can."

She had expected him to just slice off the braid and go
from there. Instead he unwrapped the rubber band that held
the ends in place and began slowly to separate the strands,
running his fingers along each section as he loosened it.

When it was undone he smoothed it over her shoulders,
than he picked up the hairbrush. She was surprised at how
gentle his touch had been, and how warmly his hands had
lingered. "You haven't changed your mind about cutting
it, have you?" she said.

"I'm just trying to get to know your hair."

"Is that necessary?"

"You're talking to an artist here."

"Just cut it, Quinn."

"Just be quiet and let me work."

She really had little choice. She could chop it off herself,
but that's exactly how it would look. "Put a bowl over my
head if you need inspiration."

"Why don't you tell me about your husband?"

He was brushing her hair now, slow even strokes all the way to the ends. Despite her best efforts, the intimacy was seeping past her defenses. "I thought you were going to write this down."

"I'll remember what you say until I can."

"What do you want to know?"

"Tell me how you met."

"We didn't, not that I remember. I grew up with Marsh. We went to the same church, had the same friends, took naps beside each other in nursery school."

He continued to brush her hair. "You knew him that well?"

"Haven't you untangled my hair yet?"

"Give me a break. I've wanted to do this every since I first saw you."

Despite herself she felt warmed by his words. "Just cut it. This isn't play time."

"I'll get it done, Hannah. Just concentrate on your story." He adjusted the towel around her shoulders, tucking it into the neck of her shirt. His hands seemed to rest against her skin for too many seconds, but how could she complain? He was doing her a favor.

He picked up a comb and began to part her hair. She closed her eyes when the teeth grazed her forehead. "I didn't know Marsh well enough, I guess. That's the problem with knowing somebody forever. You don't ask the questions you might if they were strangers. I told you he was an artist. He used to draw pictures of me in grade school, and I felt like a movie star. He made me look…beautiful."

"How hard could that be?"

Her eyes flew open. "Does flattery always come this easily to you?"

"When it's deserved."

"I'm not beautiful, but Marsh made me feel like I was. Then he joined the football team in high school, and he turned into a star. He could have had any girl, but he chose me, and that made me feel special. I never even looked at another guy. My parents wanted me to date other people, but even after I went away to college, I didn't. I came home on weekends to be with him."

He picked up the scissors. "What was he like back then?"

Despite herself, she winced when she heard the first snip.

He put his hand on her shoulder, as if he'd seen her reaction. "Trust me, I'll do a good job."

"You're a broken record, Quinn. Trust me. Trust me."

"And you're a bundle of misgivings. Tell me about Marshall."

She had tried so hard to put Marsh out of her life that for a moment she couldn't summon his image. "He's a big man. Your height but heavier. He's a linebacker with an artist's hands. What's left of his hair is light brown and curly."

He drew the comb through her hair and she heard another snip. "That's where Jolie gets her curls. Your hair's as straight as a board."

"You would know."

He snipped again. "You've told me what he looks like. How did he act? I picture a blowhard, moody, sensitive to anything that sounds like criticism, quick to anger, quick to apologize."

"Were you following us around?"

"Then I'm right?"

A sheaf of hair fell to the floor. Her heart fell with it. "You're going to leave some, aren't you?"

"More than you expect." He punctuated his words with another snip, then another. A foot of hair fell to the floor.

She could feel the pasta tangling with the knot in her stomach. "Go on," he said. "Take your mind off the scissors."

"Marsh was always moody, but he never got in fights, like some of the guys. He pushed me once when we were dating and he'd become angry, but he never hit me or even threatened to. He had a temper, but most of the time he kept it under control. He did stupid things to get even with people, but never anything violent."

He rested his fingertips under her chin and lifted it. She opened her eyes and stared into his. "Are you almost finished?"

He smiled. "Why, are you going somewhere?"

They stared at each other for a moment. She was aware how silly she must look, her hair half gone, her cheeks dusted with snippets. He didn't seem to think she looked silly, though. His gaze was warm. Then he lifted his hand and brushed his fingertips under her eyes to smooth away the wisps of hair. "What kind of things did he do to get even?"

She closed her eyes at his touch. "He let the air out of a teacher's tires when he thought he deserved a better grade. Once Marsh poured honey inside Tony's locker, then blamed it on me. The problem is he never grew up. He took the same attitude into police work. He went from letting air out of tires to giving tickets to people he didn't like, getting rough with suspects, that sort of thing. The problem was, some of his colleagues thought that made him more of a man."

She realized how much she had said and how quickly. She was trying to drown out the sound of the scissors, which were working faster now. "You're still not finished?"

"You had a lot of hair, Hannah."

Had being the operative word, she supposed. She sighed. "Not anymore, huh?"

"You'll like it." He moved around in front of her. "Close your eyes."

"Why?"

"Because I'm going to be very close to them."

She flinched and squeezed her eyes shut.

"He must have had some good qualities," Quinn said. "What did you see in him?"

He was combing her hair over her forehead again, parting and combing, then snipping. Endlessly snipping. She remembered now why she had grown her hair so long. She had always hated these moments in a stylist's chair. The suspense, the horror.

"I thought he was strong," she said through clenched teeth. "I thought moodiness was the same thing as sensitivity. I thought being loved by a man with talent like his was a great honor." She paused. "I was too young to understand what was in store."

"You said before that he went to the police academy to please his parents?"

"His dad's ex-Navy. Walt hunts or fishes every weekend and thrives on television wrestling. Marsh was a huge disappointment to him. Even star status on the football team wasn't enough for his father. He used to call Marsh a sissy because he liked to draw." She paused. "Quinn, aren't you done yet?"

His laughter rumbled close to her face. "Nearly."

"I'm glad you see the humor in this."

He was close enough that she could feel heat from his body and smell the faintest tinge of a musky aftershave. "I'd say for a woman who claims to have no vanity, you're pretty nervous about this."

"I'd shave my head in an instant if I thought it would help bring back Jolie."

"Luckily, that's not necessary." He moved away.

She opened her eyes and watched his face. "Well?"

"Nope. Not finished."

"You'll even out one side, then the other, then back to the other one and pretty soon there won't be anything left, right?"

He grinned. "How did you know?"

She closed her eyes again. "Get it over with, then."

"When did he change, Hannah?"

The comb grazed her scalp again. She sighed. "When he became a cop. He hit me the first time while he was at the academy. He'd been out drinking late with his class. He came home, I'd made chicken for supper and there wasn't enough dark meat to suit him. So he sent me sprawling across the kitchen floor."

His hand stilled. She felt his fingers clench, then after a moment they relaxed. "What did you do?"

"Went to Amanda's for the night, but I went back to Marsh the next day after he promised he would never hit me again. For a while he was fine. Then he slammed me against a wall and knocked me out. That time he thought I'd worked too late landscaping the courthouse. I stayed with Amanda for a week, then Marsh agreed to go into counseling. He only went once, but by then I was back home. The next week I found out I was pregnant. It wasn't planned, and he wasn't happy. But for the most part he kept his fists to himself."

"For the most part?"

She heard the anger in his voice. "If he *had* hit me again, I would have left him. He shoved me around a little, but I knew he was under a lot of stress with the baby coming, so I forgave him. I was a disgrace to women everywhere."

"You were trying to make your marriage work."

"There's no reason for a man to hit a woman. No excuse is good enough. We should teach it in our schools."

He rested his hand on her shoulder. She opened her eyes. "I don't need sympathy," she said.

"You have it, anyway."

"After Jolie was born, Marsh changed for the worse. When he wasn't at work, he was drinking. When he wasn't drinking, he was sleeping it off. When he wasn't sleeping it off, he was pushing me around. One night I confronted him."

"You don't have to go on."

"You asked about Marsh. Well, here's his defining moment. I put Jolie to bed for the night. She was just under a year by then. Then I told Marsh I wanted out. I thought he'd probably be glad, but he went berserk. He slammed me against the refrigerator, then threw me to the floor. Blessedly I don't remember much of what happened after that. But Amanda came to check on me later that night. I'd promised her I'd call after I told Marsh he had to leave. She found me unconscious and Jolie screaming in her crib. Marsh was gone."

He brushed a strand of hair off her cheek. His eyes were sad. "And after all that, he got off scot-free?"

"No, he lost his job, his home, his daughter, his hometown. It was enough for me. I just wanted him gone." She nudged his hand away. "Are you done?"

"I think so. You don't look at all the same. That was our plan."

Her hand went to her hair. Alarmed, she felt the short strands lying against her cheeks and forehead. Her hands followed the back of her hair to her shoulders, then just beyond.

He laughed softly at something he saw in her expression. Relief, she supposed. "I told you there would be some left."

"You're sure this is short enough?"

"You always wore it pulled back, so your face was completely exposed. Now it isn't. Go see." He slipped his fingers inside the neck of her shirt, slowly releasing the towel and wrapping it around the bits of hair clinging to it.

She stood, brushing off her legs and arms. "I'd better wait until I see what you've done to say thanks."

"I'll pour you another glass of wine."

She looked up to refuse, and saw his expression. He was looking at her with something mysterious in his eyes, something as vibrantly sexual as a kiss. Her breath caught. She had submitted to the intimacy of Quinn cutting her hair and probing her memories, because she'd had to. Now she realized exactly how things had changed. They had crossed the boundary from acquaintances to something she didn't want to name. His fingers had lingered against her skin; now his sympathy and concern lingered in her heart.

"You are beautiful," he said huskily. "More beautiful because it doesn't matter to you."

She supposed maybe it did matter to her, because his words touched the sadness inside her and momentarily warmed her. "Thanks for helping me, Quinn."

He smiled. "We'll find her, Hannah. Just have faith. Because we aren't going to quit looking until we do."

Chapter 7

Just after dawn Quinn stood in the Everests' living room and gazed at the new Hannah Blackstone.

She had bangs now, soft, wispy bangs that grazed her eyebrows. He had angled the sides of her hair so it framed her face and fell just below her shoulders. It changed her looks in the way that a shorter, more severe cut might not have. And the sophisticated curve suited Diane Everest's clothes.

"Everything fit?" He admired the peach-colored blouse and the darker skirt of the same color that Hannah had chosen from Diane's closet.

She tugged at the skirt, which ended inches above her knees. "I can't even remember the last time I wore a dress."

"Good. Then this really is a change."

"The shoes are too tight. I'm only wearing them because my sneakers would give me away. I'll need to stop for some new ones."

"Do you have money?"

"A credit card."

He shook his head. "Don't use it, Hannah. And you'd better not use your ATM card. If the police are searching for you, that's all they'll need."

She looked stricken. "Then I can't cash a check, either."

"I can. They aren't looking for me. You can pay me back."

"I can't take your money."

He grinned. "Nor will I let you."

She relaxed a little. "I'll write you a check. You can cash it the minute this is over."

"Did you get any sleep last night?"

She hesitated, then she shook her head. "Not much."

He knew better than to pity her. "Maybe you can sleep in the van."

"You're ready?"

He hadn't slept well, either. The middle of the night had never been a good time for him. For hours he had tossed and turned and worried alternately about Jolie and Jolie's mother. The armor of objectivity he had worn as a journalist had rusted through.

He searched his pocket for keys. "I'm ready. Shall we pick up something for breakfast?"

"I can't..." She grimaced as he shook his head. "Stop if you want."

"The dogs are ready?"

"When I buy shoes I have to buy dog food. They weren't all that happy last night with oatmeal and evaporated milk."

"Really? I thought they loved it."

"You don't know much about dogs, do you?"

"Even less than I know about kids."

She gave a sharp whistle, and both dogs came tearing in from the family room. Fagan—Quinn had learned which

was which—stopped suspiciously just a few feet from
Quinn and bared his teeth in a growl. Hannah called him
to her side.

"How do I make friends with them, oh, great dog psy-
chologist?" he asked.

"Well, they're probably reacting to the way you look at
me."

"They can read minds?"

Her expression softened. "Let's just say they aren't used
to having strange men around. Other than my workers and
a few old friends, Marsh is the only man they trust. I have
to keep them in the house on workdays."

"If they trust Marsh, they don't have much sense."

"But more loyalty than any human being."

"If they thought you were under threat, what would they
do?"

"I think if they'd been in the house the night Marsh beat
me, things would have been very different." She squatted
to hug them both, one under each arm. Quinn tried not to
notice how much leg and thigh her skirt exposed in that
position.

They locked up the house and left the key in the mailbox.
In the van they settled into their places. "I'll stop for break-
fast, but if you're asleep, I'll save something for you. Shall
I make up to the dogs for the cereal?"

"You're trying to worm your way into their good
graces."

"Damn right."

Hannah reclined her seat and closed her eyes. He
doubted she would sleep, but at least she was resting.

About an hour out of Cleveland he stopped for a fast-
food breakfast and fed the dogs most of a sausage biscuit
as attack insurance. By the time he'd broken off the last
bite for Fagan, he could swear they were smiling at him.
Hannah didn't even open her eyes.

Back on the road she stirred, then sat up and stretched. For a moment she didn't seem to know where she was or why. He glanced at her and watched realization dawn. "I dreamed Jolie and I were making cookies, but we couldn't find the flour. We went through the house searching. We had just reached the den, and I knew we were going to find it behind a cupboard door."

"That's a good dream. You're hopeful we'll find her."

"Is that what it means?"

"It's highly possible we'll find the place where Marshall has been living today."

She cleared her throat. "But not Jolie."

He didn't want to get her hopes up, but he couldn't let that pass. "You know, it is possible Marshall has taken her back home with him. If he just wants to scare you, then it might be the kind of thing he would do."

"You think he took her just to show he could?"

"He sounds like a man who gets a thrill out of revenge but none from taking responsibility. He knows you'll track him, so he won't make it easy. But maybe he won't make it impossible, either." He lifted the sack with her breakfast in it and handed it to her. "The coffee's hot. Drive throughs have been sued for less."

She took it, and he heard the scrape of plastic foam as she lifted off the top. She drank it black, he noted, just the way he did.

The terrain got progressively more rural and the flat landscape undulated into hills. They were off the interstate, passing farms with picturesque fields and clotheslines hung with wash. The sky had lightened gradually until now, the sun blessed pastures and newly sprouting fields of corn.

"Last night we didn't spend much time on your ex-husband's hobbies," Quinn said. "I can't imagine security guards are in demand here. Any other thoughts about how he might support or entertain himself?"

"He liked videos."

"Good. There can't be too many rental stores in a town this size. What else?"

"I'm trying, but I can't think of anything."

"Did he play sports after high school? Softball? Soccer?"

"He was on a bowling league for a little while, just a few months filling in for a friend who injured a knee."

"That's something. How about his art? Did he paint, draw, sculpt?"

"Mostly he drew. Charcoal, pastels, ink."

"You say he's too unsteady to draw now?"

"It's been six months since he visited Jolie." She paused. "No, nearly eight."

"So he might have sobered up?"

She gave a humorless laugh. "Only if he was locked away."

"That's always a possibility."

"Won't that show up in a record search?"

"It should, if Jake's thorough." Quinn planned to call him as soon as they stopped.

They were silent until they reached the city limits. They entered town on a narrow road lined with Victorian and Colonial houses. The downtown was picturesque, a slice of Mid-America that hadn't been spoiled by shopping malls and housing developments. Quinn pulled into the first gas station they found. "I'll get directions."

He tried Jake but only got voice mail. Hannah was perched on the edge of her seat when he returned. He could almost read the question in her golden-brown eyes. "We're not far," he said.

She settled back and fastened her seat belt as he pulled onto the road. He followed the directions he'd been given to a quiet side street shaded by century-old trees. He slowed and read numbers. "There it is," Hannah said. "The big brick house on the other side of the street."

The house in question was large and Gothic in style. From the street it looked as if it had been divided into apartments. "The envelope didn't have an apartment number," he said.

"We'll just knock and ask someone."

Silently he debated who should make the inquiries, but in the end, he knew it wasn't his choice. Hannah had done what she could to disguise herself. The game plan was up to her.

"Shall we go together?" she asked.

"If you think that's best."

"Okay. Then we can split up if we have to." She told the dogs to stay and opened the windows to give them air. "Okay, let's do it."

On the trip up the walk he glanced at her. He'd been attracted to the other Hannah, but this more sophisticated version pulled at him in an entirely different way. He wondered if this was the woman she might have been if she hadn't been so determined to keep men at bay. She seemed more vulnerable somehow, and after last night, more approachable.

"Let's start on the ground floor. That looks like the biggest apartment." She nodded to the left.

"What are you going to say?"

"I'm going to tell whoever answers that I'm Marshall's sister."

"Good."

"You're my husband."

"And I didn't even have anything to say about it."

"We're worried about him because the bastard hasn't gotten in touch with his family."

"I wouldn't put it quite that way."

"If they know Marsh at all, nothing I call him will surprise them."

They reached the porch. He heard her take a deep breath. "Show time." She stepped up to the door and punched the doorbell. Then she waited.

Someone was inside. They could hear a slow shuffle that grew subtly louder until at last the door opened. An old woman in vinyl house slippers and a pink bathrobe blinked at them. "S'early," she said. "You come about the apartment?"

"I'm sorry," Hannah said in a warm tone she'd never directed at Quinn. "Please don't tell me we woke you?"

"M'in." The woman opened the door. Her head was covered with a scarf, but metal curlers peeked from beneath it.

They moved inside. The apartment was musty and overly warm, even though the weather outside was pleasant.

"S'down." The woman shuffled off to an old-fashioned parlor, furnished with an ornate velvet love seat and glass lamps with fringed silk shades. She gestured for them to sit, and they took the love seat. She left the room and returned with a pot of coffee and a tray of cups.

Hannah smiled her thanks. "How nice of you. We'd love some."

She waited until the woman had set cups in front of them and seated herself in a rocker.

"My name is Hannah," Hannah said, "and this is my husband Quinn. We're looking for my brother Marshall Blackstone. Marsh lost touch with the family, and we're very worried about him. We're trying to trace him."

The sweet, friendly voice seemed to belong to someone else, but it went well with the hair and clothes. Quinn filed his approval away for another moment.

"Marshall?" the old woman intoned.

"That's right." Hannah took up her cup, as if they had all the time in the world.

"S'gone. Has been a long time."

Quinn couldn't look at Hannah. This was what they had expected, but he wished it had turned out differently. "I'm sorry to hear that," he said, giving Hannah a moment to recover. "We need to find him."

The woman didn't look convinced.

"There's illness in the family," Quinn said, lowering his voice. "We'd like to find him soon."

The woman shook her head slowly, with at least a trace of sympathy. Her eyes were open wider now, as if she was coming awake. "Can't help you. N'even a forwarding address."

"Can you tell us how long it's been since he left?" Hannah asked.

The woman piled wrinkles on wrinkles, squinting at something beyond them as if she was thinking hard. "January," she said at last. "R'after Christmas."

"And he didn't say where he was going?" Quinn said.

"Didn't talk much. Said he was going and went."

"Mrs...." Quinn waited.

"Kent. Margaret Kent."

"Mrs. Kent, did he ever tell you where he worked while he was here? We might be able to find out where he is, from somebody at his job or a friend...."

"Worked for me. Cleaning, painting. Gave him a room up there." She pointed toward the ceiling. "Money, too. Not much."

"Did he have friends you know of? Somebody who might be able to tell us where he is?"

Mrs. Kent considered, then shook her head.

"Was there a particular bar where he liked to go?" Hannah said. "I'm sorry, but I know my brother drinks."

She shook her head again. "No forwarding address."

She got to her feet. Quinn wasn't finished asking questions, and neither of them had sipped their coffee. But before he could say anything, she left the room. She was gone so long, Quinn thought she might have just expected them to let themselves out, then he heard the shuffling of her slippers again. She came back holding something in her hand.

She extended it to Hannah. "Here. Give this t'him when you find him."

Hannah took the envelope. Quinn looked over her shoulder. It was an official envelope from a city in Pennsylvania, Meadville. It was addressed to Marshall Blackstone.

"They just keep coming," Mrs. Kent said. "Sent the first one back. No forwarding address, I say. Comes another, then another. I stopped returning them. Why should I? Kept them, though. They're official."

The envelope was perforated along the sides for easy removal of the contents. Quinn knew exactly what they'd find when they opened it. "It's a traffic ticket of some sort."

"Take it," Mrs. Kent said. "Scares me, having it."

Quinn knew that the Pennsylvania police weren't planning to stage a raid and arrest the woman, but he was thrilled she'd been intimidated enough to keep Marshall's ticket.

He stood, and Hannah joined him. "Thank you," Hannah said.

Mrs. Kent hobbled to the door and let them out. They thanked her again. "S'not a happy man, your brother," she told Hannah.

"No," Hannah agreed. Halfway down the walk she added under her breath, "And he'll be a heck of a lot unhappier when I finish with him."

The van was still at the service station when Hannah exited the video store, where she had gone to ask about

Marshall while Quinn investigated the traffic ticket. The manager had remembered Marshall, and he had enthusiastically shared everything he could with Hannah. The enthusiasm had dimmed when she mentioned Quinn, her husband. "You're not wearing a ring," he'd said with disappointment.

"My fingers swell in the heat." She had thanked him for his time and left to find Quinn.

He was still at the pay phone talking either to a reporter friend in Pittsburgh or to Jake, one hand over his ear to block out traffic noise. She went inside and bought cold soft drinks, and he was off the telephone by the time she returned.

"Jake hasn't discovered anything useful so far. It looks like your ex was doing a good job of not leaving a paper trail in Ohio. Or he left the state for good."

Disappointment was just another assault on her heart. Her hands tightened around the soft drink cans. "The manager of the video store remembered him as a nice enough guy who was always bringing videos back late."

"Nothing else?"

"Marsh left town with three cop movies in his possession. Nobody knows where he went."

The traffic ticket had been issued in March. Marshall had been driving with an Ohio license and tags. And either he had been trying to hide his real address or hadn't had one. He had turned right from a left-turn lane, but more important, he had left a trail for them to follow.

"So now we go to Meadville," Hannah said.

"Not quite yet. Gary, the Pittsburgh friend, knows a cop in Meadville. He called him while I was talking to Jake. I've got to call him back now and see if he found anything."

She was fast getting used to Quinn's help. She had really believed that she could do everything on her own, that she never needed another person in her life again. Since the divorce she had even kept her girlfriends at arm's length, preferring not to accept help even when she was sick or overwhelmed with responsibility. But now she knew how foolish she had been. She was not that strong. She needed people she could trust.

And right now she really needed Quinn McDermott.

She watched him make the call and begin his conversation. From their first meeting she had noticed Quinn's easy confidence. He wasn't cocky, like Tony, or belligerent, like Marsh. He was a man who knew what he wanted and the best way to get it. She wondered why he had never married and had children of his own.

She wondered who he was deep inside. And what had made him that way.

Quinn hung up the phone and turned to her. "Our boy just can't stay out of trouble."

"What, Quinn?"

"He was picked up after a barroom brawl in a place called Cambridge Springs. He spent the night in the drunk tank and they let him go. But there's an address."

"Is he still living there?"

"Well, your friend Tony Chandler could have sent the local cops to find out. Unfortunately you and I don't have that kind of clout."

"But there's an address."

"An address as of the end of March. And it's about a two- or three-hour drive from here. Are you ready?"

Hope charged through her. She felt herself reach out and clasp his hand. She looked down and saw that he was squeezing it gently. She was surprised at her own action, and almost more surprised that he didn't comment. He just squeezed her hand once more before he dropped it.

"There's a shopping center at the end of that street—

let's buy shoes that don't pinch your feet. It's going to be a long morning.''

Cambridge Springs was a picturesque small town in the heart of the western Pennsylvania snow belt. Marshall had only lived there one month before he moved on.

Quinn and Hannah moved on in less than an hour.

"He's choosing small towns. It's his biggest mistake. People remember him.'' Quinn got back in the van, after a conversation with the caretaker of the motel unit where Marsh had been staying.

Hannah was already perusing the map. Again, Marsh hadn't left a forwarding address. But he had told the caretaker he was going to West Virginia to visit a high school friend.

"He had a buddy, Bob Jenkins, who moved to Wheeling a couple of years ago,'' Hannah said. "That has to be the friend he was talking about.''

"You didn't think of this Jenkins before?''

"No, I didn't know they'd kept in touch. Bob was kind of a quiet guy, and Marsh changed so much, they didn't have anything in common.''

"It could be somebody else, or he could have been lying,'' Quinn warned.

"No, I think it probably is Bob. He's exactly the kind of guy who would give an old friend a place to stay. This makes sense.''

"Can you call him, Hannah?''

She considered. "I could, but would he tell me the truth on the telephone?''

"It'll be night by the time we arrive. We won't be able to check this out until the morning.''

"Don't you know anybody in West Virginia?''

He gave a half smile. "Sorry. It's a long way from New

York. I can try the local paper and ask them to look through their morgue. But if he's trying to lay low…''

"Maybe he got into another brawl.''

"If we don't find him with Jenkins, we'll use whatever resources we have.''

Another night without Jolie. She couldn't imagine it. Her eyes filled with tears. "She's getting farther away. They could be out West by now. Marsh could have taken her out of the country.''

"Hannah, miles are just miles. He's careless. He'll leave a trail, and we'll follow it, whether it leads to California or Kathmandu. You've got to remember that he doesn't really want her. He wants you to find him.''

She didn't know whether she believed it, but she was more grateful than she could say for Quinn's encouragement. She realized that she was beginning to count on it— and on him—and even though that frightened her, she knew better than to push him away.

Because she needed anything Quinn McDermott had to offer.

Chapter 8

The night sky was veiled in storm clouds by the time they arrived in Wheeling. Quinn, who had driven too many miles, had a headache the size of West Virginia's mountains, with the same jagged peaks and valleys. Headaches were a relatively new development in his life, an early-warning sign of the hazards of stress. He hadn't had one in a month, but he supposed the onset of this beauty was no mystery. It had begun just after he promised Hannah they would find her daughter. It wasn't the first time he'd made a similar promise.

Mrs. Whithurst, you've got to have faith that the police will find Jeffrey in time. You've got to stay strong.

Hannah was unusually silent and had been for the past hour. They had stopped to stretch several times, and she had taken the wheel once to give him a rest. But since that diversion, she'd said little.

"We'll need to get rooms for the night," Quinn told her.

"I want to find Bob's house first."

"If we check into a motel we can use the telephone to locate him and get some directions from the clerk. But I'm beat. I'm going to have to take a break before we go any farther."

He expected an argument—and wouldn't have blamed her for insisting. But she surprised him. "Just choose someplace cheap, please. My debt to you is growing."

"I know you're good for it, Hannah. You can always work it off."

She made a noise that didn't need further explanation.

"I'm talking about landscaping," he said. "Unless you have something better in mind?"

She surprised him again. "Well, if Marsh's opinion in that area meant anything, I'd be in debt for the rest of my life."

"Are we talking about the same thing?"

"I suspect."

He was silent a moment, trying to process that. "Let me get this straight. Your abusive ex-husband told you that you weren't…" He was in too much pain to find a gentle way to phrase it.

"Worth a nickel in bed? Yes, that's what I'm saying."

"And you believed him?"

"Forget it. We were both trying to be funny. I must be tired to be talking about this with you."

She must be brimming over with doubts and fears. This was so unlike Hannah that for a moment he faltered. Then he exploded. "Damn it, did you believe him?"

"Quinn, it was a joke. A pathetic attempt at humor. You know, it's better to laugh than cry?"

"You did believe him."

"The truth is, I don't care. It's not my job to please a man. Whether I could or did is irrelevant."

"You know, there are men out there who would like to

please you. Not because it's their job, because it would be an honor.''

"Honor?''

He scowled. "I speak with a certain amount of personal knowledge.''

"You're saying you would find it an honor to give me pleasure?'' She sounded incredulous. "That sounds like I'm some sort of charity case.''

He pulled into the parking lot of a two-story brick motel complex that looked clean and inexpensive. Planters in front of each unit were filled with riotous red geraniums, and the concrete walk had been swept clean. He parked before he turned to her.

"Charity begins at home. Don't you get it? Giving a woman pleasure gives any man in his right mind pleasure, too. Sex is a mutual thing. What makes one person feel good makes the other feel good, too.''

"Sex 101? I was a married woman, remember?''

"You remember too clearly.''

She had a blonde's complexion, and he watched her cheeks warm with color. "I don't know how this came up.''

"Neither do I. But since it has, try this on for size. I think you're one of the sexiest women I've ever known. And last night while I was cutting your hair, I had one hell of a time not touching more of you, because the parts I did touch felt wonderful.''

"For your sake, I'm glad you controlled yourself.''

"Hannah, no one could ever convince me that making love to you wouldn't be the best experience of my life. And when Jolie's safe at home in Port Franklin, I intend to convince you it might be one of the best of yours.''

"Jolie's not safe at home, and your ego knows no bounds.''

"She will be. And when she is, sex won't be payment

for anything. I hope it'll be a celebration." He tore his gaze from hers and opened his door. "I'll get rooms."

Inside he asked for adjoining rooms in the back of the building and got them. Hannah was composed when he returned, as if they hadn't just catapulted their relationship into an entirely new direction. They parked in front of their rooms and unpacked. The accommodations were plain but neat, and there were telephone directories in each room.

Hannah flopped down on her bed as Quinn waited in the doorway. As he expected, she immediately thumbed through the phone book and scanned the listings. "Two Robert Jenkins," she said. "Now, how do I figure out which it is?"

He was glad she was consulting him, as if nothing else had happened. "Will you recognize his voice?"

"I might."

"You can always pretend you're from your high school alumni committee collecting addresses for a class reunion."

"That came easily to you. You've used that before, haven't you?"

"I told you, reporters aren't always honest."

She was already dialing the first number. He watched as she asked for Robert Jenkins then grew silent. "I'm sorry," she said politely, after a moment. "I have the wrong number." She listened a moment more, said her thank-yous and hung up. "No go. That Bob Jenkins is about eighty."

Quinn's head felt as if it were about to blow off his shoulders. "Try the other one."

"I didn't think of it before, but what if Marsh answers? He'll know my voice."

"Not mine." He held out his hand for the receiver. "Dial."

She did. A young woman answered on the fifth ring. He asked for Bob Jenkins, then listened to her explanation.

"I'm sorry," he said. "I'd forgotten. Thanks." He hung up.

"What?" Hannah said.

"It was a woman, and Bob Jenkins is her father-in-law. He's out of town at a Shriner's Convention."

She looked stricken. "But those were the only two in the book."

"Start at the beginning of the listing. Spell it every way you can think of. Look for Bob, Robert, R., B., Bobby, Robby."

Her hair fell forward and hid her face as she searched, then it swung back and forth as she shook her head. "Nothing. I'll try directory assistance." She did, asking for listings for all the possible permutations of Bob Jenkins and for a listing for Marshall as well. She looked defeated when she hung up. "Nothing. There's an R. Jenkins, but that number's unlisted."

Quinn's head was throbbing so hard he could barely think. "If he has a roommate or girlfriend the phone might be listed under their names. Or maybe his home and business number are the same. What does he do?"

"I don't know. I don't even remember why he left Port Frank. I just know he came here."

Quinn realized they should have called directory assistance first to make sure that Jenkins was living in Wheeling. "At least we know Marshall headed to West Virginia in April. Maybe we're in the right state at least."

"Amanda will know where to find Bob." She looked up. "She keeps track of people. She's a nurturer. Plants, pets, everybody she's ever met. If she doesn't have Bob's address, at least she'll know what he's doing and why he's here."

"Good. Call her. Let me know what you discover."

"Quinn, are you all right?"

He had a prescription at home that would have knocked

out the headache. But home was one state away. He grimaced. "Just a headache. I'm going to lie down for a few
minutes." He crossed in front of Fagan, who bared his
teeth—proving that one sausage biscuit did not guarantee
loyalty.

"Unlock your side." She gestured to the connecting door
that separated their rooms. "I'll unlock mine. That way I
can check on you when I'm done."

He supposed it was a good sign that she trusted him
enough not to barricade herself. "If I'm asleep just
wake—"

"I'll take care of things. Get some rest."

He didn't have the strength to argue.

Hannah hung up after her conversation with Amanda.
She fed the dogs and washed her face before she went to
find Quinn. A knock on the interior door didn't rouse him,
so she opened it and peeked in his room. In the glow of a
light from the parking lot she saw that he was lying facedown on the bedspread. And he didn't twitch when she
crossed to check on him.

"Just a headache," she said softly. Sympathy tugged at
her, and she considered her options, all of which began with
tiptoeing back to her room.

An hour later she knocked on the door once more, and
this time she heard a mumbled "Come in."

She did, to find him sitting up in bed. He snapped on a
lamp, then winced at the sudden glare.

"I've got the strongest painkillers the drugstore would
sell me and a pepperoni pizza hot from the oven."

He blinked at her. She watched him putting his brain
back together in reluctant stages. Finally he said, "Don't
tell me you hot-wired the van?"

"You threw the keys on the dresser before you conked
out."

He ran his hand through his hair, and she watched it slide back over his forehead the moment his hand fell to his side. "I didn't expect to sleep so long."

"You don't have anything to be sorry about. It's a killer headache, isn't it?"

He shrugged. "I wish it were."

She whistled softly. "I've set up the pizza in my room. Do you think you can eat something?"

"What did you find out from Amanda?"

"Bob's here all right, and he's managing a pizza franchise."

Despite the headache he seemed to put two and two together. "The one you went to?"

"No, but it's a branch. And they told me which location Bob manages. I drove by, but I didn't see him inside. I'm going to call now and see when he's expected."

"I'll be up in a minute."

She disappeared, then reappeared with a glass of water. She handed it to him and took a bottle out of her pocket. "My treat."

He opened it and shook out a couple of tablets. "This should help. Thanks."

"Why didn't you say something earlier, Quinn?"

"You have enough on your mind."

She couldn't remember a time when a man had put her first. Quinn had been worried about *her*. The experience was undeniably seductive. "That was nice of you," she said softly. She touched his forehead, pushing his hair off it with one deft motion. "Next time, though, remember I'm a big girl. I would have been happy to stop at a drugstore before it got this bad."

He gave a half smile, obviously an effort under the circumstances. "I hope to avoid a next time."

She rested the backs of her fingers against his cheek in consolation, then left him to finish waking up.

* * *

By the time Quinn walked through the door, Hannah had scooped the pizza onto paper plates and poured canned cola into glasses filled with ice. He noticed she had kept the lights low, too, and he was grateful.

"You're moving. That's a good sign."

"Keep me informed of my progress." He lowered himself to the only chair in the room.

She served him, then took her slice back to the bed, sitting cross-legged at the end.

"Did you find out when Jenkins will be in?" he asked.

"There's a staff meeting at ten tomorrow morning. I asked for his phone number, but they said they couldn't give it to me."

"We should intercept him in the parking lot. What else did Amanda tell you?"

"You're sure you feel good enough to listen?"

He nodded, which under the circumstances seemed like a small victory. His head did not roll off his shoulders.

"Amanda says that Bob had a serious drinking problem, and he got fired from a white-collar job in Port Franklin. He came here because an uncle offered him a position manning telephones at his pizza shop. That was two years ago, and now he's the manager."

"So either he got a handle on his problem, or he hides it better."

"Amanda was surprised Marsh knew where to find Bob."

"Are you?"

"No. Don't you see? Before Bob left town they were probably drinking buddies. I never went to bars with Marsh, so I wouldn't have known."

"It seems possible."

"The trick now will be to get Bob to talk to me."

"If he refuses, we'll follow him home and talk to his

neighbors. Somebody will remember your ex. What did Amanda say about the investigation?''

Hannah looked away. "They're dragging the lake in front of my house.''

Quinn's response was profane and to the point. "Are they also looking for Marshall?''

"Faye came by again to question her. Amanda tried to find out what's happening, but Faye didn't tell her much. Just that they still want to question me. Nothing about my pushing Tony.''

"Did Amanda ask her directly about Marshall?''

"Faye said that the police have filed reports with all the appropriate agencies and missing children's clearing houses and that, in the course of the investigation, someone in authority will be questioning everybody with connections to Jolie.''

"Police mumbo-jumbo.''

"Mandy thinks Faye is simply doing what she's told right now. She's one of the few women on the force and making her way through a good-old-boy jungle. She has to step carefully, but Mandy thinks she'll be a help when we really need her.''

Quinn filed that away in his aching head. So far the pain-killers had dulled the throbbing just enough to allow an occasional thought to slip through.

"Quinn, try to eat something,'' Hannah said. "It might help.''

He gave a wan smile. "That's my line.''

"And a sensible one it is.''

He picked up his plate and stared at cheese melting into paper. He couldn't take a bite.

"Look, this has gone far enough.'' Hannah got to her feet and removed the plate from his hands. "Get up a min-ute.''

He was on automatic pilot; he did what he was told. She dragged the chair to the middle of the floor. "Sit."

He did. She came to stand behind him and rested her hands on his shoulders, positioning her thumbs at the apex of his spine. "No wonder you have a headache, you're one big muscle spasm."

"You don't have to do that."

"Good. Requirements are a turnoff."

He closed his eyes as she began to rotate her thumbs. "I must be hard as a rock. That hurts."

"Is it taking your mind off the pain in your head?"

"Uh-huh."

"Good." She increased the pressure just a little. "My father got headaches like this whenever he was under a lot of tension. This was the only thing that really helped him."

He didn't expect miracles, but her hands against his skin were enough of a pleasure to make suffering worthwhile. "Your parents are living?"

"In Arizona."

"Have you told them about Jolie?"

"I called them after you went to bed last night. The police had already called, and so had about half a dozen old friends. They're frantic. They want to fly to Ohio, but I told them to wait until I get back to Port Frank. My father had a mild heart attack last year, and I don't want him under more stress."

"Do they think it was Marshall?"

"Unquestionably. They want to hire a private investigator to find him. I asked them to wait and see how we do, first. It might scare him farther away."

"They sound like good parents."

"You know, Quinn, I'd love to hear about *your* family."

A lightning bolt seemed to split his brain in two. He held his breath a moment and her fingers stilled. "You're tensing up again," she said. "We don't seem to be getting anywhere."

He reminded himself to relax. "Keep trying."

She began to rotate her thumbs again, moving them lower on his spine. "I forgot to mention something else about my conversation with Amanda."

"What's that?"

"She did some checking on you."

He didn't breathe or speak.

Hannah dug her thumbs in harder. "She found out something interesting. Care to guess what it was?"

"Sorry, but I don't have the stamina for guessing games."

"Through the years Tina told several people in town that she was an only child. No sisters, no brothers. Yet you claim to be her nephew."

"This is called kicking a man when he's down."

"This is called getting information."

There were other things Amanda could have discovered that Quinn would have been even unhappier to explain right now. He thanked the universe for small favors. "What do you want to know?"

"Who you are."

He was silent, then: "I'm the man Tina left her house to. Nephew or not, she wanted me to have it."

"I'm trusting you to help me find my daughter. Don't you think I deserve to know your past?" Now she was digging her fingers into his shoulders. Releasing, digging, releasing. "I was close to her. We were friends, but she never mentioned you, never displayed your photograph...."

"She was a stranger to me," he said at last.

"Then why did she leave you her house?"

"Because she was also my mother."

He expected an outburst, instead she continued to knead

his shoulders, and oddly, almost at the moment he said the words, the pain in his head began to recede.

"Why don't you tell me about it?" Hannah said at last. "It's quite a secret to hold inside, isn't it?"

He found the story came easily. "There's not a lot to tell. I was born out of wedlock. Tina was thirty-five when she got pregnant. She had taken a year's leave from teaching and gone to Europe. She had a brief fling in Italy, and I was the prize. She knew that if she kept me, she would lose her job, and teaching was everything to her. That was over thirty years ago, and people in small towns like Port Franklin weren't forgiving of single mothers."

"I'm sure that's true."

"So Tina asked her parents to raise me. I was to be told that my parents had died. My grandparents were very strict, very upright. They agreed, but they told Tina that she was dead to them. She would not be allowed to have any contact with me, and in return, I wouldn't be told anything about her. And that's how the whole thing played out."

Hannah's thumbs moved slower and more gently. "I knew her so well. She was a wonderful woman. I can't believe she abandoned you."

"She didn't leave me in a fast-food rest room, Hannah. She knew I'd be cared for, but I don't think she realized how rigid my grandparents had grown or how intolerant they had become of all human failings. She expected them to relent and let her be my loving 'aunt.' But they never did. Of course, since I didn't know anything about her, when I came of age I didn't look for her. After high school I left home against my grandparents' wishes. They're both alive, but when I call them, they still refuse to speak to me. They don't forgive easily."

"And Tina never got in touch with you?"

"I think Tina was ashamed, not of having me, but of turning me over to her parents. After her death an attorney gave me a letter explaining everything. And that was the first I knew of her. She left me everything she had.''

''Why didn't you tell me this right away?''

He had asked himself the same question, but the answer was finally clear to him. ''Because I was bound by her shame. I couldn't expose her. Not to you, because you were her friend, and not to the people in Port Franklin who might gossip about her.''

''And now?''

''Now Tina's shame is the least of everything, isn't it? You need the truth so you can trust me.''

She was silent so long he thought she wasn't going to answer. ''Hannah?''

''Take off your shirt, Quinn.''

''Excuse me?''

''Take off your shirt. I'll get better leverage. I'm not going to do all this work for nothing. I've seen half-naked men before.''

He crossed his arms and lifted his shirt over his head in one easy motion, tossing it to the bed. He waited for her to touch him, but she didn't. Then she spoke, and he realized she had crossed the room. ''I think they have lotion in the bathroom.''

She returned and her hands were slippery and floral-scented when she pressed them against his skin. ''Close your eyes and try to relax. We'll lick this.''

The pain in his temples was no longer the most emphatic sensation in his body. ''I should be taking care of you.''

''You've been doing a good job. You've been taking care of Tina, too, but I'm glad you told me the truth.''

Hannah had strong hands and long, talented fingers. She did hard work with her hands, so they weren't particularly soft or feminine. They were capable hands with short, well-cared-for nails and calluses on her palms. But they were part of the package, and they excited him.

Every touch, every sweep of her palm, every probe of her fingers excited him.

"I wish you could have known Tina," she continued. "Would you like me to tell you about her?"

His neck was beginning to feel like cooked spaghetti. Other parts of him were not nearly so limp. "Go ahead."

"Well, she had a great sense of humor. She could make anybody laugh. As a teacher she could make her students do anything she wanted just because she understood them so well. Not just kids, either. She went to city council meetings on a regular basis and convinced them to clean up the public beach or erect stop signs. They hated to see her coming."

He laughed, then he sobered. "She kept a scrapbook. I found it in the attic."

"Of her exploits?"

He remembered his own surprise on finding the album. "Yes, and mine."

"Yours?"

"She subscribed to the weekly newspaper from the town in Michigan where I was raised. Every time my name was mentioned she cut out the article. Every time my photograph was there, she cut that out, too. I don't know how she got them, but she had more photos, programs from recitals or school concerts. She even had copies of stories I wrote for my school paper. I think she had somebody in my hometown who knew the truth and took pity on her."

"She lost her only child." He heard Hannah take a deep, shaky breath before she went on. "It must have been hard."

"She wrote letters on each of my birthdays. She kept them together on the very last page of the scrapbook. It meant something to know that she had never really forgotten me."

"A mother never forgets her child, Quinn."

He knew they weren't talking about Tina now. He placed one hand over hers. "Not everyone's like you."

"I'm sure Tina mourned losing you every day of your life."

Just the way Hannah would mourn her daughter if they didn't find Jolie. He didn't think about his next move. He did what he'd wanted to since the moment he discovered Jolie was missing. He stood and wrapped his arms around her in a comforting embrace. "Your story will turn out better than hers did, Hannah."

She rested her cheek against his shoulder, and she didn't pull away. He could feel her heart pounding against his bare chest. He wondered if in all the hours that Jolie had been missing, Hannah's heart had sped just this way, if the misery inside her had congealed into a mass so solid she could barely swallow or breathe.

"I want her back." The words emerged on a sob. "I want my little girl."

"I know." He stroked her hair and wished his stock in trade was miracles.

"She's been gone...almost two days!"

"Two days too many."

She was crying now, not silent, gentle sobs, but sobs that shook her entire body. He guessed she rarely cried, that the experience was so new to her that she couldn't protect herself against the intensity. She couldn't release it a little at a time. It was a deluge, a tidal wave, and his arm tightened around her for support.

"Hannah, go ahead." He kissed the top of her head gently. "This is long overdue."

"Where...is she?"

"Somewhere we'll find her."

"How did Tina...stand it?"

Quinn knew that if his mother had loved him the way Hannah loved her daughter, that no school board, no small-town gossips, could have separated them. The woman in his arms had such a fierce bond to her child that without thinking, she would lay down her life to protect her. Any lingering doubts that he'd been a fool to involve himself in Hannah's search disappeared. All doubts that he would survive this unscathed skyrocketed.

He was not objective. He was not an observer. Somewhere along the way his emotions had become entangled with Hannah's.

Somewhere along the way he had begun to fall in love with this woman.

There was nothing he could say to ease her pain. He had uttered all the platitudes, but they both knew that's all they were. They could search forever and have nothing but missing posters and receipts from shabby motels to show for their efforts.

He held her instead, simply held her and felt her breasts pressing against his chest, her hair caressing his collarbone. She moved away at last, spent and heartbroken. He let her go, although he wanted to hold her forever.

"I'm sorry…" She gasped the words.

He touched her hair. "Don't be."

"I just…Tina…never found you again…."

"Tina knew where I was. This is different." He touched her chin, lifting it so that she was staring into his eyes.

She didn't move farther away, which surprised him. Her eyes were red and weepy, but her gaze didn't falter. "You…deserved better. You deserved to be loved."

His heart slammed against his rib cage. He had never thought about his life that way. But now he realized that in his thirty-two years, he had never allowed love to happen. There had been women, but he had never let them slip over that invisible line. Love was uncharted territory, and now he felt himself wandering through emotional old-growth forests that closed behind him with every step.

He didn't know where he was, but he knew he could never go back.

"I still do," he said at last. "I still deserve it."

"I can't...I can't think of anything but Jolie."

He knew it was a lie. Because she was thinking of something else. Of *someone* else. He saw it in her eyes, and saw the guilt that followed on its heels. She was as aware of him as he was of her. They were immersed in this together, and searching for Jolie had only heightened and hastened the pull they had felt toward each other right from the beginning.

He leaned forward. She was so close that he had only to move scant inches. He kissed her lightly on the lips, a gentle, lingering kiss that was salty with tears and sweet with emotion. Then he stepped back. "Nothing you feel for me will take anything away from what you feel for your daughter. There's no trade involved."

She didn't answer. He saw that she couldn't.

"Go to bed, Hannah." He retreated still farther. "In the morning we'll be one step closer to Jolie."

Hannah, nodded, then he turned and crossed the room. He stopped in the doorway, watched her for a moment, then disappeared into his room and closed the door behind him.

He waited for the click that would lock him securely on his side of the search for her daughter.

The room remained silent.

Chapter 9

Hannah was learning to live without real sleep. Soon, if she wanted to be any help to her daughter, she would have to resort to taking a drugstore aid. She remembered now that when Amanda had undergone fertility treatment, she had been afraid to add sedatives or sleeping pills to the mix of hormones and drugs already in her system. So she had gone to the local health food store for tea and vitamin supplements. Hannah resolved to ask Amanda about it during their next phone call.

But tea and supplements would not bring back her daughter.

After what seemed like hours of staring at the ceiling she rose and went into the bathroom. The motel was clean, but the walls were paper-thin. Over the din of a noisy air conditioner she could hear the television coming from the room to the north. Now, as she ran the tap to fill a glass of water, she was surprised to hear a voice from Quinn's room, too.

At first she thought she was listening to his television,

then she realized she was listening to Quinn himself. She turned off the tap, wondering whom he was talking to.

"Well, I'm glad you finally got home. Enjoying my car?"

In the bathroom the words were as clear as Port Franklin's air, although she knew that back in her room they would have been a faint rumble.

There was a pause, then: "Well, that's why I'm calling. I want you to park the Lexus in your garage and leave it there." Pause. "No, I'm not kidding. Rent something, Jake. I'll pay you back. But I checked my voice mail a little while ago, and there's a threatening message from the Port Franklin cops. Chandler himself, in fact."

Hannah lowered herself to the edge of the tub so she was even closer to the wall that separated them.

Quinn continued. "He wants to talk to me. He's obviously suspicious. Hannah disappears on foot half a mile from my house, and an hour later I suddenly leave town. By now Chandler may even realize what I do for a living. Hannah has trouble believing I don't want to do an article about this. Maybe he does, too."

Hannah closed her eyes. At no point along the way had she really considered that helping her might hurt Quinn.

"So, park the car," Quinn continued from the other room. "Rent anything you want. I'm good for it. But if someone does trace the car to you, tell them I asked you to lend me your van so I could do some camping, and we switched. Don't admit to seeing Hannah with me."

There was silence, then a humorless laugh from the other room. "Camping, Jake? You know, when you go out in the woods and sleep in a tent?"

She listened to the rest of the short conversation. Quinn quizzed Jake about the database search. From Quinn's side of the conversation it sounded as if little progress had been made.

"Keep trying," Quinn told him. "And see what you can do here in West Virginia. Check with the Wheeling paper. Have them look through their morgue." There was a significant pause. "I don't know. We've made some headway, but it's a wing and a prayer. We could find him tomorrow, or the trail could turn cold." He paused to let Jake say something, then he continued. "No, look, I'm in it for the long haul. You don't have to remind me I could be in trouble. But finding this kid is more important."

You don't have to remind me I could be in trouble.

The room next door was silent now. She sat quietly for a few minutes, but obviously the conversation had ended.

She'd wondered if Quinn had his own agenda, or if he and Jake were going to step on her to boost themselves up their professional ladders. Now she realized Quinn was risking his reputation to help find her daughter. The police were suspicious. If he returned Tony's call, Tony would insist he return to Port Franklin for questioning.

For years she had insisted on doing everything alone. Now she knew she was going to have to insist again. It was only ten o'clock. She had to find Bob Jenkins, and she had to find him tonight, then she had to follow the next lead by herself, and the next. She would leave Quinn a note telling him to go back to Port Franklin. If he wanted to protect her he could refuse to cooperate with Tony, but she could handle it alone from here.

Now how did she start?

She pictured the pizza shop Bob managed. It was delivery and take-out exclusively. She couldn't take her time over a late-night dinner, pumping the server for Bob's address. There had to be another way to approach this, another way to discover where he lived without waiting for tomorrow's meeting.

The shop was in a neighborhood that teetered between residential and shabby commercial. The shop itself was positioned between a bar at one end of the block and a church at the other, convenient enough if the local booze hounds needed a snack on their way to confession.

A bar.

Hannah realized why she hadn't made the connection before this. Bob had come to Wheeling because he had a drinking problem. There was a bar at the end of the block where he worked. Surely someone there must know him and be able to tell Hannah where he lived.

She dressed quickly, slipping into a slinky green jumper she'd borrowed from Diane Everest. She folded everything else she had with her and placed it in the plastic shopping bag her shoes had come in. Then she started for the door, nearly tripping over a snoozing Oliver.

The dogs. She hadn't even thought of them. What would Quinn do with Oliver and Fagan? She had to ask him to take them to Amanda.

The note was short, but she didn't lie. She told him what she had heard and why she was leaving. She stared at the three sentences she had written, then she added: "Don't look for me. Thank you for everything you've done. You've helped me more than you know."

She almost struck out the last part, but it was true. Quinn had gotten her as far as Wheeling, but he had done something even better. She was nearly a stranger. He had helped her, anyway. Not for what he could gain. Just because she needed him. She'd almost forgotten that kind of help existed. She'd almost forgotten that a man could nurture as well as abuse.

She had almost forgotten what it felt like to be held and petted and kissed when her heart was breaking.

She had almost forgotten what desire felt like.

She dropped the pen on top of the note. She would get the reception clerk to call a taxi, then she was on her own. She had a little cash, but despite Quinn's warnings, she would have to use an automated teller. Since Wheeling was just a stop on the search for her daughter, she wouldn't be here by the time the cops were alerted. She would be one step closer to Jolie.

She quietly closed the door behind her, waiting tensely for the dogs to howl. When they remained silent she started toward the office.

Quinn wasn't sure what made him part the drapes that covered his window. One more check of the van before he turned out the lights for the night. One more glance at the moon. Maybe he'd heard something and only registered it in the dimmest recesses of his mind. But whatever the reason, he peered out at the parking lot making one final visual sweep.

Hannah was walking swiftly toward the office. She glanced over her shoulder, but apparently Quinn wasn't as visible to her as she was to him, because she kept walking.

"Ice, Hannah? A newspaper?" He spoke the words out loud, since now there was no one in the next room to hear him.

He wondered if he had scared her away. By holding her, touching her, kissing her. She hadn't seemed frightened or angry. Far from it.

She stepped under a light, and its soft glow illuminated something in her hand. He recognized the bag her shoes had come in, and it was bulging.

She was definitely not looking for a newspaper.

Quinn had come this far on faith, taken risks, and for what? She was leaving at the first opportunity to find her daughter on her own.

Then a terrible thought occurred to him. Maybe she wasn't going to find Jolie at all. Maybe Hannah knew where her daughter was. Maybe Tony Chandler had been on to something, and Hannah and Millie's talk of police harassment was a lie. Quinn hadn't bothered to investigate, although even the greenest reporter would have. Instead he had taken the word of a waitress who might have been fooled by Hannah herself.

On the surface Hannah looked like a great mother, but Quinn knew from experience that relationships within families weren't always as they seemed.

For a moment he wallowed in this new possibility. He had been duped, emotionally persuaded into helping a woman who might have harmed her own child.

Then he remembered the woman trembling and sobbing in his arms, the woman who could not even fathom that his mother had loved him less than Hannah loved Jolie. A woman who couldn't admit to the possibility of maternal neglect in another woman.

"Where in the hell are you going, Hannah? And why?"

He was going to find out. But he wasn't going to ask her. This time he would see for himself and be done with doubts once and for all.

The taxi driver dropped Hannah off at the pizza shop, but she saw that she was already too late to get help here. The taxi had taken half an hour to arrive, and now it was just a few minutes before eleven. She made it inside before the night manager locked the door, but the small staff was already wiping down counters and cleaning the wide steel oven.

"Oh, I'm too late for a pizza, aren't I?" Silently she kicked herself for not trying this before, when she might have had time to wheedle Bob's phone number or address. She had been in a hurry to return to the motel to check on Quinn, and now she regretted it.

"Sorry," the manager said. He was in his early twenties, long-haired and lanky, with just a few remaining traces of acne. "We're cleaning up."

"Darn, I'm starving." She smiled up at him. "You don't have anything else, do you?"

"Nope. We got cleaned out tonight. Talk about busy."

On the ride over she had considered how best to ask about Bob. "Bob Jenkins tells stories about how busy you get. We went to high school together. Do you know him very well?"

"Sure, he trained me."

"He's not here right now, is he?"

"Nope, but he'll be in tomorrow morning."

She winked at him, and the attempt felt stiff and unnatural, but she must have pulled it off, because he flushed. "I was hoping to find him *tonight*," she said. "If you get my drift...."

The young man cleared his throat. "I bet he'll be sorry he missed you."

"I'd call him, but I've lost his number. You don't happen to have it, do you?"

"He asked us not to give it out."

"He did?" She gave her best imitation of a giggle. "Who's chasing the poor guy?"

"I dunno. You're the first woman who's asked for it, that's for sure."

The Bob she remembered was sallow and stoop shouldered. He had never been good-looking and was probably even less appealing now. "Well, under the circumstances, wouldn't you hate to have him miss out?"

"I could call him for you..."

She put her finger on her cheek, as if she were considering his offer. She shook her head, as if she'd made a difficult decision. "Tell you what, I think I'll just drive over to his house. Is he still living on Hillvale?" She made up the street name, hoping the young man would slip and give her the real one.

"I've never been to his house." He turned to one of the girls cleaning the oven. "You know where Bob lives?"

The girl shrugged.

He faced Hannah. "Want me to call and tell him you're coming?"

Hannah struggled not to show her frustration. "No, I'd rather surprise him."

The manager walked to the door and unlocked it to let her out. "Good luck. I wish somebody would come looking for me."

She made her exit and heard the lock snap behind her. She suppressed a string of words Jolie would never be allowed to say and started toward the neon sign advertising Tico's, the bar at the corner.

Tico's took up the bottom floor of a dirty, slab stone building with high, glass-block windows and a front door thick enough to ward off bazooka fire. She didn't frequent bars, and for years she had blamed them for Marshall's decline. But as bars went, this one seemed decent enough, judging from the absence of men loitering in front of it.

Inside, the air was blue with smoke. In the corner a young couple danced to country music from the jukebox, and just in front of them half a dozen men laughed and poked each other as a waitress in a tight, fringed dress placed a pitcher of beer in the center of their table.

The bar running the length of the room was a fifties reject of peeling, black linoleum tacked in place by cheap chrome strips. The stools were vinyl, backless and too high. She climbed up on one at the end closest to her and waited for the bartender to serve her.

Tico's was undoubtedly rowdy on weekends, but tonight it was subdued. When the song ended, no one rose to prime the jukebox. The men at the center table were arguing good-naturedly, but quietly enough.

"What'll it be?"

The bartender had a handlebar mustache and tattoos on his biceps, but he also had an air of great patience. Hannah ordered a draft beer and waited until he brought it before she began to question him.

"Seems like a quiet night."

"More money flowing when it's not."

"I guess." She lifted her glass in a mock toast. "I've never been here before."

"I know."

"Really?" She took a sip.

"I'd remember."

She smiled for the first time. "Bob Jenkins told me about it. Do you know Bob?"

"Old Coca-Cola Jenkins."

"Is that what you call him?"

"Since he went on the wagon, yeah…"

She couldn't believe her luck—unless they weren't talking about the same man. "Bob's on the wagon?"

"Must be a long time since you've seen him."

"Longer than it should be. We…we had a fight." She tried to look pensive. "I want to find him and make it up to him. I thought maybe I'd catch him here tonight."

"He doesn't come in anymore. He did for a while after he stopped drinking. That's how he got the nickname. We didn't see him for a long time, then he started coming in again a couple of months ago."

"Oh? He fell off the wagon?"

"No, but he had a friend who never hopped on it. Bob came in after work sometimes to drive him home." The bartender started toward the other end of the bar.

"The friend, is he here now?"

"Hasn't been in a while."

"You wouldn't remember his name, would you?"

He shook his head and moved out of conversational range.

Hannah pondered this revelation. Marshall had come to Wheeling to live with Bob. Despite Quinn's doubts, she was sure of it. Could Marshall be the friend? And if he was, why had he quit coming to Tico's?

She nursed the beer, considering what to do next. The problem was solved when a dark-haired man in his thirties settled himself on the next stool. He was dressed in a navy sports jacket and starched dress shirt. "I haven't seen you here before," he said. He had a deep voice and a pleasant enough smile to go with it.

She told him everything she had told the bartender. "I'd call him, but I didn't bring his phone number."

"I know Bob. All the regulars do."

"You're a regular?"

"The only one tonight. I have an office down the street. Name's Ralph Green. I'm an attorney. I stop by most nights if I work late. It's a nice break between work and home."

She wondered if Ralph had a wife waiting. As well dressed as he was, there was something not altogether respectable about him. "The bartender told me Bob doesn't come in anymore. I guess if I want to see him, I'll have to try to remember where he lives."

"I've been to his place, but I don't have the address. I could show you."

She hated to admit she didn't have a car, but she didn't seem to have a choice. "I'm on foot tonight. My...roommate borrowed my car."

He brightened. "Oh, I can take you. No problem."

Not for him, perhaps. But a problem of magnificent proportions for her. She knew better than to get into a car with a strange man. But if he really could take her to Bob's house, then she would be one step closer to Jolie.

"I don't know you," she pointed out.

"Tico'll vouch for me. Tico?" he shouted down the bar. The bartender, obviously Tico himself, plodded back in their direction. "I told the lady I'd take her to Jenkins's house," Ralph said, when Tico was standing in front of them. "Tell her she'll be safe with me."

Tico didn't speak. Hannah's heart sank.

"Tico," Ralph chided.

"You look strong enough to wrestle off a slimeball ambulance chaser," Tico said at last.

"Can you tell me where Bob lives?" Hannah asked Tico point-blank. "Because I can take a taxi."

"You'll be safe enough with Ralph, I guess. He knows I saw you leave together."

She had heard more enthusiastic endorsements of ax murderers. Frustration welled inside her. Ralph Green might be able to give her what she wanted, but Jolie needed her mother alive and well. "Would anyone else know where Bob lives?"

Tico shrugged.

Hannah could see that she wasn't going to get anywhere. She would have to go back to the pizza shop and ask the manager to call Bob. Then she would have to throw herself on his mercy. "Thanks, both of you, but I guess I'm on my own."

She slid off her stool, laid a five-dollar bill on the bar and started toward the door. Outside, when the door opened behind her and she felt a hand on her shoulder, she realized she hadn't gotten away with her rejection.

"I don't know what game Tico's playing," Ralph said, not nearly as pleasantly as he had before, "but I've got what you're looking for, lady. You don't have to look any further."

Hannah sighed. She suspected Ralph wasn't talking about an address. "Take your hand off me, please."

Instead his fingers dug deeper into her flesh. "You know, sometimes you have to play nicey-nice to get what you want."

She turned and looked him straight in the eye. "And sometimes, you don't."

"What makes you think you can just walk away from me?"

She sighed again. "Ralph, I'm going to tell you one more time to take your hand off me."

It was one more warning than she'd given Tony Chandler.

Tracking the taxi had been simple. Wheeling wasn't New York and a taxi was an uncommon sight. Quinn had kept a respectful distance, parking at the end of the block behind a pickup truck when Hannah got out and went inside the pizza shop. She hadn't looked in his direction then or later when she'd emerged and started toward the bar on the corner. At that point he'd gotten out of the van and trailed her, although by now it was clear what she was trying to do. She was trying to find Bob Jenkins. Whether she was planning to return to the motel afterward was another matter.

At Tico's he had chosen to wait in the shadows in a small lot on the building's west side where he had a view of the front door and an ear cocked for trouble. He didn't want to follow Hannah inside, because he was more interested to see what she might do next.

Not more than ten minutes later he saw and heard her come back out. He heard a man's voice and moved closer, wondering if she had found Jenkins so quickly. But that possibility was quickly dismissed.

"You think you're better than me, blondie? You think a gal hanging out in bars asking questions about losers is somehow better than me?"

Quinn rounded the corner just in time to see Hannah's hand shoot high. She ducked, spun and slammed her palm against the chin of the man in front of her, all at the same moment. The man, nearly as tall as she was but a good sixty pounds heavier, stumbled backward toward the door, falling against it with a resounding thud.

"If you touch me again," he heard Hannah say in a low voice, "you'll need your own ambulance chaser, Ralph."

"You made me bite my tuggg..." Ralph spit out the words like a wounded man. Before he could recover, the door opened, shoving him back in Hannah's direction. She sidestepped smoothly.

A big tattooed man stood in the doorway, smoke from the bar oozing onto the sidewalk like the sulphurous fumes of hell. "I don't tolerate fighting on the sidewalk."

Hannah stood her ground. "Then you might want to keep the troublemakers inside, Tico."

She started to turn away, as if she was planning to leave, but the man named Tico stopped her. "Why are you really looking for old Coca-Cola, lady? What's he ever done to you?"

As Quinn watched from the shadows Hannah faced Tico. "Look, I'm going to tell you the truth, okay? I'm looking for my ex-husband. I have custody of our daughter, but he disappeared with her two nights ago. I'm desperate. I've known Bob since high school, and I think he knows where my ex is living."

The wounded Ralph was tenderly touching his tongue with his fingertips. "And you thought I'th get involfed in thomething like that?"

Tico leaned forward. "Coca-Cola lives on the corner of Fairfield and Holly, behind a big white house with a chain-link fence. When he was really on the sauce I had to take him home a time or two. Last time I passed that way there was an old junk car up on blocks in the driveway."

"You knew all the time?" Hannah said.

Tico glared, and his mustache drooped an extra inch. "I know how to keep secrets, lady. That's why this place is still in business. But I've got a little girl of my own."

Hannah stared at him a moment, then she gave a short nod. "May I come back inside and call a taxi?"

Quinn knew his moment had come. Hannah hadn't needed a protector; she'd done a damn fine job of watching out for herself. But she did need a ride.

"I'll drive the lady anywhere she wants to go," he said, stepping out of the shadows.

Hannah looked up and even in the sputtering light of a streetlamp he could see her cheeks color. "Quinn..."

"You know this guy?" Tico said.

"The lady and I are old friends," Quinn said.

"I guess I won't need the taxi after all," Hannah told Tico.

"What in the hell were you thinking of, Hannah?" Quinn said once they got in the van.

"Those self-defense classes I took after the divorce worked. I handled myself, didn't I?"

She had, and reluctantly he realized how much he admired her for it. Hannah Blackstone was a strong, confident woman who had taken control of her life. She did not need a knight in shining armor, just a partner and friend.

But when his voice emerged, it was stern. "You didn't want to wait for tomorrow because you wanted to disappear faster? You knew I'd be waiting in the pizza shop parking lot tomorrow morning."

"I heard you talking to Jake tonight. Now Tony's after *you.*"

She was exhausted and increasingly desperate. He could see it in her eyes. But she wasn't guilty of anything else. He realized that any doubts he'd had were gone. She had risked the search and her own safety to protect him.

"I can handle Tony Chandler," he said. He brushed a strand of hair over her ear, and she didn't jerk away. "I can't handle worrying about you. Promise you won't take off by yourself again.''

"I don't need you."

"Maybe not. But you do need my van, my contacts and my warm, accepting presence." He risked a grin. "Especially the last part."

"I'm handling enough. I can't worry about you, too."

"Then let me do that part, okay? Hannah, no cop in his right mind goes after a reporter."

"Tony's not in his right mind."

"No, but somebody on the Port Franklin police force is, and they'll be sure Tony doesn't star in an eyewitness newspaper account of police brutality."

She turned to him for the first time. "I hurt you. I'm sorry. I didn't mean to."

He wanted to take her in his arms, but he knew better than to push his luck. "On the contrary, it means a lot that you were that worried about me."

"I want this over! I want Jolie, I want my life back. I don't want to worry about anybody else again."

She thought she was telling the truth, but he knew differently. When this *was* over, she would not have her life back. She might have her daughter, she might have her house and business, she might even have a life free from police harassment. But it would not be the life she had known. Because for the first time in years she had trusted a man, and now she had sacrificed for him. The shell she had built around herself had cracked wide open.

And that changed everything. For both of them.

Chapter 10

Bob's house was simple to find using Tico's instructions. Quinn parked the van on the street, and they skirted the broken-down Chevy that was still in the driveway, heading straight to the stairs that led to an apartment over the garage.

The house was old, with the apartment a more recent addition. The apartment looked small and plain, but the stairs were new and the location private. Unfortunately no lights were burning, and no television screen glowed in the darkness.

"You've thought about what to say?" Quinn asked.

Hannah steeled herself for the upcoming encounter. "I'm just going to tell him the truth."

He stepped back to let her go ahead. "Just don't be disappointed. Whatever happens, it's another step on the road, even if it's not the last one."

She didn't, couldn't answer. How many disappointments could she take before she fell apart?

At the top of the stairs she rapped on the door, glad that Quinn was on the steps just below her. Despite anything she had said, she was relieved he had found her.

A light flicked on in the apartment, and her heart sped in response. She waited, hardly daring to breathe.

Bob Jenkins opened the door. He was heavier, and better looking than she remembered, which surprised her. He looked healthier, perhaps even happier. He stared at her for a long moment as she stared back.

"Hello, Hannah," he said at last. "Come in."

"I've brought a friend."

"He's welcome." Bob stepped back so that Hannah and Quinn could enter.

The apartment was plain with few frills, much as she had expected. It was almost painfully neat, as if Bob spent too many restless hours cleaning and straightening.

She introduced Quinn, and Bob motioned to a sofa. She perched on the edge with Quinn sitting beside her. "I've come about Marshall," she said.

He didn't ask how she had found him. He didn't even seem surprised. "How is he?" he asked.

She drew a startled, painful breath.

"He's not here in Wheeling?" Quinn said.

"I haven't heard from him in about a month."

Hannah tried to remember what Quinn had said as they ascended the stairs. One more step, but maybe not the last one. "A month?"

"What's going on, Hannah? Why are you here?"

She told him the entire story.

Bob frowned. He had a stern face, and frowning, he was formidable. "This is all so hard to believe."

"What was he doing here with you?" Hannah asked, "Why did he come to West Virginia?"

Bob sat down on the only chair in the room, as if he had just realized they were going to be there awhile. "Marsh asked if he could come to Wheeling and stay with me. Somebody told him I was a recovering alcoholic, and he thought maybe I could help him."

Hannah just stared at him, trying to decide if he was making a bad joke. "Marshall Blackstone?"

"I gather that comes as a surprise to you?"

"Yeah, to me most of all."

"I know what he did to you. I'm sure not excusing him. But he's a sick man, and he needed help."

"And did you help him?" Quinn asked.

"I took him to AA meetings. He stopped drinking for a while and got a job as a dishwasher. Then he started drinking again and stopped going to meetings and work. Under those circumstances I couldn't keep him here. I found him another place to live about six weeks ago and about four weeks ago he left town."

Hannah had no reason to doubt anything Bob said. Obviously he was a man with no time or stomach for deceit, a man who had simply tried to help an old friend. "I have to...find him."

Bob leaned forward. "I'm sorry about your little girl, but this story is hard to believe. Marsh hardly talked about her. He's so wrapped up in his own problems, I don't think he even thought about her very often."

"He's punishing me."

"Hannah, I don't think he really blames you for anything. Maybe he did at first, but while he was sober, he was taking some responsibility for the things he had done. He even talked about sending you child support."

"When I find him, I'll find Jolie," she said stubbornly.

Quinn interrupted. "Does he have a car? Do you know his license plate number?"

"He never had a car while he was here."

"Do you have any idea where he might have gone?" asked Quinn.

"I checked around. He didn't tell anybody where he was headed." Bob was silent a moment, as if he was thinking. "He doesn't like cities, though. I can tell you that. He claimed he would do better in the country. He talked a lot about living in the mountains, far away from everybody. I told him he'd be taking his problems with him, but I don't think he heard me."

"Anyplace in particular?"

"We went camping one weekend, near a little town east of Morgantown called Mountain Creek. He really liked it, even talked about moving there one day when he straightened out his life." He paused. "I remember he said it might be a good place for your daughter to visit. He talked about it a lot, like it was something he could hang on to when things got rough."

Hannah drew in a sharp breath.

"It's just a possibility," Bob warned. "There are a thousand little towns, and for all I know he went to another city where he could find a bar whenever he needed one."

She tried to stay calm. She had known from the beginning that this wouldn't be easy, but she could feel Jolie slipping away. "Can you think of anything else? Please, you're all we've got." She had said the *we* before she stopped herself. Quinn was such a part of this now that she thought of *we* and *us* instead of *me* and *I*.

"His parents were helping for a while, sending money care of some address in Ohio. It was always forwarded from there because he never told them where he'd moved. He would call them once in a while, but he got into a fight with his father. He started drinking again after the fight. I doubt they know where he is, either."

"What was the fight about?" Quinn said. "Do you know?"

"I don't know how that will help."

"It's the little things that do. Every time."

He sounded so convincing that Bob nodded. "They wanted Marsh to visit Jolie more often, so they could visit her, too."

Quinn turned to Hannah. "They aren't allowed to visit on their own?"

"They can visit whenever they want. They just can't take her out of town." She shook her head sorrowfully. "I was afraid something like this might happen if they did."

"You were afraid they might not bring her back?"

"I told you before, they despise me. I just wanted to keep an eye on things."

"How would it help if Marsh visited her more often?"

"They were always more comfortable when he was there and they were visiting as a family. When he wasn't there, they never seemed to know what to do with her, or with me, either."

"I think the pressure to be a better father knocked him off the wagon," Bob said. "Marsh was barely holding it together. He wasn't ready to think about anybody else."

"And maybe the pressure finally got to him and he decided to become a full-time father," Quinn said.

Bob stood to let them out. "I can tell you something. If he did take Jolie, he'll be regretting it about now. He'll want to be found."

He wrote something on a piece of paper and handed it to Hannah. "That's my number," he told her. "It's unlisted. Too many of my old drinking buddies had the old one."

She held out her hand. "I can call?"

"If Marsh has Jolie, he'll get in touch with me somewhere down the line. Call me every night to see if I've heard from him. But you need to find your daughter. Because even if he's not drinking now, the stress of caring for a child will send him back to the bottle. And then he won't be able to care for her at all."

* * *

Quinn was pensive on the trip back to the motel. Hannah waited for him to tell her what was on his mind, but when he didn't, she filled in the blanks. "You're wondering if Marsh really has her, aren't you?"

"I am." He pulled into the lot and parked in front of their rooms.

"And you're wondering if we've hit a dead end...."

"That, too." He removed the key from the ignition, but he didn't get out. "From everything Bob said, this is not a man who could pull off an abduction. Kidnapping takes a clear head."

"You don't have to go any farther, Quinn. I can rent a car tomorrow morning and make the trip to Mountain Creek by myself."

"You know I'm coming."

"I know...."

"Are you going to get any sleep tonight?"

She shook her head. "How about you?"

He shrugged.

They sat there, too tired to move, too wrought up to go inside and sleep. "How's your headache?" she asked after a moment.

"Sitting beside me."

She punched him lightly on the arm.

"They have cable movies." Quinn rested his hand on the door handle. "Do you want to see what's coming on?"

It sounded like just the thing to put her to sleep. Inside she greeted the dogs who had taken her absence as a signal that they could sleep on her bed. She shooed them down, then opened the connecting door to Quinn's room. His television was on. "Any luck?"

"There's a new movie coming on, but I haven't heard of it. *Magical Interlude?*"

She shrugged. "I'll try it."

"Why don't you come over here and watch it with me?"

"Why?"

"For company."

She lifted an eyebrow. "I have the dogs."

"Stiff competition."

"I'll see you in the morning. Bright and early."

"Make sure you're still here."

She closed the door and changed for the night. She hadn't thought to borrow nightwear from Diane Everest, so she had adopted the dress shirt that Quinn had given her when he'd released her from the trunk of his car. She pulled it on now and settled in bed with the remote.

The television didn't work. She got up and tried the buttons on the set itself, and she managed to turn it on. Unfortunately there was no picture. Apparently the problem required a repairman.

She knocked on the door to Quinn's room and waited until he called "Come in" before she poked her head inside. "Is your television still working?"

"Perfectly. Yours isn't?"

"I thought maybe the cable was out."

"Then I have something to offer that the dogs don't."

"An opposable thumb?"

"A picture on my screen. Come on, Hannah. Make yourself comfortable. It's about to start."

She considered. She could sit in the straightback chair at the table in the corner and crane her neck, or she could lie down in the bed beside him. He was under the sheet, but she could see that his chest was bare. She wasn't sure what else might be.

As if he could read her mind, he threw off the sheet to reveal a pair of perfectly respectable, striped boxer shorts. "I'll put on a T-shirt if you'll join me."

She was not a prude. Until her life with Marshall completely fell apart she'd believed she had a normal sexual appetite and a healthy outlook. Now her outlook was "look out!" And that's exactly what all systems were screaming.

He got up and pulled on a shirt he'd thrown on the floor beside his bed. "It's up to you now."

She gazed down at her exposed legs. The shirttail hid her bottom and the tops of her thighs, giving more coverage than a modest swimsuit. She was exhausted. She couldn't risk another night of staring at the ceiling.

Despite Quinn's doubts, she was sure that tomorrow she would be one step closer to holding Jolie in her arms.

"Ground rules," she said. "You below the sheet, me above."

"Sure. On the birth-control scale that's at least a step higher than the rhythm method."

She couldn't help herself, she smiled. His expression changed, surprise followed by frank admiration. "You really are beautiful when you smile, Hannah."

The smile disappeared, but not the warmth that had ignited it. "You'll see more smiles when Jolie's safe."

"I know." His expression was enigmatic. He got back into bed and pulled the sheet over him. "All suspicious male body parts covered." He patted the bed. "It's about to start."

She crossed the room and lay down beside him, fluffing her pillow self-consciously. "Have I mentioned the dogs are trained to attack?"

"Give me a few more sausage biscuits, and they're mine for life."

"Watch the movie, Quinn." She pulled the spread over both of them and settled in.

The last thing Quinn thought as he drifted off to sleep was that he was grateful Hannah had fallen asleep first. She had remained awake for the only part of the movie that wasn't X-rated—the first three minutes.

The movie's hero was a magician who seduced statuesque young women and used them as assistants, conveniently finding ways to make them "vanish" when he found another buxom beauty he liked better. Quinn had been amazed at the ingenuity of the screenwriter, who had engineered sexual encounters in a coffin, in chains and a straitjacket underwater and—the tour de force—in the center of a blazing ring of fire.

He *might* have turned off the movie if he hadn't been afraid that the absence of noise would wake Hannah. As it was he tried to fall asleep, too, but his curiosity continued to get the best of him until the conclusion, when the hero and final heroine made love in a cage of snarling tigers. He drifted off to sleep acutely aware of his own arousal and the impossibility of doing anything about it.

Soft sunlight was seeping through the heavy drapes when he awoke from a dream that he was making love to a passionate blonde at the bottom of a cobra pit.

In the first few moments of awareness he thought he was back in his New York apartment. Apparently Angela had spent the night because he could feel her warm body snuggled against his. He opened his eyes when he realized that this couldn't be right. Angela never snuggled. She was all sharp angles and delicate bones, a runway model who ate as infrequently as a snake and exuded the same amount of personal warmth. They had suited each other because both had so passionately pursued their careers, their mutual obsession had seemed like a bond. They had never cuddled after sex or shared their feelings. In retrospect he wasn't sure she'd had any except ambition and a horror of weight gain.

The woman in his arms was the blonde he had dreamed of. The cobra pit was not a knock-off of last night's movie but a reminder of what he and Hannah faced. And the love-making...well, that part was as clear as the reasons it was impossible. He wanted Hannah and had since the first moment he'd seen her. But now he wanted something more than the elusive, self-contained woman he had believed her to be.

He was turned on his side, and she was resting against him, her lips lightly parted against his shoulder. Her legs were curled and one knee nudged the inside of his thigh. Her hair was spread over the pillow and along his arm. In sleep the haunted expression that seemed as much a part of her as her brown eyes had disappeared. Her cheeks were flushed with sleep, and her dark eyelashes curled against them in sharp relief.

Heat kindled inside him at the sight of her. He was torn between a need to protect and a need to lose himself forever in her flesh. Her breath was warm against his shoulder, her hair was cobweb light and soft against his arm. With an economy of movement he could pull her closer, feel her breasts against his chest, unbutton her shirt and feel them even more intimately.

And if he did, he could lose her forever.

That thought was like ice water, and it brought with it all memories of why they were here together.

He wondered how he could extricate himself before she woke up. He didn't want to move away and risk waking her. But neither did he want to risk the fallout if she found him holding her in his arms. He could certainly explain about the cobra pit, but he doubted it would do the trick.

He was spared decision making. Her eyes opened. Not gently, but like window shades wrapping sharply around a roller. She looked startled, and for the briefest moment, frightened.

"You missed some movie." He tried to smile, but he knew his eyes were watchful.

She didn't move away, which surprised him. "I just shut my eyes for a few minutes."

"It's morning."

She frowned. She didn't look frightened now, just perplexed. "No... It can't be."

"And just for the record, I did not gather you in my arms like this. You insinuated yourself."

He expected outrage. Instead, she laughed softly. "Baloney."

"Well, I'm not sure how it happened, but that would be my guess."

"Where's the sheet?"

He hadn't thought of that. He felt for it with his free hand, but it was nowhere to be found. "The sheet monster came while we were sleeping."

"Are you always this jovial when you wake up?"

"I would be if I always woke up with you."

She stirred, just enough to see his face more clearly. "So, what did I miss?"

"You don't want to know."

"I insist."

"Sex."

Her eyes widened. "I missed it? After all these years, it was over like that? I didn't even wake up?"

His laugh was a low, hoarse rumble, but the image of them together was anything but funny. "Sex on television. In every conceivable position and setting. This motel might look genteel enough, but the entertainment is strictly adult."

"Just the entertainment, huh? I didn't miss anything else?"

"I can guarantee that you won't sleep through it when we make love."

Her expression sobered. She was fully awake now, and he could almost see worry descending. "We're just lying here. I should be up getting ready to go."

He brushed her hair off her cheek, and it clung to his

hand. "Hannah, it was good to sleep and even better to sleep until dawn. You won't bring Jolie home any quicker by making yourself sick."

"For a moment...I forgot."

The mind was a funny thing. Hers had taken a brief break from terror, but now guilt was rapidly destroying any good that had been done. "You didn't forget. You relaxed. You recharged a little so you'd be ready to find her."

"Quinn, what if she's not with Marsh?"

He knew it was early-morning vulnerability talking, and yet the possibility seemed very real to him. He'd been uneasy all along that Hannah's assumptions might be false. Now, after talking to Bob Jenkins, he was more concerned. The picture that had emerged of Marshall Blackstone was not of a man intent on revenge, and certainly not one who loved his daughter so much he couldn't be without her. The picture was of a wounded and self-absorbed soul who had little energy for anything except drinking his way from one hour to the next.

"We'll cross that bridge when we have to." He raised himself high on his elbow and gazed down at her, hoping for some objectivity. "Let's find him first."

"You're sure I didn't miss anything except a movie?"

Objectivity fled. With a groan he leaned down and kissed her. Her lips were so soft he was afraid he might not find his way back. She clung to him a moment, as if kissing him might ward off the terrors of the day.

"You missed that," he said pulling away at last. "But only in my dreams."

Chapter 11

Mountain Creek wasn't much more than its name, a crossroads on a mountaintop with an incomparable view and a gas station. Undoubtedly there was a creek somewhere, too, but Hannah and Quinn discovered it was unlikely they would find Marshall camped beside it.

"Nope, nobody like that livin' 'round here," the old man at the gas station told them. "Nobody's moved up here in a coon's age. We get campers now and then, but not so many this year. Too much rain. They move on after a night or two. Cain't blame them."

Hannah swept the rest of the town with her eyes. Across the road there was a tiny grocery store that also served as the post office and video rental center, a picturesque log café with boarded-up windows and a concrete block laundromat big enough for about half a dozen washing machines. Half a mile away an old barn advertised "antiques," but the only other buildings in the vicinity were houses—and only a few of those.

The old man left to circle the van, kicking the left rear tire suspiciously as he went.

"In a town like this all the jobs go the locals," Quinn said under his breath. "Marshall couldn't earn a living."

"Maybe someone's supporting him."

The old man returned, and Hannah moved closer. "I'm curious. How many people live around here?"

"Here, or around here?"

"Around here."

He shrugged.

From experience she knew that country people protected their own. If Marsh were here, this old man wasn't going to tell them outright.

"Well, I can't help but notice there couldn't be a lot of jobs," she said patiently. "I just wondered what people do."

"Oh, some farm. Some drive in to Morgantown. Left tire needs some air. Want me to tend to it?"

"I'd really appreciate it," she said, before Quinn could answer.

Fagan and Oliver vied for a place at the passenger window. "Good-lookin' dogs," the man said as he went to unhook the air hose.

Quinn rolled his eyes, and she glared at him. "Smart, too. The black one's part hound."

"Ever hunt him?"

She almost said no, but something stopped her. Maybe one more lie could be forgiven. "As a matter of fact, that's why I'm trying to find my ex-husband. Now that he's living up here somewhere, he'll want them when hunting season opens. I don't have a place to keep them anymore."

The old man was silent until he'd plumped out the tire. He checked the pressure, then he straightened. "You're so friendly with this fellow, how come you don't know where he's at?"

"The dogs are a peace offering. We have a little girl. We can't be fighting over every single thing."

He did not look convinced. "Air's free. Fifteen for the gas."

As Quinn paid him Hannah struggled to be philosophical. It was too much to expect that they would find Marshall on their first stop. They could try the store, the laundromat, even the houses. And there were other little towns. Someone would help if they asked enough people.

If he was here.

If he had ever been here.

"Haven't seen nobody like the man you're talking about," the old man said. "And that's a fact. But if it was me, I'd try Morgantown. This ain't the only little town 'round here. He might be livin' in one, but he'll be workin' in the city."

"Good advice," Quinn said. "That's what we'll do."

"Why do you really want to find him?" the old man asked Hannah. "You won't be givin' those dogs away. You think I cain't tell?"

She decided to level with him. "My daughter disappeared three days ago. She may be with my ex-husband. If she's not, he needs to know she's gone."

He shook his head as if the state of the world weighed heavily on his shoulders. "Me, I'd look in Morgantown."

Hemmed in by hilly terrain, Morgantown was a small city that housed a big university. The few roads in and out clogged quickly. It was nearly noon by the time they got to the center of town. They stopped for sandwiches and ate them in a parking lot.

Quinn had been making mental notes along the way, and they had already called directory assistance to see if Marshall had a telephone listing. "We don't have much of anything to go on. I'm hoping Jake gets a lead, but in the meantime, I think we should check out possibilities here.''

Hannah leaned against the hood and fed most of her sandwich to the dogs, splitting the remains carefully into two equal pieces. ''What were you thinking?''

She was wearing the green jumper over a paler green T-shirt. She had washed her hair before they left the hotel that morning, and it gleamed like gold in the afternoon sunlight. As he answered he admired the picture she made. ''We know Marshall was a dishwasher in Wheeling. Unskilled labor's a good bet for somebody who doesn't want to show up on tax records.''

''In a city this size there could be a lot of restaurants.''

''So far it's been a fairly easy trail, but this could be where it takes a turn for the worse.''

She fed the last bite to Oliver before she looked up. ''I don't care how hard it is if we find him—or at least find out he was here.''

''Let's start with employment, because if he goes home to one of the small towns around here at night, he wouldn't frequent the Morgantown bars.''

''It's a needle in a haystack, isn't it?''

''It's something to do until we get a better lead.''

''Okay, dishwasher first. Maybe art supply stores next. Then what?''

''He could be doing simple maintenance work somewhere, like he did for the lady in Millersburg. Or possibly construction?'' The list was growing. Quinn was afraid that by the time they finished brainstorming they would have to visit most of the businesses in town. ''It's possible he might be working under an alias, too.''

''He might, but so far he's been using his own name. I don't know why that would change if he moved here.''

''I think we should cover the downtown first, then fan out.''

She brushed the crumbs from her hands. "I'm ready."

They sized up the downtown, street by street, and took different sides of each. They tried restaurants, video stores, and one family-run bowling alley. Quinn used the same technique he instructed Hannah to use. He smiled and asked for Marshall Blackstone, and when he was told that no one by that name worked there, he described Marshall, acting surprised when the person in charge still claimed not to know him. "I could swear this is where he told me he worked," he said each time. "But I guess I got it wrong."

By four-thirty they were back in the same parking lot, sipping Cokes and sharing notes. "No one was the least suspicious," Hannah said. "Most of the time they seemed genuinely interested in helping. I would have been happier if they acted like they were hiding something."

Quinn's experience had been just as frustrating. Additionally, he hadn't been able to connect with Jake. His own voice mail had yielded another summons from Tony Chandler, but nothing better.

"We need a break before we start in another area. Let's have an early dinner and find a motel for the night. Then we'll map out the rest of the search."

Surprisingly, she didn't protest. "Let's try a restaurant we haven't checked yet. We can kill two birds with one stone."

They settled on an Italian restaurant in a strip mall near the university. It was small and dark, but it smelled marvelous inside, as if somebody's old-country grandmother was hard at work whipping up family favorites in the kitchen. Not surprisingly, the dining room was already half-filled with students in town for the summer session.

When it was clear the hostess had never heard of Marshall, they settled in with their menus, both choosing spaghetti with meatballs. Hannah played with a slice of bread while they waited for their dinner.

"Spaghetti is Jolie's favorite." She picked the bread apart until it was a sizable pile of crumbs.

Quinn wished he knew how to bolster her morale. "Tell me about her, Hannah. Not talking isn't making you feel any better."

"I don't know very much about you. I just assumed you don't have children...."

"You assumed right."

"Do you want them?"

One moment the blood coursing through his veins was warm, the next it was cold as ice.

I never really wanted children. Jeff always had a nanny, of course, and I tried to do right by him. But I never got all goggle-eyed over him the way some mothers do. Can you understand that, Mr. McDermott? Or are you one of those men who can't wait to have a son?

"The world is an unkind place," he said, looking away. "And I've never been sure I'd be very good at fatherhood."

"It's natural to be scared. But that's not the same thing as not wanting a child, is it?"

"I'd have to be sure I'd be a good father before I could take that step." He looked up and saw what she was thinking. "Yes, I want kids. And no, I may never be sure enough of myself to have them."

"There's a lot of room for mistakes, Quinn."

"Some things can never be forgiven." He didn't elaborate, but how could he? Sometimes the truth was the cruelest blow of all.

She picked out another slice of bread, but this time she buttered it, pulling the knife back and forth slowly as if she was determined to fill every air space. "I married a man who was still a child himself, and when I got pregnant I was terrified. The birth was harder than I expected, and I was so exhausted I wasn't even sure I wanted to look at

Jolie afterwards. Then they put her in my arms." She shook her head.

"What did you feel?"

"The most astounding magic." Her voice caught. She cleared her throat. "And it never went away. Oh, when she was a baby I'd be so tired in the middle of the night I'd wish I didn't have to get up with her. Or I'd be annoyed sometimes when she clung too hard or when she was angry and pushed me away. That's normal, I guess. But I never got over the magic. Someday I'll be an old woman, and I'll look at her with her own children, and I'll still feel it."

He felt a lump in his throat as big as his doubts that Hannah would ever see her daughter again. "Tell me more about her."

"She's almost always sunny tempered. She loves being outside, just like me. When she goes on a job she likes to help. She's been known to instruct my customers on the care and feeding of their gardens." She laughed a little. "Amanda says some of them hire me just so they can play with Jolie."

"Does Amanda have children?"

"She and Dan are trying, but it's not likely they'll ever conceive, so they're looking into adoption. In the meantime, she spoils Jolie whenever I let her."

"This must be particularly hard on her."

"Mandy's holding up. She knows I need her."

Their salads arrived, and Hannah abandoned fiddling with the bread to fiddle with the salad. Quinn ate his without speaking. He wasn't sure how wise it had been to ask about Jolie. He wasn't sure about anything.

As if to distract them there was a stir at the door and a coed came barreling into the room amidst giggles from a group of her friends at the table closest to Quinn and Hannah. The girl squeezed a chair between two of her friends, and the noise level rose. Quinn listened idly and saw that Hannah was listening, too.

"I locked my keys in the car. I'm such an idiot!"

"Doofus! Don't you have a spare?"

"I locked my purse inside, too. The spare's in my purse."

Giggling ensued, and Quinn looked at Hannah. They both smiled wryly.

"Well, how'd you get here then?" the group spokesman demanded.

The latecomer giggled louder. "The guy upstairs dropped me off. But I have to call a locksmith. Do you believe it?"

Quinn didn't have to look at them to know they were all rolling their eyes.

Hannah leaned across the table. "Too bad we don't have more time. I could open it for her."

"Your ex taught you to break into cars *and* hot-wire them?"

"I told you, picking locks is Marshall's greatest skill. He can bypass any security system. He'd make a great burglar or car thief."

"Or a locksmith," Quinn said slowly. "In a college town filled with empty-headed coeds."

They stared at each other, then rose as if they'd planned their mutual exit in detail. Quinn threw a twenty-dollar bill on the table to cover the spaghetti they wouldn't be eating. In a moment they were on their way out the door.

The last locksmith in the yellow pages was a middle-aged man named Sigmund Zimmerman, who insisted they call him Ziggy. His shop was in Star City, a nearby community of neat, comfortable homes. He was just closing for the evening when Quinn and Hannah arrived, but he didn't seem to be in any hurry.

"So, what's your problem? Locked out of your house?"

"Nothing like that," Hannah said with a smile. Quinn had let her do the talking in each of the other places they had tried first. "I was just looking for Marshall. Is he in tonight?"

Ziggy looked surprised. "Is he expecting you?"

For a moment Hannah couldn't speak. Her heart beat double time, and she knew better than to even glance at Quinn. She leaned on the counter, because her knees had suddenly grown weak.

"Not really," she said, surprised that her voice sounded normal. "We wanted to surprise him."

His voice frosted over. "You're not drinking buddies, are you?"

Now Hannah was sure they had the right Marshall. "Lord, no. Old friends. With everybody's best interests in mind."

He examined her, as if determining her sincerity. "I'm just surprised he told anybody he was here."

Hannah held her breath, and Ziggy went on. "I'm glad he did, though. Every man needs company."

"Is he in the back, Ziggy?" Quinn said.

"I let him off early tonight. He seemed in a hurry to get home."

"Darn." Hannah knew exactly whom Marshall had been in a hurry to get back to. Her heart sped even faster.

"Tell you what, he doesn't have a phone, but why don't you go see him? Do you know how to get to his place?"

"He gave me directions." Quinn patted his pockets. "But I don't remember where I put them."

"I'll draw you a map." Ziggy began to draw on the back of an invoice. "But listen, don't take any booze out there, you understand? He's still pretty shaky, and he doesn't need temptation."

"Marshall's succumbed to temptation one time too many," Hannah said.

"Ain't that the truth?" Ziggy handed Quinn the make-shift map. "Go cheer him up, why don't you?"

Quinn folded it carefully. "I'm sure he'll feel like a different man by the time we leave."

Quinn knew Hannah was quivering with anticipation. He wasn't sure he believed in divine guidance, yet here they were, closing in on Marshall Blackstone. They had followed an increasingly shaky trail, and at any point along the way they could have been thwarted.

"He could be armed," Hannah said out of nowhere. "He was a cop."

"Does he like guns?"

She was silent, as if considering. "Not the way Tony does. Tony won't go to the bathroom without his service revolver. Marsh locked his up the moment he got home and never took it out again until he had to. He never threatened me with it. I guess I can count myself lucky he preferred his fists."

Quinn's hands tightened convulsively. He was surprised that over the past few days the steering wheel hadn't snapped in two. "This could be a trap, Hannah. If he's taken Jolie to get even with you, he might have even worse revenge on his mind."

"No."

He glanced at her and saw that her jaw was set in a way he recognized now. "Why not?" he said.

"This will sound odd."

"I don't care how it sounds. Why not?"

"Because he's not a violent man, not unless he's drinking."

"Hannah..." He shook his head.

"I told you it would sound odd. I think he's capable of

grabbing Jolie to make a point, but not of putting a gun to my head.''

"And you didn't believe he would beat you when you told him you wanted a divorce.''

"I did learn a thing or two from that experience.''

"I know you—''

"Listen, Quinn, I'm not asking you to risk your life, and I'm not going to risk mine, either. Okay? *I* mentioned a gun, after all. We need to be careful.''

According to Ziggy's map, Marshall lived halfway back to Mountain Creek on a dirt road winding through a pine forest. Marshall obviously had to have a car to make the trip every day, and cars cost money. He continued that train of thought out loud. "He didn't have a car by the time he got to Wheeling. How do you suppose he managed to buy one now?''

"With money he saved from selling the last one?''

"A man with a drinking problem doesn't save money.''

"Well, maybe his parents helped him.''

"Bob seemed to think they're estranged.''

"Somebody in the family always bails Marsh out. That's why he's the way he is.''

"That somebody may have warned him you're looking for him.''

"And maybe they just told him I'm running from the police.''

"If he has Jolie, he'll put two and two together.''

"All right. We need to be *very* careful.''

They made the rest of the trip in silence. By the time they turned on to the forest road, the sun was no longer visible. The trees barely cast a shadow.

"When we get to the turnoff, we'll pass by and walk back,'' Quinn said.

"And then?''

"Then we'll decide how best to get him out of the house."

"We have the ultimate distraction."

Quinn wasn't sure what she meant.

"The dogs," she said.

"Turn them loose?"

"They'll be wild with joy the moment they catch his scent. He'll come out to investigate…"

"And I'll be waiting for him."

"He's a big man, and he's good with his fists."

He smiled without humor. "Not as good as I am."

Marshall's house was little more than a neatly kept clapboard shack with a tin roof. Hannah was surprised to see a garden behind it with newly emerging plants in carefully cultivated rows. An old Pontiac was parked beside the house under the shelter of a lean-to. The yard had been recently mowed, and sections of snow fencing had been placed along the eastern perimeter to hide a makeshift dump of rusting appliances.

Quinn carefully made his way along the fence until he was positioned beside the narrow front porch. He signaled to Hannah, who was hiding with the dogs behind a clump of trees at the roadside.

She took a deep breath and released her hold on the dogs. They stayed beside her at first, sniffing the ground as if they expected this to be just another pit stop. Then Oliver trotted off, and when she didn't call him, he began to range farther away, followed quickly by Fagan. With her heart in her throat she watched them drawing closer to the house.

Oliver began to howl.

The porch light flicked on. A man who was as familiar to Hannah as the taste of betrayal stepped outside and peered into the darkness.

The dogs bounded toward Marshall, and he leaned over

the porch, staring at them. Quinn took that opportunity to spring.

The scuffle was over before she could emerge from the trees. Quinn had Marsh on the ground with his arm twisted behind him, and Quinn, who was sitting on Marsh's back, didn't even look winded.

Hannah didn't waste words or sympathy. She sprang up to the porch, warding off Fagan who was snapping at Quinn. "Where's Jolie?" she demanded.

Marshall turned his head to look at her. "Call off the bodyguard, Hannah."

She was surprised he wasn't struggling, but maybe he had more sense than she'd given him credit for. Quinn was obviously not someone to fool with.

"I'll call him off when you tell me what you've done with my daughter," she said.

"You're the one with custody."

"I want Jolie. Either you turn her over or I call the cops and have you arrested for kidnapping."

"You're the one they're looking for."

"Where is she?"

"I don't know. I wish to God I did."

She stared at him, and suddenly she wanted to cry. Because she had been married to this man. He had beat her in a drunken rage, but as far as she knew he had never bothered to lie to her. He had been incapable of lying because that took self-control.

He wasn't lying now.

She put her fist to her mouth to keep from crying out.

"Hannah?" Quinn said. "Are you going to check inside?"

She emerged from the house after a few minutes. The rooms were tiny, and there was no place to hide anyone or anything. Jolie wasn't there.

"If you let me up, we can talk about this calmly," Marshall said.

Quinn didn't move. "Are you capable of a conversation without using your fists?"

Hannah had noticed something else in her brief search. There were no whiskey bottles in the cupboard, no beer in the battered refrigerator. And even under these trying circumstances, Marshall was as calm as she'd ever seen him.

"Quinn, please let him up," Hannah said.

Quinn got to his feet, and after a moment Marshall got to his, dusting the knees of his faded jeans before he straightened.

"How did you know about Jolie?" Hannah said.

"Tony called me the morning she disappeared."

"So he knew where you were all along."

"He's the only one who knows. He loaned me the money for a car and the first month's rent on this house. How'd you find me?"

"You left a trail."

Marshall was heavier than he'd been the last time she'd seen him, and he had lost more hair. He looked like a man who'd been through hell and wasn't finding his way back fast enough. "After a while, I didn't care if you found me or not. You can't get blood out of a stone."

"Or a man who's stoned all the time. But I never wanted your money, anyway. I just want my daughter."

His face seemed to shrink in on itself. "And I don't, but I don't want anything to happen to her, either. I may not be much of a father, but I've never wished my little girl any harm. I thought the best thing I could do for both of you was to get as far away as possible."

"You showed good judgment there," Hannah said.

"Tony thinks you killed her," he said.

"What do you think?"

''I told him it wasn't possible.'' He met her eyes. ''And I told him I was the one who beat you.''

She just stared at him, hardly comprehending what he'd said.

''I'm sorry.'' His voice was so low she wasn't sure she'd heard him.

She was so battered by emotion she could hardly breathe. Marshall was here, but he didn't have Jolie. And he was sorry.

''I was so scared, Hannah... All the time. Every single minute I was a cop. I was mixed up. I drank...for courage. I couldn't tell you. I was afraid you were like Dad, that you wouldn't...that you would think I wasn't much of a man.''

''Where's Jolie?'' she said at last. ''What's your best guess?''

He shook his head.

''Have you spoken to your parents since Jolie disappeared?''

''I can't. I'm sorry, but I'm living my life one minute at a time. Mom and Dad suck me under, and next time I might not come back up.''

She chewed her lip. ''Could they have her?''

''I thought of that.''

''And?''

''I don't think they'd go that far.''

She thought of everything she knew about Marsh's family. His father had made him the man he wasn't. His doting mother had assisted. Now the only way Marshall could climb out of the black hole of his life was to stay so far away from them that he couldn't even risk a telephone call.

The Blackstones were capable of stealing her daughter.

''I'm going to find out for myself,'' she said. ''Please don't warn them.''

''I don't think she's there.''

"Somebody has to look for her."

"If there was anything I could do, I would."

She believed him. Deep in Marshall's heart, there was a flicker of feeling for their daughter.

She whistled for the dogs. When they were dancing beside her she spoke. "I'll tell you what, Marsh. Just work on staying sober. Then maybe someday when you're ready, you can be some kind of father to Jolie. Because I don't care how long it takes, I'm going to find her, and you're going to have that chance, whether you take it or not."

Chapter 12

"**I** know what you're going to say," Hannah told Quinn when they were in the car. "I don't want your sympathy. So Marshall doesn't have Jolie, but his parents might. They've been in and out of my house dozens of times. For all I know they even have keys. The dogs know them, and Jolie would have gone with them without a fuss."

He couldn't even imagine the torment she must feel, but he had to challenge her, because time might be running out for Jolie.

If it hadn't already.

He tried to ease into it. "Hannah, think about this. Why *would* they take her? It's easy to understand why you suspected Marshall. But from everything you've told me, his parents would have everything to lose if they got caught. You've said yourself they can visit her whenever they want—"

"But they can't take her home with them. Don't you see? They want more than an afternoon in my living room. You heard Bob. They were putting pressure on Marsh."

"But do they want to be locked away for kidnapping? Would they risk jail just to spend a cozy weekend with their granddaughter?"

"They want to get even. They blame Marsh's disintegration on me. And Lolly thinks I'm a bad mother. For all I know she might think she's saving Jolie from a life of drop-in day care and store-bought cookies."

"Hannah…"

"I know them! They're capable of this. They're probably frantic because Marsh dropped out of sight, and they blame me for that, as well. Or maybe they're trying to scare him back into the open."

He didn't remind her she'd been wrong once. "I think you have to go back and work with the authorities," he said when the silence had stretched a mile. "It's not a parental abduction anymore, Hannah. The FBI will certainly be involved by now, whether Tony wants them or not. You can tell them your story."

"I can't go back. You heard Marsh. Tony still thinks this is murder."

"There's no body. He can't arrest you."

"He can keep me from leaving town to conduct my own search. Then there's that little matter of assault.…"

"Maybe he's decided to forget that. Didn't Amanda say he didn't mention being pushed?"

"Don't kid yourself. He'll use anything against me."

He tried one more reminder. "Marshall told Tony the truth about beating you."

She had one more rebuttal. "So he'll feel like an even bigger fool for believing Marsh's previous story, which will make him even more determined to prove I'm no good."

More miles passed while Quinn pondered what to do next. He was heading back toward Ohio but he had no clear destination in mind. Marshall's parents seemed like such a long shot to him, but there was a small chance Hannah could be right. If they were crazy or angry enough, one of them might have cracked. He didn't know the Blackstones—and had no desire to change that. But someone had taken Jolie, someone with easy access to Hannah's house, someone familiar enough to calm the dogs.

"Tell me again where they live," he said at last.

"Maple Ridge. It's a little town just north of Columbus. Walt bought a gas station. Marsh has three brothers who live nearby."

"Could one of the brothers have taken Jolie?"

"They all answer to Walt and Lolly. They wouldn't act on their own."

"Then we'll start with the senior Blackstones and go from there."

He felt a hand on his arm. Her eyes were haunted, and when she spoke, her voice was hollow. "Thanks, Quinn."

If nothing else he knew that Hannah needed a transition from the certainty that her ex-husband had taken Jolie to the terrible uncertainty of a stranger abducting her. If Jolie was living with her in-laws, then she was safe. Hannah had to believe in that possibility right now, because the alternative was so unthinkable.

Quinn covered her hand and squeezed it. He didn't know what else he could do.

They stopped for food, then drove nearly to Columbus before they pulled into a motel for the night. He had hoped to go farther, but he was too worn-out to drive safely, and he didn't dare ask Hannah to take the wheel. Her mind wouldn't be on the road.

"I'll get rooms," he told her. "We're in a good position to bypass Columbus in the morning."

When she didn't protest, he went inside to make the arrangements.

He returned a few minutes later and went directly to her

side. She opened the door and stepped down, as if that was the first time she'd thought about getting out of the van. She leaned against her seat, a dog on each side.

"We're out of luck," he informed her. "There's a convention in the city, and every motel room is booked. This place had a cancellation while I was standing in line, so they have one room. I grabbed it, but that's it."

"Can't we make it to Maple Ridge?"

"I've got to get some rest. And neither of us is thinking clearly enough to be effective tonight."

She didn't argue. He wondered if at least some part of her was reluctant to find out she was wrong about the Blackstones.

"I'll sleep in the van." She lifted her chin in an attempt to look stubborn. "This is my search. You've already done too much."

"It's a king-size bed, Hannah. We can share it. We shared a bed last night. Remember?"

"I saw the way you threw Marsh to the ground. I guess it wasn't fear of retaliation keeping you in your place in Wheeling."

"College wrestling. That's how I put myself through school. It's come in handy a time or two since then."

"But not tonight, Quinn."

She was struggling to sound normal, even casual. He wanted to fold her in his arms. He wanted to tilt at windmills for Hannah Blackstone. But all he could do was play along and let her make the calls. "Not tonight," he said.

"Okay. If you promise we'll be on the road early."

"We'll get a wake-up call as early as you want one," he said as he started to unpack the van.

The room was large, which made things easier, with a separate sitting room at the entry where the dogs could sleep. In the bedroom he and Hannah didn't bump into each other as they circled the bed. The toilet and bath were separate, which was another plus, and there was a second vanity. As they carried in the essentials Quinn told himself this would work out. If Hannah was too uncomfortable with the arrangements, he could sleep on the narrow sofa flanked by Oliver and Fagan—as long as he didn't drape an arm over the side too close to canine teeth.

He made the offer, but she declined. "I thought of that, but you need a good night's sleep."

He wondered if either of them would sleep. Since leaving Marshall he had thought of little except where Jolie might be. If he was haunted, how must Hannah feel?

"I'm going to take my shower now, so I won't have to worry in the morning." Hannah disappeared into the bathroom and closed the door, and he stripped down to clean boxers and a T-shirt. He washed up at the sink, then fed the dogs to save Hannah the trouble—and garner some doggy bonus points. He supposed they were warming up, since neither snapped at him as he put paper plates of dog food in front of them. At this rate they would be wagging their tails in his face by the millennium.

He was in bed with the covers to his waist by the time Hannah came out. She was wearing his shirt again, and she looked drained, but she didn't look as if she'd given in to tears.

"I want to stop on the way to Maple Ridge tomorrow." She pulled the covers back on her side of the bed. "Jolie loves orange soda. I want to get some to have in the van. And pretzels. The little ones. The big ones are too easy for her to choke on."

"We'll stop."

"And a coloring book and crayons. She'll need something to do in the van."

His heart was breaking. "That's a good idea."

"Of course she'll have the dogs to play with. Now I'm glad we brought them along. They'll be so glad to see her."

"Maybe she can teach me how to get along with them."

"They're dogs. They don't have good judgment. Look how much they love Marshall."

"I saw hints of the man you thought you'd married, Hannah. Maybe that's the man they love."

She clamped her lips, and he realized he'd made a mistake. She was skating on such thin emotional ice that she couldn't feel anything, or she would feel everything.

"It's been a long time since we ate," he said quickly, changing the subject to something less dangerous. "I could call out for a pizza."

"Not for me."

"Then maybe you'd like to watch television? It put you to sleep last night."

"I'd just like to turn off the light, if that's okay."

He could hear the strain in her voice. He was sure she needed the cover of darkness, the anonymity of her grief. He snapped off his lamp and turned on his side away from her. "I asked for a wake-up call at six. I hope that's okay."

"Perfect."

A family passed by their room, laughing and chattering. There were small children in the group, because he could hear the unmistakable stomping of sneakers on the pavement and a child's happy screeching.

"Jolie loves motels," Hannah said, when the sound had died away. "She loves to swim in the pools and bounce on the beds. She'd be so happy here."

His eyes were wide open in the darkness. "Instead of rushing right home tomorrow, maybe we can stop along the way. We could find a place with a playground and a pool. Would you like that?"

"It has to be near a Tasty Burger. The first thing I want to do is take her there for a hamburger, just the way…she likes it."

He closed his eyes. They were suspiciously moist. "That sounds perfect."

She began to weep very softly. At first he wasn't absolutely sure. Then he realized she was muffling her tears in the pillow.

The sound nearly destroyed him. He lay without moving, undecided about what to do. He wanted to comfort her, but he was afraid it would make things worse. She was a strong woman who had held up miraculously well. Now he realized how much of her strength had been a fierce conviction that Marshall had their daughter.

When the sobbing didn't stop he moved across the bed and put his arms around her. He could not ignore her suffering any more than he could have ignored her quest to find Jolie. "Hannah," he soothed, "we'll find her. We won't stop looking until we do. I promise. You have to believe it."

"She's...gone. She's not...with Marsh."

"I know, sweetheart." He tightened his arms and pulled her closer. "But maybe she is with his family. You listed a lot of reasons why they might have taken her. Don't give up yet."

"I'm not...but I'm afraid."

He was afraid, too. He had used every comforting word in his vocabulary, but he hadn't been convinced by any of them. Neither had she.

"Someone has her.... They might hurt her...or worse."

He squeezed his eyes closed. "Children *are* returned to their parents, Hannah. Alive and unharmed. It happens...."

"Where is she?" She pulled away from him, but only to face him. She was so close his lips nearly brushed her hair. "Who has my little girl?"

He brushed her hair off her face, then he pulled her head to rest against his shoulder, cradling her in his arms. "I don't know, but we're going to follow every lead. I promise. Starting with the Blackstones."

"Maybe...she did wander outside. Maybe...she went down...to the lake."

"The doors were still locked when you got up, remember?"

"Maybe I was wrong about that. Maybe...she got outside."

"That kind of thinking won't do you a bit of good. Trust what you know, and you know the house was locked up tight the next morning. Somebody took her while you were checking the sprinklers, then they locked the house again, so you wouldn't be suspicious when you returned. It's the only thing that makes sense."

"I should have checked on her!"

"You had no reason to." He rubbed her back through the shirt. It felt perfectly natural to hold her in his arms this way. Everything about her seemed familiar and right to him. The circumstances were wrong, so terribly, terribly wrong. But the woman was absolutely right.

Hannah took a deep, shaky breath. "She trusted me to take care of her."

"You can't control everything and everyone else. You took every reasonable precaution to protect her."

"I'm...sorry you're involved, Quinn. You don't...deserve this."

"And you do?"

"She's my child."

"And my neighbor. And her mother is a friend of mine."

She looked up at him, and through the pale light seeping in their window he could clearly see the devastation in her eyes. "No man ever has been as good to me as you have these last...three days."

He had not considered the intimacy of taking her in his arms. She needed comfort; he had comfort to give. Now he was aware of a feeling more intimate than a need to console her.

"You deserve good things," he said. "Only good things. Always."

"The world doesn't work...like that."

"No." If it did, Hannah would be lying beside him for an entirely different reason. Jolie would be safe, and the three of them would be on their way to becoming a family.

The thought astonished him because it was so unfamiliar. Yet it, like the feel of Hannah against him, was absolutely right.

He realized he had to move away. His need for Hannah wasn't simple desire. It was mixed up with wanting to reassure her and wanting to become part of her life. Desire was the most complicated part of what he felt, and the most dangerous.

He was gathering himself to ease away from her when she stopped him. "Quinn?"

"Uh-huh..."

"Don't go."

"I'm not going anywhere except the other side of the bed."

"I know. Don't. Please?"

He stroked her hair, but he stopped when she took his hand and kissed his palm. His heart began to pound. He told himself he had misunderstood, that the kiss was a gesture of thanks. Gratitude for the simple gift of kindness.

"I need...your arms around me," she whispered.

"Hannah, I would do anything for you. But maybe...it's not such a good idea," he said, after an emotional struggle. "I trust myself, but I have limits."

"Not here, not now." She framed his face with her hands, and her eyes filled with tears. "I know you can't make this go away. But I need you... More than I'll ever...need anyone again."

He knew how desperate she must feel, how hungry she was to ease the loneliness and sorrow inside her. He knew it even more when she kissed him.

And then he didn't know anything, he only felt her breasts pressed against his chest, her hair sliding along his cheek, her hips rocking against his. He knew that she felt everything, too, and that his arousal must be as obvious to her as it was to him. He could not deny how she made his body ache with desire any more than he could bring her daughter home by wishing.

He tried once more to be gallant, to prove that this was never what helping her had been about. "If I've made you feel...you owed me this...."

"No!" She kissed him again, and the scent of her skin, the lush give of her lips, wrenched a groan from deep inside him. He needed her, too, needed to feel the warmth of her flesh, the ferocious beating of her heart. At this, the lowest point since Jolie's disappearance, he wanted nothing more than to hold life, at its most elemental.

He circled her with his arms and lifted her to his chest. She dug her fingers into his hair and kissed him harder, murmuring his name as she did, as if she needed to say it over and over again to convince herself that unlike the child who had been torn from her, he was really there. His hands found the hem of the shirt and lifted it. Her skin was taut and warm. He could feel the clean outline of her spine. Her body was womanly, but not soft. She labored hard, using and honing her strength, and the result was a curving, feminine sculpture that gave him greater pleasure than he could even have guessed.

She rose above him and stripped off her shirt in one impatient movement. Then she took his hands and placed them against her breasts. Her eyes were closed, and her cheeks were still wet with tears, but she swayed when he traced her nipples with his thumbs.

"I said you were beautiful. I had no idea how very..."

"Let me...undress you."

She moved just far away enough to let him sit up. She smoothed his shirt over his chest and head, dropping it to the floor beside her own. He pulled her down to lie beside him. Under any circumstances but these he would have felt compelled to slow their pace, to use every skill he had to give her pleasure. But it wasn't pleasure they craved so much as contact. They needed to drown in each other.

And they did. Someday perhaps they would find the time to learn each other's bodies, but not tonight. He skimmed his hands over her again and again, desperate not to be separated from the feel or heat. When she moved away to finish undressing, he kept an arm around her. When he sat up to do the same, she draped herself against his back, her breasts pressed firmly against him.

Face-to-face again with the long length of her legs pressed against his, the soft swell of her breasts against his chest, he could feel her heart pounding and her body growing supple with desire. He understood her need for what it was, but it didn't diminish his own passion. That he could give her something, anything, now, when she was in such despair seemed the greatest test of love.

There was no time and no inclination to prove themselves. He sank into her with one deep thrust and found her more than ready for him. He wrapped his arms around her, unwilling even in the midst of intimacy to be separated.

They moved together, as if they had moved that way since the beginning of time. There were no adjustments, no instruction. They took what they needed, legs entwined, hands greedy for each other's flesh, until passion had stretched to a breaking point.

Quinn couldn't let the moment pass without some word of love, some acknowledgment that for him, at least, this encounter meant more than comfort.

"Someday," he whispered, straining to hold himself back from release, "someday you won't be sad and you won't need to forget. Someday we'll be together this way with no thought of anything except each other."

"Someday," she whispered. "To someday, Quinn."

He closed his eyes because the vulnerability in hers was too hard to bear. He felt her move beneath him, and suddenly he was vulnerable, too. To love, to sadness, to the joy of merging with this woman.

With a fierce certainty, he knew that if he had to, he would take on the whole world for Hannah Blackstone and her child.

He would be certain there was a someday for all of them.

Chapter 13

When the wake-up call came, Quinn sat up in bed with the telephone in his hand, aware that Hannah was no longer in the bed beside him.

Slowly he became aware of more. The rumpled sheets, the unmistakably twisted covers, the scent of a woman and a man who had not merely slept.

He sat perfectly still, the receiver dangling in his lap. He had known better than to let the emotions of last night blossom. He had known better than to touch Hannah, and surely better than to make love to her.

The bedroom door opened and Hannah appeared in the doorway. She was wearing his shirt again, but nothing else. Her expression was inscrutable. "You're awake?"

"The front desk just called." He watched her carefully hide whatever she was feeling.

"I got up to take the dogs outside, then I took a shower. I'll dress while you take yours."

He was stumped for a reply. When he didn't move, she

took the matter out of his hands. "Quinn, what happened last night just did. You didn't take advantage of me, and I don't regret it. But I don't want to talk about it, either."

Staring at her, he could see that their relationship and all its implications could be the straw that broke the camel's back. She was emotionally overloaded, and she couldn't think of anything now except survival. "All right," he said gently. "Whatever you want."

"I just want to find my daughter."

So did he, in the worst possible way, but the futility of their search gnawed at him. He rose from the bed and went to stand in front of her, resting his hands lightly on her arms.

"I want you to give some serious thought to working with the authorities, Hannah. You can get an attorney to advise you, but I've known a fair number of FBI agents, and I think they'll treat you objectively. They won't have Chandler's prejudices, and they won't listen too closely to his ravings. They have a way of asking questions that could trigger something you haven't thought of before."

She didn't quite meet his eyes. "I've been thinking, too. We'll check out Marsh's family, then I'll call Amanda. She promised she'd talk to Faye again and see what she could find out. But there's no point being free to search for Jolie if I don't know where to go next. I had to be sure it wasn't Marshall, and now I have to be sure it's not his family. But if it's not, I—" she cleared her throat "—I don't know where to go or what to do."

"I don't know how involved the FBI is at present, but they won't let Chandler pursue this vendetta against you."

"We need to get moving."

He dropped his hands. She didn't move away. He leaned down and kissed her, then he straightened before she could protest. "I'll be ready in a few minutes. Whatever happens today, it's another step toward bringing her home. Even if we're only eliminating possibilities. Remember that. Okay?"

She didn't smile. "It's my mantra."

He wanted to do so much more for her, but the best he could do was step around her to take his shower.

In the past few days Hannah had seen more small towns than a second-rate carnival, but Maple Ridge, at least, was familiar. After her in-laws had moved here, she and Marshall had made the trip from Port Franklin for Blackstone family gatherings. In her naiveté she had believed that being with his family might encourage Marshall to try harder at being a husband and later, a father.

They reached the outskirts in less than an hour. She hadn't known what to say to Quinn on the drive because she wasn't sure what she felt about last night. She had needed him, and she wasn't ashamed of their lovemaking. But what had any of it meant? For now she had no time or emotional reservoirs left to consider it.

"I'm going to pull over so we can make some plans." Quinn turned into the parking lot of a sprawling white frame church.

She had thought little about how to accomplish their task. Most likely if the Blackstones had Jolie, they had her here with them. But Hannah couldn't walk up to the front door and ask to see her daughter. Neither could she and Quinn wait for Jolie to skip down the front walk or play on the swing set. If Jolie was here, Lolly and Walt would be careful that she stayed hidden.

If Jolie was here.

"First, we have to figure out if she's really with her grandparents," Quinn said, turning off the engine. "Then, if she is, we have to figure out how to get her away from them. That might be a good time to call the Maple Ridge police."

"If Lolly has Jolie, she's keeping her inside." Hannah stared at the church steeple casting its shadow over the parking lot. "One of us has to go in there and find out."

"Then we can break in, lie our way in, or go to the front door and tell the truth."

"That last one's out. They'll call the Port Frank cops before we open our mouths."

"You seem to have some expertise at breaking in...."

"And you have some at lying." She made a face. "We're a pretty pair, aren't we?"

"Does your father-in-law go into his station in the morning?"

"Every morning about seven. Lolly's mortified because he even goes in on Sundays. He never goes to church."

"Is she a churchgoer?"

"Not really, but she likes to blame her poor attendance on Walt. In fact I think this is her church."

"What does she do while her husband works?"

"Cleans. Cooks. Cleans some more. You could do sterile surgery in any room of the house."

"Hobbies? Clubs or meetings?"

"None that I know of."

"So Lolly should be at home and Walt should be at work. I'm assuming Jolie would stay with Lolly?"

Hannah's heart was sinking. It all seemed so incongruous. Yes, the Blackstones disliked her, but enough to abduct their granddaughter?

She met his eyes. She would not be defeated. "If Jolie's here, that makes the most sense."

"Then here's my suggestion."

Quinn examined the tan brick ranch house as he strolled up the walkway. He listened for a dog's barking, but was relieved when none greeted him. Hannah had warned that the last she knew, the Blackstones owned an aging Chihuahua. Either the dog had passed on or it was too old to note his arrival.

The street was sparsely populated, and even though there were neighbors in hailing distance, at least they weren't thirty feet from the front door. He climbed two steps to the porch, a narrow concrete affair with a roof supported by metal grillwork pillars. A welcome mat read "The Blackstones" and pictured a garden of colorful flowers. It was the only garden on the starkly landscaped property.

He wore a discount store tie he'd bought just half an hour before, and his sports coat was buttoned. He had considered buying a Bible, too, but even these desperate circumstances weren't enough to excuse that. He might impersonate a minister, but he had no intention of using sacred props to do it. He pulled the collar of his dress shirt away from his throat, then he knocked. He waited, but not long. The woman who opened the door could only be Lolly Blackstone.

"Yes?" she said warily.

Quinn smiled warmly. "Mrs. Blackstone?"

"That's right."

She was a tiny woman, rail thin and prematurely wrinkled. Her iron-gray hair was a lacquered helmet, and her cat's-eye glasses had been popular in the fifties.

He held out his hand. "I'm Ron Creston, the new associate minister at Ridge Road."

Lolly narrowed her eyes, then she extended her hand. "I don't know anything about a new minister."

He smiled again. "I guess you weren't there on Sunday when they introduced me?"

She shook her head.

Quinn had discarded the possibility of using Jolie's disappearance as an excuse for this visit. If he seemed unaware of the kidnapping, then she might not be as worried about the "new minister" glimpsing her granddaughter.

He smiled again, and his teeth ached from the effort. "I'm just in the neighborhood visiting church members and friends. Did I catch you at a bad time?"

"Every time's a bad time these days."

"I'm sorry to hear that. Is there something I can help you with?"

She seemed to consider. "Not likely, I guess."

She backed up, as if she was going to close the door, so he stepped forward just enough to make that difficult. "You know, sometimes talking to another person is the best thing, Mrs. Blackstone. And I'd like to know more about you, anyway. That's the only way I can do my job."

"I'm afraid I'm busy."

He had been listening for sounds from the house, and now he caught what he thought might be voices from a television set. "Did I interrupt one of the talk shows, maybe?"

She actually blushed. "I don't watch those kinds of shows. One of my little neighbors is here watching cartoons."

The words echoed momentarily in his head. He schooled himself not to react. "You're baby-sitting."

She scowled. "I promised I would."

"You know, I promised myself I'd sit down over a cup of coffee with you this morning and find out about your family. But if it's inconvenient, we can make another appointment when your husband's at home. That way I can find out what he likes about coming to our church, and I'll recognize him when I see him on Sundays."

As he had calculated, she was mortified. "No! I mean, I guess you'd better come in now. Walt's awful busy."

He was happier than she could know. There was a "neighbor" child in the other room he wanted to take a look at. "I won't keep you long," he promised.

"Coffee's all made."

He followed her through a small but immaculate house. Neither dust nor child would survive happily here. He had grown up in a house as pristine and colorless as this one, and he knew. He noticed that the smell of ammonia and bleach wafted after Lolly, as if she dabbed it behind her ears like perfume.

"Have a seat," she said, gesturing to the living room sofa.

"Mind if I meet your little neighbor first?" He started toward the sound of the television. "I really love children."

"You won't love this one. He's a little heathen. I only keep him so he'll know what it's like to be in a Christian home."

"He?"

"Sammy. Not after anyone in the Bible, I'm sure."

Quinn swallowed disappointment as he crossed through the dining room into a darkly paneled family room. A little boy of about six sat cross-legged on the floor in front of a big-screen television that was too large for the room.

Lolly was busying herself in the kitchen. Quinn could hear the clatter of dishes. He crossed to the little boy, who hadn't even turned at his approach. He squatted beside him and put his hand on the boy's shoulder, keeping his voice low.

"Sammy?"

Sammy turned. "Yeah?"

"I'm a friend of Lolly's. Are you all alone in here?"

"Uh-huh."

"No playmates?"

"Uh-uh."

"No other kids in the house? Just you?"

The little boy screwed up his face in an expression only a child could manage. "I'm bored."

"Have you been in any of the other rooms?"

"Yeah."

"Nobody there, either? No little girls younger than you?"

"How come you're asking questions?"

Quinn rocked back on his heels. "Oh, I just thought one of Lolly's granddaughters might be here, that's all."

Sammy stuck out his tongue. "I don't like girls."

Quinn spared him a smile. "You will, believe me."

"My mom's coming home in a while, then I'm going to find somebody to play with."

Quinn got slowly to his feet and ruffled the little boy's mop of hair. "Good luck, sport."

Disappointment settled heavily over him. It was inconceivable that Sammy and Jolie could be in the same house and not know it. Unless Jolie was with her grandfather at the station—and that scenario was improbable—then Jolie wasn't in Maple Ridge. He and Hannah could check the homes of Marshall's brothers, but even Hannah had found that possibility unlikely.

Jolie Blackstone had been abducted by a stranger.

He closed his eyes for a moment as he thought about how to tell Hannah the awful truth. She had believed so sincerely that her daughter was being cared for by someone with strong connections to her. No matter how reprehensible any of the Blackstones, they were, at the very least, family. And as family there would have been some measure of comfort and protection offered the little girl.

"Mister, don't you feel good?"

Quinn opened his eyes and realized that the little boy had given him an excuse to leave. "You know what? I don't."

Lolly came into the room as he finished the sentence, but Sammy rushed to tell her. "He's sick. He's sick."

Quinn shook his head, anxious to be gone. "I'm sorry, Mrs. Blackstone, but I'm afraid Sammy's right. I felt fine when I knocked on your door, but there's some sort of fast-acting flu going through my family. I might have picked it up, too.''

"Should I call someone?"

"No. I'm certainly well enough to get home, but I shouldn't stay here and expose you. I'd rather you didn't mention it to anybody, if fact. The church staff fusses like a flock of mother hens. I'll let them know later in the day.''

She nodded, tight-lipped, as if she were trying to decide which room to disinfect first.

Quinn started toward the door, hobbling his usual long strides. "I hope you'll let me call on you again.''

"When you're all well.''

"In the meantime, we'll see you in church.'' He opened the door before she could, and he visualized her running for a rag to wipe it down before his fingerprints turned cold.

"Do you have someone with you?''

He was surprised by the question, but he followed Lolly's gaze toward the van and he saw the passenger door click shut. As he wondered what Hannah had been doing, he cast around for an answer. "I brought one of our lay leaders along to visit a family at the end of the block. He must be finished, too.''

"Oh, and who would that be?''

He managed a deferential grin. "I'll be honest, Mrs. Blackstone, I'm still stumbling over names.''

"I didn't mean which neighbor. You don't know the name of the man in your own car?''

He used his creativity and turned the tables. "Well, yes. That's Mike Stevens, a retired pastor from Grand Rapids. He's almost as new in the church as I am, but he's quite an old hand at visiting. We're lucky to have him. You've met Mike, of course? He's been here several months.''

She looked dismayed, which is just what he'd hoped for. "I'm sure I have.''

Satisfied he started out to the porch. "I'll look forward

to seeing you again." That was probably the biggest lie he'd told all morning.

"You say a prayer or two for my baby granddaughter."

He stopped. "Granddaughter?"

"My son's little girl. She's been missing for three days. Nobody knows what happened to her."

He tried to sound surprised. "Nobody knows?"

"Well, her mother took off right after she disappeared. The police think she's involved."

He couldn't think of anything appropriately pastoral to say.

"But I don't think so," Lolly went on. "I don't like my daughter-in-law, you understand. And I sure don't think she was any good for my son. But Hannah, well, she loves little Jolie. I'll give her that. She would never hurt her."

Now Quinn really *was* at a loss for words.

"The police have been hanging around asking questions about where Hannah might have gone, you know? But I don't know how that's going to bring my grandbaby home."

"Do you have any idea who might have taken her, Mrs. Blackstone?"

Lolly shook her head. "You'll say a prayer?"

For the first time he could be perfectly honest. "I promise I won't stop praying until this is over."

"She's not there," Hannah said, the moment Quinn got behind the wheel. "Now we have to check the station."

"Hannah, she's not there, either." Quinn turned, and Hannah saw from the expression on his face that he had been trying to find a way to soften the blow.

"How do you know?"

"First, what were you doing outside the van?"

"While you and Lolly were occupied, I went around and looked in all the bedroom windows."

"You didn't trust me to find out the facts?"

"I had to make sure."

He let out a long breath. "I guess I would have done the same."

She swallowed tears at his gentle tone of voice. "What makes you sure she's not at the station?"

"Lolly told me that she doesn't know where Jolie is. She also said she knows that *you* didn't hurt her."

Hannah knew she should feel gratified for Lolly's support, but she didn't have time to feel anything except dismay. "Maybe you're wrong. Maybe she's lying."

He shook his head slowly.

She couldn't give up. Not now, and not like this. The alternatives were too terrifying. "Quinn, I have to see for myself."

He turned the key in the ignition. "Then that's what we'll do. Tell me about the station. Is there anywhere Jolie might be hidden?"

"Not really. There's a garage with a couple of bays, but that door's always open. And there's an office where you pay for gas. Walt goes back and forth from one part to the other."

"Back rooms?"

"No, and the storage area out back wouldn't be an appropriate place for a child."

"Then will you be satisfied if I buy gas and go inside to pay for it? If I don't see her, we'll know she's not there?"

It sounded so simple and so impossible, but Hannah had to give it a try. "That will be fine."

He pulled out on the road and started toward the center of town. "Lolly also mentioned the police have been asking questions."

"Which police?"

"She didn't say, and it wasn't an appropriate question to ask. I was afraid she might get suspicious."

"You turn right at the next light, then make your first left. The station's one block down."

She watched as Quinn followed her directions. He was patiently following her lead. "You've been great, Quinn." She cleared her throat. "I...appreciate it."

He didn't look at her. "I would walk over hot coals to find her."

She believed him. Somewhere along the way her search had become his, too. His interest had moved beyond one neighbor helping another, a man helping a woman who attracted him, even a lover helping a lover.

She did not have time to think about Quinn. But his presence had become as important to her as the air she breathed. Without him beside her, she knew she would never have gotten this far.

"There it is." Quinn slowed and crossed the quiet street to pull into the station parking lot. "Maybe you ought to slip into the back while we're here, in case someone gets close enough to see you."

"I've had it with hiding."

"Then will you at least stay in the van? Maybe you're tired of hiding, but I'd rather we choose the place and time to end it. I'll pump my own gas and pay inside."

She nodded, vaguely ashamed of her outburst. "I'm sorry. I'm not looking for trouble."

"You don't need to. It found you big-time."

He got out and slammed the door. Hannah felt a sharp pain in one palm and realized she was digging her fingernails into it.

As she waited she admitted to herself that Quinn would not find Jolie here with Walt. She closed her eyes as the realization that she might never see her daughter again washed over her. She couldn't get beyond that thought. She knew she would later, that the most terrifying possibilities would engulf her. But now the struggle to cope with the horror of never holding her daughter, never tucking her into bed at night with her favorite doll, was all she could manage.

"Annie!" Her eyes flew open, and she looked around wildly. Annie, Jolie's one-eyed, nearly bald rag doll was missing, too.

She didn't know how that fact had escaped her attention until now. Jolie, a restless sleeper, always started the night with Annie in her arms, but without fail, in an hour or two the doll landed on the floor beside her bed. Part of their morning ritual was to find and rescue poor Annie and place her in a doll cradle for the day.

When Hannah had discovered that Jolie was missing, she had pulled the covers back and peered under the bed in case Jolie was playing hide-and-seek. But neither the child nor any toys had been hiding there. She had been so agitated that she hadn't thought to look for Annie.

Whoever had taken Jolie had taken Annie, too.

Although she didn't know what it meant, she wanted to spring from the van to tell Quinn, and she nearly did. Instead she peered out her window to locate him.

Straight into the face of her former father-in-law.

"I thought it might be you," Walt said.

She watched Quinn striding toward the van looking angry enough to throw Walt across the island of gas pumps. She held up her hand to stop him.

"How did you know?" she asked Walt.

"Lolly called a few minutes ago. She got to thinking there wasn't something right about his visit." He cocked his head toward Quinn.

Walt was a large man. His son had gotten his strength and physique from his father. Walt resembled Marshall in other ways, as well, although not the chastened, remorseful Marshall she had confronted yesterday.

Now Walt leaned on her door, his fading blue eyes narrowed. "What have you done with my granddaughter, Hannah?"

"We came to ask you the same question."

"She's not here."

"I wish to God she were."

"You're pretending you don't know what happened?"

"Walt..." She cleared her throat, then shook her head. "I woke up and she was gone. It's the truth. Somebody has her."

"You going to blame this on my boy, too?"

"No, Marshall doesn't have her. I found him yesterday and saw for myself."

"Where is he?" Walt demanded.

"I'm sorry, but I can't tell you that."

"I'm his father!"

"And Marshall's an adult. He'll contact you when he's ready."

Walt assessed her. "I think you're lying," he said at last. "I don't think you know where Marshall is, and I think you did something with little Jolie. I think you're just what Tony says you are!"

Before she could answer, Quinn nudged the older man away from the door with his shoulder. "Hannah, roll up the window. We're getting out of here. She's not inside."

Walt's hand shot out as if to grab for her, but Quinn intercepted him. Hannah realized there was no longer a chance of dialogue. She rolled up the window to keep Walt at bay as Quinn rounded the van and climbed into the driver's seat.

"You know who this man is?" Walt was shrieking now, through the closed window. "Tony told me all about Mr. Quinn McDermott. You think I'm stupid? This is the man who covered the Whithurst kidnapping, Hannah. He stood right there and watched that little Whithurst boy get himself killed. Took notes while the gunman was loading bullets. What's he paying you for your story?'' He slammed his open palm against the glass but it didn't break. ''You gonna tell him what you did with my granddaughter? Maybe he'll put you in the newspaper, too. Maybe he'll take you apart and put you back together again the way he—''

His final words were cut off as the van screeched out of the service station parking lot.

''We have to get out of here,'' Quinn said. He didn't glance at her, but a muscle in his jaw jumped erratically. ''He'll report us to the local cops.''

''What was Walt talking about, Quinn? What did he mean?''

''There's no time for that.''

''What was Walt talking about!''

He clamped his jaw shut, and she knew what that meant. He made the first left, then a right, picking up speed as they drove farther from the center of Maple Ridge. He wove through side streets and across parking lots until they were clearly out in the country, then he chose a road that looked sparsely populated and made a right, following it as it twisted and turned until he came to a gravel driveway winding up a low slope to a farmhouse. His wheels spun as he pulled the van into the drive, but he slowed as they neared the shelter of giant maples swaying serenely in the morning breeze.

Quinn parked under the maples and shut off the engine. ''The game's up, Hannah.''

She stared straight ahead. ''Which game? The one that features me? Or the one that features you?''

''The one that features us. Walt will report us to the local sheriff. In a matter of minutes the Port Franklin cops will know we're driving this van. It's time to turn yourself in.''

"I want to talk to Amanda first."

"I suppose that makes sense."

The van had grown overly warm. She rolled down her window, and the smell of newly mown grass filled the van. She could see honeybees flitting from flower to flower in a patch of fading daffodils, and somewhere a cardinal sang.

Jolie loved cardinals best of all. Red was her favorite color.

"Suppose you tell me what Walt meant," she said at last.

"I'm trying to think of the best way to do it."

"The truth would be a nice change."

"I've never lied to you. I just didn't want to burden you with my past."

"Burden me?" She looked at him for the first time since they had stopped. Her voice rose. "Do you think that *any-thing* about you could be a burden compared to what I'm going through already?"

"This could."

Tears welled in her eyes. "Tell me!"

"I never wanted to be anything but a reporter, Hannah. Maybe it was because there were so many secrets in my own life. Maybe I needed to discover other people's to make up for that. I don't know. But from the moment I left home, I knew that's what my future held."

"Stop it! I didn't ask for a biography."

"Can you give me a moment to work into this?"

She gazed at him. This was the man she had made love to last night, the man who had touched her with such care and such passion. The man who had held her as she sobbed, held her as desire and sorrow and all the myriad emotions in between shattered into a thousand pieces.

She looked away. "Go on."

"I was ruthless, Hannah. I didn't think much about any-body else. Not the people I went after for stories, not the people in my own life. I found a woman who cared as little about me as I did about her, and I was perfectly happy. I worked myself into a frenzy and right up the ladder to the top stories. I made a name for myself, so when a really juicy story broke, I was the obvious choice to cover it.''

"The Whithurst kidnapping."

"I was never glad little Jeff Whithurst was kidnapped. I'm not that kind of monster. But I remember that after I heard about it, after that first jolt of dismay hit me, I thought, 'This is some story. Somebody's going to make a name on this one.'''

"And you did." Her voice was hollow.

"Obviously not in Port Franklin, which is half the reason I moved there."

"Right. The hicks in Port Franklin didn't know we had a bonafide celebrity in our midst."

"I never, ever thought of it that way. I thought of Port Franklin as a chance to get away from a nightmare."

"I guess you'd better tell me about the nightmare."

"You don't know the story, do you?"

She still didn't look at him. "I remember that a little boy was kidnapped. A senator's son, right? It happened about the time my father had his heart attack and Jolie and I flew to Arizona. I was there a couple of weeks, and I hardly saw the papers or the news."

"Jeffrey Whithurst was taken by his nanny and an accomplice. His parents spent so little time with him they didn't even realize he was gone until they got the ransom call late that night. Neither of them had ever really wanted children, and they had turned him over to this woman, pulling him back into their lives for photo ops, then pushing him away again when the cameras were gone."

She closed her eyes and rested her head against the seat. Despite her anger she heard the genuine sadness in his voice. "Go on."

He was talking slowly, trying to find his way. "I had an inside track with the family because I'd covered the senator's last campaign. Howard Whithurst had courted me because he was considering a run for the presidency in the next election. I won't say that he wasn't sorry his son had been kidnapped, but mostly I think he saw it as a chance for publicity. He was the worst of the two, but his wife wasn't much better. Through the entire ordeal she only talked about how carefully she would choose the next nanny, how many references she would require, how many security checks. She never once mentioned the possibility of spending more time with Jeff herself."

Hannah realized she was crying when she felt tears on her cheeks. She brushed them away. "He died, didn't he?"

He rested his hand on her shoulder until she shrugged it away. "It's nothing like what's happened to Jolie, Hannah. Jeff was kidnapped for ransom. The payment was made, but agents followed the man who intercepted it. I was with them...."

She finally looked at him. "And?"

"They tracked the man to an old house on the city's east side, and they surrounded it. They were afraid to wait for the kidnappers to come out with Jeff. So they used their bullhorns and demanded the kidnappers release Jeff. That if they did, everything would be all right. There was a gunshot from inside. The FBI was afraid to wait any longer, and they stormed the house. I was behind a barricade at the rear. The back of the house was boarded up, and no one thought there was any chance they'd exit that way, which is why I'd been able to get that close. The agents with me ran around to the front, and I started to make my way to the front, too."

"Started to?"

His face was haunted now, as if he was viewing the scene in his mind. "The door closest to me crashed open, and a man came through, dragging Jeff behind him through the splinters and wood shards. He froze when he saw me.'' Quinn swallowed hard. "I was afraid he might shoot me, then I was afraid…he might not, because he turned the gun on Jeff. I pleaded with him not to shoot, that if he did, he would be tried as a murderer. But he didn't seem to hear me. Later it became clear he was on heavy-duty drugs, that any judgment he'd ever had was gone by then. Jeff began to scream and tried to pull away.…''

"Don't!" Nausea filled her, and her head began to whirl.

"I couldn't save him, Hannah." Quinn rested his elbows on the steering wheel and put his head in his hands.

"So you wrote about it, instead?"

"I wrote about it. Yes."

"Why? Because that was your job? Because the senator wasn't the *only* one who wanted publicity? Did you use little Jeff Whithurst's story to make a name for yourself, Quinn? Is that what you've been planning to do this time, too?''

"I owed Jeff Whithurst that story, Hannah." He raised his head wearily. "It was the only thing I could do for him. Because there are terrifying people in the world, and some of them are parents. Because there are people who use children for whatever sick purposes motivate them. Because nobody ever really loved Jeff, but over the week he was being held for ransom I learned to.''

Her heart squeezed painfully in her chest, but she could not forgive him for keeping the truth from her. "Why didn't you tell me this before? You were involved in the most important kidnapping case of the decade and you didn't tell me!''

"I didn't tell you because I didn't want you to think about Jeff and how that story ended. This is a different story, Hannah. You thought Jolie was with her father, then her grandparents. You didn't believe she had been taken by a stranger, and I didn't want you to think about the consequences if..." He didn't go on.

She still couldn't think about it, because if she did... "You couldn't save Jeff, and now you're trying to save Jolie."

"Should I ask for forgiveness?"

"You lied to me. You lied by omission."

"I'm not looking for absolution, Hannah. I can't bring Jeff back. But ever since that day I've wondered if I had just tried harder, followed more clues, dug a little deeper, if I might have found Jeff before the situation got so desperate. Maybe I could have offered myself as a go-between or found a way to free him. I know it's not possible. There were no clues that the FBI hadn't already plumbed. I tell myself that, then in the quiet hours after midnight, I start to wonder all over again."

She purposely hardened her voice to keep it from breaking. "And when I came to you and told you I had to find my daughter, you wondered even more."

"I'm not writing for any paper now. I never lied to you about that. I am thinking about a book on the Whithurst kidnapping, using some of the articles I wrote as a framework. But never, at any point, have I considered bringing you or Jolie into it. That has *nothing* to do with the choice I made to help you."

She believed him. She had no proof that his account of what had happened was true, yet she knew in her heart that it was. And now she knew something more important. This man *would* do anything to bring her daughter home, because he had his own demons to slay.

She stared straight ahead, because she couldn't look at him anymore. "I want my daughter, and you want forgiveness. We both have our own agendas, don't we? But we should never have let this become personal."

"Because I didn't tell you the entire truth? Because I tried to spare you?"

"No. Because you didn't tell me why you cared so much. And I believed...it was something different."

"Nothing I've told you changes the way I feel about you, Hannah. This became personal right at the start."

Her head was whirling. This was one more thing to handle, the ultimate straw that was going to destroy her. She took a deep breath and tried to push this new burden away. "I need to get to a telephone. I have to call Amanda. I have to find out if Faye will help us."

He took her shoulders and gently turned her to face him. "Did you hear what I said? This is personal. I care about you."

"I can't hear you! I can't think. I can hardly breathe! Please." She saw how deeply she'd wounded him. But there was no time to make amends. No time to think. No time to compose herself.

He dropped his hands. "All right. We'll get to a telephone."

"Thank you." She knew she sounded as if she were thanking a stranger. And maybe she was, despite all they had shared.

Chapter 14

They stopped at a gas station just off the interstate, and Hannah made her phone call from a booth littered with cigarette butts and candy wrappers. By the fourth ring she was afraid she had missed Amanda, by the eighth, she was sure of it, although Amanda's answering machine didn't pick up.

She was just about to hang up and try the number again when a man, breathless but familiar, answered.

"Mandy?"

Hannah debated whether to hang up or talk to Daniel. Mandy's husband was a good man, solid and dependable, and he had always been her friend.

"Daniel," she said at last. "It's Hannah."

"Hannah, for godsake, where are you?"

"I may be on my way back to Port Frank. I need to talk to Mandy. If she thinks I have any chance of making the cops or the FBI listen to me—"

"You haven't found Jolie?"

"Mandy told you?"

"As a matter of fact she didn't, but I guessed you were searching for Marshall."

"I found him. Jolie's not with him, and she's not with his parents." She cleared her throat. "Daniel, I don't know where else to look."

"Mandy's not here." He paused, as if he was searching for the right words, then gave up. "Hell, she hasn't been home since yesterday afternoon."

Hannah leaned against the grime-streaked glass. "Where is she?"

"I don't know. There was a message on the machine last night when I got home from work. She said she'd gone off for a while to do some thinking. She didn't say where, and she didn't say for how long."

"Mandy's gone away?" She could hardly believe it. "Now?"

"She hasn't been herself, Hannah. This thing with Jolie hit her hard, right on top of..." His voice trailed off.

"On top of what?"

"The news that the last *in vitro* didn't work."

Hannah was stunned. Amanda was her best friend, but she hadn't told Hannah that she and Daniel were trying to conceive by *in vitro* fertilization. "Daniel, I didn't know. I'm so sorry."

"Maybe she's just gone off to pull herself back together, but I'm worried about her. She knows you need her. It's not like Mandy to take off when somebody else needs her. And she wanted a baby so badly...."

Hannah knew that Mandy wanted to be a mother more than almost anything, but she had believed her friend was looking forward to adoption. As fond as Amanda was of Jolie, it had seemed clear that she would love any child placed in her home.

As fond as she was of Jolie.

For a moment the glass walls seemed to move toward her, squeezing the air from the booth and then from her lungs.

"Hannah?"

She opened the folding door, letting in the noise from the interstate as well as a soft, reassuring breeze. "Just how upset was she?"

"I honestly don't know where one thing stopped and the other started. It's just been too much for her."

She closed her eyes. *Where one thing stopped and the other started.* "She's always loved Jolie so much."

"You don't need this now. Look, my advice is to come back home. Try to work with the police and the FBI. If Tony Chandler continues to try to pin anything on you, we'll protect you."

"Daniel, have you tried the cottage on Kelley's Island? Could Mandy have gone there?"

"No, her parents rented it out for the month of June to make a little extra cash. She wouldn't be there."

Hannah tried to remember if Amanda had mentioned the rental to her. If the Longs, Amanda's parents, had indeed rented out the cottage for a month, then this was the very first time. Between the elder Longs, Amanda and her three siblings, the Kelley's Island cottage was always in demand by family during the summers. Amanda and Daniel had even discussed buying their own place once they had children.

She had to be sure that Daniel's story about the rental was true. Because if it wasn't...

She pulled herself together as best she could. "I'll...I'll probably be home tonight or tomorrow. When I get in I'll come to your house, Daniel. Maybe Mandy will be home by then."

He sounded as if he was trying to force optimism into

his voice. "I know she will. She'll be here by the time you come home, and together we'll figure out what to do next."

Hannah thanked him and hung up. In the van she turned to Quinn. "Mandy's disappeared, but I think I know where she might be."

"Disappeared?" His face mirrored his surprise.

"Yes, just the way Jolie did."

"Where are you leading with this, Hannah?"

But Hannah was thinking out loud. "Mandy would *know* how important Annie was to Jolie. Mandy would scoop up Annie and take her, too."

"Annie? What are you talking about?"

"Quinn, hand me the road map. I'll tell you as we drive."

"We're not going to Port Franklin?"

"Not yet."

Quinn watched the wind from the lake lift Hannah's hair and blow it against her cheeks. There was no bridge to tiny Kelley's Island, which, according to Hannah, was why it was such a charming place to visit and rarely overcrowded. Only a limited number of cars could cross on each ferry from the picturesque port at Marblehead, and car reservations had to be made weeks in advance. Instead most day visitors took bikes or rented them once the ferry landed.

"We'll be there in a few minutes." He could see the island growing larger, and he knew what Hannah must be feeling. "It's still light, Hannah. What do you want to do?"

They had talked this over at length, choosing to board one of the later ferries so they could do their investigation of the Longs' cottage under cover of darkness. But the sun still hovered above the horizon, and it would be at least another hour before their risk of being seen diminished.

At Quinn's feet Oliver growled in annoyance as Fagan

jostled him. The dogs had come on the ferry, too, since they couldn't be left in the van.

"We might be caught whatever we do," Hannah said. "But I think we'd better risk renting bikes and riding over to the other side of the island. We'll find a place to wait."

"You haven't eaten in hours. We'll get sandwiches."

She didn't protest, but he doubted she would eat. In the few days of their search she had lost weight, and her face was growing gaunt.

"Hannah, you know this is a long shot, don't you?"

"It's the only shot I have right now." She pushed her hair back over her ears and faced him. She wore round sunglasses and the Yankee baseball cap she had escaped in, along with leggings and a bright pink T-shirt she'd bought along the way. He wasn't sure her own mother would recognize her.

"You've known Amanda all your life," he said.

"And I know how much she wants a child. Something might have snapped inside her, Quinn. Maybe one day Mandy woke up and decided she deserved Jolie more than I did."

"But she's been at home every time you called except today. Would she have left Jolie here on the island by herself?"

"I don't know what she did, and I can't believe I'm even suspicious of my best friend. But maybe she hired a babysitter. Maybe somebody helped her. Maybe she drugged Jolie when she couldn't be here to watch over her."

"Why would anybody help her? Jolie's picture must be all over the local papers. And Kelley's is hardly deserted."

"I don't have the answers. I just have the questions. Where did Mandy go? Why now, when she knows I'm counting on her? Why didn't she tell me about the failed infertility treatment? Why has she taken off without Daniel?"

Quinn knew he had to rely on Hannah's instincts. If she felt that Amanda's behavior was so uncharacteristic as to be suspicious, then he had to accept that as a given. "Well, whatever questions you have, we'll have some answers as soon as it gets dark."

"I wish we didn't have to wait."

"We run the risk of having her see us if we don't. And if she has Jolie…"

"One thing I know for sure. Mandy would never hurt Jolie."

"Would she hurt anyone else? You or me, for instance?"

Hannah shook her head, and he knew if he could see her eyes, they would be bleak. "That's the part I don't know. And that's why we have to be careful. She owns a gun, Quinn. Mandy's father is a collector. Daniel worked nights for a while, and Mr. Long gave her a handgun for protection and taught her to use it."

Near the bike rental office they bought sandwiches—fast proving to be Quinn's least favorite food—and soft drinks. Hannah tied the dogs' leashes to her handlebars and Quinn carried the food. On the side of the island opposite the Longs' cottage they found a field where the skeleton of a new house rose from a tangle of brambles, and they settled themselves in its shadows to wait for the sunset.

They hardly spoke, although Quinn knew there was so much that needed to be said. Hannah forced herself to eat a few bites and finished most of her drink. The dogs devoured the rest of her sandwich and one that Quinn had bought just for them.

By the time a spectacular sunset had streaked the sky, they were ready to go.

"I'll lead the way," Hannah said.

"We could tie up the dogs and come back for them. We don't want them barking at the wrong moment."

She debated, but in the end, she agreed. To their credit, both dogs were silent as Hannah and Quinn pedaled away.

The ride took about fifteen minutes. Close to the Longs' cottage Hannah got off her bike and propped it against a tree. "I think we ought to go on foot from here."

Quinn propped his against hers and followed her along the side of the road. They had seen few cars but a fair number of pedestrians and bikers. Now as they passed a house with a second-story deck, somebody called hello.

She slowed, and when he caught up to her, she put her hand on his arm. It was the first time she had touched him voluntarily, and he realized how much he had missed that.

He had already grown used to her touch.

Hannah spoke softly. "The cottage is around the next curve. On the right."

"How often have you visited here?"

"Jolie and I have been here both summers since the divorce plus I came a couple of times as a teenager."

"Tell me about the house."

"The layout?"

He nodded and listened to her description. "Jolie would probably be sleeping upstairs," Hannah finished. "Where her presence wouldn't be noticed by anyone passing by."

It made sense to him. "How are you going to get inside to check?"

"I think we have to watch the house for a while. If Mandy's in there, then we'll decide."

"If she's in there with Jolie, she'll almost certainly have the curtains drawn."

His warning was prophetic. They made the rest of the trip in silence. Hannah's description had been so detailed that Quinn recognized the Longs' house immediately. It was sided in graying cedar, and in the light from the front porch he saw that the trim was painted a soft peach. Flowers grew along the sidewalk and in window boxes on the ground-floor level.

The curtains were all closed tight.

They stood together behind a row of poplars that shielded one side of the house from the road. "Someone's at home," Hannah whispered. "The lights are on."

Even that much was difficult to tell. The curtains were completely opaque, as if privacy was a much-valued commodity of the Long family. "We can stand here and wait for something to happen, or one of us can march up to the front door and demand entrance," Quinn said.

"We've got to stand here."

Quinn slapped a mosquito on his arm. "At least we have company."

Hannah was silent. He knew how ambivalent she was about her suspicions, but he also knew that loyalty wouldn't keep her from following every lead, no matter how distasteful or obscure.

Fifteen minutes passed, then twenty. A light went on upstairs, but the lights downstairs stayed on, too. "It looks like someone is going to bed," Quinn said.

"And someone's still up."

"I could knock on the door and ask for Mrs. Long. If the house is rented, they'll tell me she's not there."

"Would you recognize Amanda?"

"No."

"She would recognize you. That's tipping our hand."

"Look." He pointed toward the house. The front door was opening, and a man stepped out. He was about fifty, dressed casually and the proud bearer of an aluminium watering can. As they watched he stepped around the front of the cottage and began to water the window boxes.

"Amanda's father?" Quinn whispered.

"No, I've never seen him before."

He took her arm. "We're just passing by, Hannah. Come on."

There was no time to argue. They stepped out from behind the trees as if they'd been strolling from that direction. "Hi there," Quinn called. "Are the Longs home tonight?"

The man looked up as if they'd startled him. "The Longs? Oh, I see. No, they'll be here next month. My family's renting the cottage."

Quinn didn't glance at Hannah because he didn't want to witness her disappointment. "Then I guess none of the rest of the family is here, either," he said.

"One of the daughters is staying on the island somewhere. Are you friends of the family?"

"Yes," Hannah answered for him. "I—we were hoping to catch up to them. Are you enjoying the house?"

"Yes, it's lovely. Would you like me to leave a note for Mr. and Mrs. Long?"

Hannah paused, as if she were considering. "That's not necessary. I'm sure we'll see one or the other of them before then." A heartbeat passed. "You say one of the girls is here? Maybe we'll run into her."

"Dark-haired and pretty. About your age. I'm sorry, I can't remember her name."

"Sounds like Amanda," she said casually.

"That's it."

"You wouldn't know where she was staying, would you?"

"She didn't mention it. She came by this morning to pick up something from one of the upstairs bedrooms. She left with a small bag."

"Did she have her daughter with her?" Quinn said. "A cute little towhead?"

"No, she was alone."

Quinn was sure the man had reached his tolerance. "Well, maybe we'll run into her. Thanks for your help."

The man nodded and raised his hand in goodbye. "Oh, you know what? I just remembered. She said something that made me think she was staying on the other side of the island."

"What's that?"

"Well, she stayed upstairs a long time. I don't know what she was looking for. It's the room the Longs use for their grandchildren, the one with bunk beds and toys on the shelves. But when I walked by the room, she was staring out the window. I asked her what she was looking at, and she said, Nothing much. That the view was just different here from the one where she was staying. I guess that's what made me think she was living on the other side."

"You're sure it's Amanda?" Quinn said, once they were out of earshot. "Not one of her sisters?"

"She's the only brunette." Hannah was frantically trying to think where Amanda might be staying. "If she has Jolie, she'll want to be somewhere isolated, Quinn. Especially if she's leaving Jolie alone."

"That's the part that doesn't make sense. From everything you've told me about her, she wouldn't leave a child that age on her own."

Hannah didn't think so, either, but then she had never imagined that her best friend might steal her daughter. "He said Mandy was up in the room where the grandchildren stay. That's where Jolie always sleeps when we visit. Mandy left with a small bag. I bet she took toys for Jolie to play with."

"How are we going to find her?"

"I don't think she'd be staying with friends. Not if she has Jolie."

"Maybe we ought to start there, anyway, Hannah. Even

if she's not staying with friends, they may have seen her and know where she's living.''

"Mandy knows somebody in every cottage. Everyone loves her.''

They had reached their bicycles. Quinn pulled his out on the road. "Let's get the dogs, then we'll make a list.''

"The last ferry's going to be leaving soon.'' They had expected to know something before the ferry left, but neither had guessed this outcome.

"Is there any hope of finding a place to stay for the night?''

"With the dogs?''

"If we find Amanda and she doesn't have Jolie, we can stay with her. If she does, the local police will find the three of us a place to stay. They might even fly us back to the mainland.''

She was glad one of them was thinking straight. She was running on nothing but adrenaline. "You're putting up with a lot of uncertainty. Thanks.''

"You don't have to thank me.''

She realized it was true. Nothing he had said or done anywhere along the way pointed to a desire for gratitude. And even now, after discovering his connection to the Whithurst kidnapping, she still believed, deep inside, that Quinn really cared about more than a new chapter for his book and absolution for a crime he had never committed.

They rode back to get the dogs in silence, getting off their bikes and walking them through the field to the skeletal house. But the dogs weren't tied where she had left them. Instead Fagan came bounding toward Hannah, tail wagging furiously, and Oliver skidded to a stop right behind.

She squatted on the ground and held out her arms. Both dogs greeted her as if she'd been away for years. "Somebody let them go. Look, there's no sign they chewed through their leashes.''

She felt Quinn's hand on her shoulder, and she glanced up. A figure was outlined against the house, the familiar figure of a woman who was holding something dark and compact in her hand and pointing it in their direction.

Hannah stood slowly. "Mandy?"

Amanda started toward them. "What are you doing here, Hannah?" She sounded genuinely puzzled.

Hannah's gaze dropped to the object in Amanda's hand. Her heart beat faster as Amanda drew closer. She felt disembodied, as if this couldn't really be happening, as if she might wake up any moment and find herself at home with Jolie sleeping soundly in the room next door.

"Binoculars," Quinn said softly. "She's carrying binoculars, Hannah."

Chapter 15

"The Hancocks, the people who own this place, are old friends. I called them after I got to the island last night and asked if I could use the cottage for a couple of days, since they're in Toledo for the week."

Amanda threw open the side door of a lakeside cottage just down the road from where Quinn and Hannah had left the dogs. Hannah turned the dogs loose in the yard and followed Amanda into a musty kitchen which, judging from the age of its appliances, hadn't been renovated in a quarter of a century.

Amanda leaned against an old-fashioned white linoleum counter and crossed her arms. "Okay, we can talk here. You first. What are you doing here? If I hadn't heard the dogs howling and gone to check on them, I wouldn't even know you were on the island. Boy, was I surprised."

"No, you go first," Hannah said. "What are *you* doing here, Mandy? Daniel's worried sick. And I—"

Amanda waved that away. "I know, I feel awful about Danny. But he'd have a fit if he knew I was here and why."

"Suppose you tell us what the reason is," Quinn said.

Amanda continued to focus her attention on Hannah. "I waited for you to call, Hannah. I was desperate for you to call me again, but you didn't."

Hannah stepped toward her. "Mandy! Just get on with it."

"I think Jolie's here."

"Here where?"

"I've got to back up."

"Take your time and get it right," Quinn said.

This time she looked gratefully at him. "I'm sorry we're meeting like this, Quinn. I'm not usually such a basket case."

"Mandy..." Hannah's impatience was barely in check.

"I decided to talk to Faye after my last phone call with you. I told her that you had left town so you could search for Marshall, and I begged her to find out if Tony knew anything about where Marsh had gone. I wanted to know if we could count on her to turn the investigation in a better direction."

"And?"

"Well, she was great. She told me she was doing everything she could, that she was sure someone had taken Jolie and that you hadn't had anything to do with her disappearance. She even said that she'd been at Tasty Burger the night Jolie was taken, and she'd seen for herself how controlled you were."

"She was there?" Hannah was surprised. She hadn't noticed Faye that night, and during the interrogation nothing had been said.

"She was *there*," Amanda repeated. "But more important, when I asked her if Tony knew where Marsh was living, she said absolutely not. Then she said if you were on his trail, you ought to *stay* on it. That you shouldn't come back until you'd found Marshall."

"It's not true," Hannah said. "Tony knew where Marsh was all along."

"Well, I believed her, until I talked to Millie. Millie's cousin Latrelle told Millie that Marsh wasn't even a suspect, because Tony had spoken to him the morning Jolie disappeared, and he didn't know a thing about it. In fact Tony even followed up and sent the local cops to snoop around Marsh's house, just to be sure."

"Marsh doesn't have Jolie. We found him. But maybe Faye didn't know any of this." But as she said it Hannah realized it couldn't be true. If Latrelle, who was only a police dispatcher, knew what Tony had discovered, then surely Tony's partner had known first.

"I nearly gave Faye the benefit of the doubt." Amanda pushed her dark curls over her ears. "Right up until the minute I found out she'd quit her job."

"What?" Hannah was trying to put all this together, but Amanda had just thrown her biggest curve. "Faye quit?"

"According to Millie, Faye told the chief that she was tired of the way she was treated, that the job had pretty well destroyed her marriage, and now the other cops were trying to destroy her. So she handed in her badge and left town. Without her husband."

Hannah felt Quinn's arm come around her for support. She hadn't even realized she was sagging until then. "Mandy, I don't understand...."

"Neither did I. But I got to thinking about Faye, Hannah, and I couldn't get her out of my mind. Her mother still has the family cottage here, and I've known Faye a lot longer than you have. But I've never been able to figure out what makes her tick. When we were kids, none of the kids on the island really liked to play with her. She was always off in her own little world, and when we did play with her, if she didn't get her way she'd do things to get even. I liked her better as an adult, but not a lot."

"You never told me that."

"People change when they grow up. Besides, I try not to judge people. You know that. It always comes back to haunt you."

Hannah knew it was true. She remembered thinking that Amanda's outspoken denunciation of Tony Chandler had been highly unusual and a mark of how much she disliked and distrusted the man. "What does this have to do with Jolie?"

"I think Faye took her," Amanda said bluntly. "Remember I told you that she miscarried several years ago? Well it was just about the time Jolie was born, and right afterward Faye told me that the baby she lost was a girl."

"That's hardly proof of anything," Quinn said.

Amanda went on. "I know that, but I'll tell you what I think. Faye saw you carrying Jolie out of Tasty Burger the night she disappeared, Hannah, and something just snapped inside her. Her marriage was about to end. She hated her job. Then there you were, with a little girl who's almost the same age her daughter would have been, and it didn't look as if you were handling things very well. So I think Faye decided to start over somewhere else with your child. She pretended to support you, while all the time she was lying to me about Marshall and the investigation to keep you away. And I bet she brought Jolie here to stay with her mother while she finished making her plans."

Amanda had known better than to report her suspicions about Faye to the Port Franklin Police Department. She had come to the island on her own to find evidence, and she had visited her family's cottage on the pretext of needing something from the upstairs bedroom. In reality she had taken her binoculars and settled herself at the window, which had a view of Alice Duncan's cottage on the next street. Alice Duncan was Faye's mother.

"And you didn't see anything?" Quinn asked, going over Amanda's story for the second time. They were sitting at the kitchen table over freshly brewed tea that nobody was drinking.

"No. But I asked around. Nobody mentioned seeing a child, and nobody's seen Faye, either. But they all commented that Alice hardly came out of the house this week, and they're getting concerned about her. Her closest neighbor took her cookies, just to be sure she was all right, and Alice didn't invite her inside. The neighbor seems to think that's a little odd. She's usually very sociable."

"Well, that fits," Quinn said. "If she has Jolie with her, she wouldn't want anyone to know."

"Why would Mrs. Duncan go along with this?" Hannah seemed to be struggling to make sense of everything. Quinn knew she was close to tears, exhausted and raw with worry.

"She's a nice enough woman," Amanda said. "Ditzy, but nice. She's the kind of person who would buy ten years of magazine subscriptions over the telephone or give a panhandler with a good story a fifty-dollar bill. If Faye told her even the foggiest lies about Jolie she wouldn't question them."

"But the news..."

"Hannah, lots of people on the island come here to get away from the news. They don't have televisions, they don't subscribe to newspapers. For all I know, Mrs. Duncan might be one of them." Amanda sat back. "I can't believe you thought I'd taken Jolie." She sounded more mystified than upset.

Hannah bowed her head. "I didn't, not really, but I had to check it out. Daniel told me about the *in vitro*. I thought you might be despondent."

"You mean you thought I'd cracked up. I didn't tell you we were doing more infertility stuff because I didn't want you to worry. It's such a long shot, but the adoption lists are longer. We're just so tired of waiting.''

"Can you forgive me?"

"When this is over you'll owe me." Amanda gave Hannah's shoulder a quick squeeze. "What are we going to do next?"

Quinn was still searching for the right answer. "We haven't even considered how Faye might have done this. What about the dogs? Why didn't they bark that night? What about the locks?"

"That part's easy enough," Hannah said. "For one thing, the dogs aren't as suspicious of women. But more important, when Marsh was still on the force he tried to train Fagan and Oliver as search and rescue dogs. Faye and some of the other cops were helping until it was clear Marsh didn't have the patience to continue. They did the training at our place, and Faye was in and out of the house with the others. She got to know Jolie, and after the divorce she stopped by occasionally just to check on us. If she woke Jolie up that night and told her she had to go somewhere, she might have gone without a fuss. Especially if Faye took Annie, too.''

"Annie's gone?" Amanda said.

Hannah nodded.

"Did you have extra keys lying around?" Quinn asked Hannah.

"They were always there if somebody looked hard enough."

Quinn decided this possibility was no more of a long shot than any of their other suspicions. And Amanda had been suspicious enough on her own to worry her husband and come to the island. The time had come to act.

"I doubt there's much of a police force on the island, but *somebody* has to be in charge. We could go there and ask them to investigate." But Quinn discarded that possibility the moment he said it. If Faye had taken Jolie, she would be desperate to keep her. And even though she would have turned in her service revolver when she resigned, she could still be armed. Provoking her with an all-out search—providing they could convince the local cop or cops to make one—might be dangerous for everyone.

"Look, we can go back to my parents' cottage and level with the renters. Then we can camp out in the upstairs bedroom with the binoculars and see if we can spot Jolie," Amanda said.

"No." Hannah pushed her chair back and stood. "We wouldn't see anything until tomorrow when it's light, and I can't wait. I have to know right now. I can't just sit still and hope Jolie moves into view."

Amanda and Quinn exchanged glances. He could see that Amanda understood Hannah was on the brink of collapse. "I have another idea," he said, "but it means you have to hold yourself together a little longer, Hannah." He took her hands and rubbed them. They were as cold as ice. "You can do it, can't you?"

"I can do anything to get my daughter back. You know I can."

"Here's my plan." He lifted her hands to his lips and kissed them. Then he told her.

The Duncan house was one story and snug, set off by itself at the end of a shady side street. A sunporch ran the length of the back, and a patio surrounded that. There was a narrow patch of woods behind it and a vacant lot on one side. Quinn had to admit it might not be a bad place to hide a child.

"You've thought about what you're going to say, Mandy?" he asked.

"Listen I could chat about nothing until the stars fall out of the sky," Amanda said. "Ask Hannah."

He glanced at Hannah and saw that she had a death grip on the tools they had found in the house where Amanda was staying. A screwdriver set, a file and wrench and a collection of everybody's credit cards.

"Tell me again where the bedrooms are," he said.

"I'm going on childhood memory, but from the back door you'll go left, through the kitchen. There are two." She pointed to the correct side of the house. "Then there's a door going down to a finished basement. There might be another bedroom down there."

"I'll try the basement," Hannah said. "You try the bedrooms."

Quinn repeated their plan, just to be sure. "If Jolie is there, and if Faye isn't, then we retreat through the back door. By the time Mrs. Duncan figures out what's happened, it will be too late to do anything about it. We'll go straight into town and find a cop."

"If Jolie's not there, we still exit by the back," Hannah said. Her voice was strained, but she seemed to be holding up.

"If Faye's there?" Amanda said.

"If Faye's there, we'll reason with her," Quinn said, even though all of them knew how impossible that would be. "But the main thing is to get Jolie out of there."

"No one's seen Faye on the island," Amanda said.

Quinn couldn't let that pass. "She has to be somewhere. And we know she left Port Frank."

Amanda was stubborn. "I think she's gone off to make plans for another place to live."

Hannah exploded. "She may have gone off with my daughter."

Quinn squeezed Hannah's shoulder. "Easy. One step at a time. First we check out the Duncan house, then we look for Faye."

"I never thought I'd be grateful to Marshall for anything," Hannah said tightly. "But he did teach me how to pick a lock."

"Remind me never to try to hide anything from you." The joke fell flat, as he'd known it would. The three of them were wound to the snapping point.

"Okay, here I go," Amanda said. "Wish me luck."

"And the same to us." Hannah started through the vacant lot with Quinn right behind her. They rested behind a tree at the edge of the Duncan's backyard. Quinn looked at his watch, but as it turned out, he didn't need to. Amanda's voice rang clear in the quiet evening air.

"Mrs. Duncan? How are you?"

Faye's mother's voice was muffled. Quinn couldn't make out her words, but he motioned Hannah forward. In a moment they had slipped across the lawn to one of the sliding glass doors of the sunporch. Gently he edged it open.

There were two steps up to the main part of the house, and Hannah got to them first. She tried the back door and found it secure. She reached for a credit card and slid it along the door's edge above the lock. Then she began to wiggle it carefully.

Quinn watched her work. She was biting her lip, concentrating so hard he was sure she wouldn't notice if she drew blood. Here inside the sunporch Amanda's voice wasn't as loud, but he could still hear the occasional word, an indication that the conversation was progressing.

He was listening for noise in the house, too. A child's voice, a woman's voice. But if anyone else was inside, they were silent. He remembered the night the Whithurst kidnapping had come to a head. No one, not even the most skilled investigators with the most innovative equipment had been able to save Jeff. They had gambled on their strategy and lost, and he wondered now if he and Hannah were repeating that tragedy.

If Faye did have Jolie, she wasn't going to give her up easily.

"Got it," Hannah whispered.

Kelley's Island was the sort of place where security was never a major issue. The fact that the door was locked at all seemed suspicious.

The door swung inward and Hannah entered first, even though he tried to stop her. As they had expected they stepped into a family room, but the kitchen was just beyond, and the door leading down to the basement was obvious. She pointed, and he nodded. He had chosen to check the two bedrooms on the first floor because there was a better chance of getting caught. Now he hoped he'd made the right call and she would be safe.

When the door closed behind her he started down the hall past the kitchen to the bedrooms. He passed a bathroom first, but a quick look revealed no evidence of a child. Neither did the first bedroom, which obviously belonged to Mrs. Duncan. It contained a double bed with a flowered comforter and several pieces of heavy, dark furniture, but little else.

The door to the second bedroom, which was closest to the front and most dangerous to investigate, was closed. He could hear Amanda chatting away, and from this vantage point he could hear Mrs. Duncan, too.

"I really have to go, dear. Next time I see Faye I'll be sure to tell her you were asking about her."

"Well, I'm not sure you ought to tell her that, Mrs. Duncan. Do you remember the time she was ten and we…"

He hoped he was never stuck in a corner with Amanda at a party.

The door wouldn't budge when he turned the knob, and for a moment he was afraid it was locked. But when he applied more pressure it swung open and he stepped inside, closing it behind him again. This room was smaller than the first bedroom, furnished simply with a single bed neatly made up with an old white chenille bedspread. The shades were drawn, and it took his eyes a moment to adjust to the darkness.

He was alone.

He hadn't expected anything different. There were too many unanswered questions, too many "might haves" to point decisively to Faye as the kidnapper. But he had hoped a miracle would occur.

He did a perfunctory investigation of the room. No toys on the dresser top, and the open closet door revealed neatly laid-out shoes and summer dresses hanging from the rod. The room had probably been Faye's.

He was turning to go when a shadow on the floor caught his eye. He turned back, squinting hard at whatever was peeking out from under the hem of the bedspread. He could hear Amanda's voice, and the more petulant sound of Mrs. Duncan's. She was rapidly losing patience, and at any moment might close the door in Amanda's face. Still, he had to check. He strode across the room and knelt to look under the bed.

He was face-to-face with a balding rag doll who was staring at him from one button eye.

Quinn tried to remember what Hannah had told him about Annie, the doll Jolie slept with. He rose and turned to the door, holding the doll at his side. He realized he could no longer hear voices, but he did hear footsteps in the hall outside the bedroom.

The footsteps paused outside the door and the knob began to turn.

"Mrs. Duncan, one more thing…"

He heard Amanda pounding on the front door, and her voice was loud enough to wake the dead.

The knob snapped back into place, and in a moment the footsteps faded away. Silently he blessed Amanda and opened the door himself, slipping into the hallway and through the kitchen.

The door to the basement was closed, and there was no sign of Hannah even though they had arranged for her to wait for him in the kitchen. Either she was still downstairs or she had been spooked by the end of Amanda's first conversation and had exited through the sunporch, hoping that Quinn might find his own way out.

He was torn between checking the basement and going outside to look for her there. In the end the doll helped him make the decision. If Jolie really had been here, then Hannah might very well have found something in the basement. He opened the door and started down the steps.

There was no light, only the faintest tracings of moonlight through two casement windows. He hadn't risked flipping the switch at the top of the steps because the light would seep under the door, and he suspected Amanda was not going to keep Mrs. Duncan occupied much longer.

He edged carefully down the steps, feeling his way. At the bottom he started toward the left. The basement had been carpeted, and his footsteps were muffled. He had taken only two steps when he heard a noise behind him. Before he could turn, something slammed against the back of his neck, and he fell forward into oblivion.

Hannah saw Faye materialize from the darkness to club Quinn with what looked like a wrench, but there was nothing she could do. She was trapped in a corner behind an entertainment center with a small television set and a stereo. She had barely avoided detection herself. In the midst of searching the recreation room she'd heard a woman singing softly in the other section of the basement behind a closed door. Then the door had creaked open, and Hannah had slipped behind the cabinet to hide, just in time.

Faye had started up the stairs, then she had stopped on

the second step. Even here, Amanda's voice calling loudly for Mrs. Duncan was audible and Faye had frozen. She had descended again to disappear back into the room from which she had come. Before Hannah could escape to warn Quinn, he had appeared at the bottom of the steps, and Faye had knocked him out.

Light suddenly trickled down the steps, then lights came on just above Hannah, and a voice called from the top of the stairs. "Faye, was that you, honey? Is the baby all right?"

"She's fine, Mom. She's asleep again. I just dropped something. Don't bother coming down."

"I think her cold's getting better, don't you? Maybe we should cut back on that cold syrup."

"Mom, who was at the door?"

"It was that Mandy Long, or whatever her married name is. What is it again?"

There was a long pause. Hannah could barely see Faye now, but what she could see of her, a hand and a leg, went absolutely still. "Amanda Taylor," she said finally. "What was she doing here?"

"She said she was worried about you, and wanted to know if you were here. I told her no, because I know you're trying to stay out of sight. But she's an odd one, isn't she? She told me she'd heard that you had quit the Port Franklin Police Force. I don't know where she got a story like that."

"You know small towns," Faye said, and although Hannah had withdrawn farther into the shadows and couldn't see her, she suspected Faye was shaking her head. "Nothing but rumors and more rumors."

"I thought I'd never get rid of her."

"Are you sure she's really gone?"

"I saw her heading down the road."

"Mom, I think she might know about Jolie. I think she

might suspect Children's Services placed her temporarily with me.''

"How would she know that?"

"I don't know. But Amanda is good friends with Jolie's parents. I told you we had to hide Jolie until we could find a good foster family out of the area. Well, this is just the kind of interference the social workers were afraid of.''

"Mandy Long...Taylor?" Alice Duncan didn't sound convinced. "She's always been a good girl. She's a friend of these people?''

"I told you, not only are Jolie's parents abusive, they're well connected. That's why everybody at the Welfare Department insisted the police get involved in hiding her.''

"Well, that baby's a sweet little thing, considering what she's been through. I wouldn't mind keeping her forever.''

"Thanks, but I made that phone call I told you about, and it looks like Children's Services has found a better place for her. When it's good and dark I'm going to take her back to the mainland, and they'll take over from there.''

"Faye, do you think you ought to risk taking the boat out in the dark again? You know the lake, but it's different at night.''

"I'll just have to be careful. I can't take Jolie out of here in daylight, not with Amanda snooping around. It's too dangerous. There's no telling what her parents might do if they get hold of her.''

"Poor little thing.''

"I'll be up in a few minutes. I'm just getting her stuff together now.''

"What little there is," Mrs. Duncan said sadly.

"Well, we'll send along the things I bought for her. At least she'll have something.''

"Don't forget that old doll.''

"It's not down here. Can you find it, Mom?''

"I'll look." The door closed.

"Busybody," Faye muttered.

Hannah was simultaneously experiencing a spectrum of emotions. Jolie was here, sleeping soundly just yards away. Jolie was alive and well! But Quinn was lying facedown on the carpet, just inches from where Mrs. Duncan's view of the basement must have ended. And although he was lying very still, Hannah knew that he would regain some semblance of consciousness soon and Faye would have to deal with him.

Faye had abducted Jolie and told her mother a story so improbable only love and blind faith could have made it believable. Unfortunately Mrs. Duncan herself had supplied those ingredients.

Frantically Hannah tried to decide what to do. She knew that when she and Quinn didn't show up at the designated meeting place down the road, Amanda would go for the local police. But by the time Amanda convinced them to talk to Mrs. Duncan, Quinn might be dead and Jolie might be heading for the mainland in a madwoman's powerboat.

Quinn groaned once, then fell silent. Faye moved toward him, and when she was standing over him, she kicked his shoulder. He lay perfectly still. She kicked him again as Hannah searched frantically for a weapon she could use against Faye. Faye still had the wrench in her hands, and she tested it against Quinn's shoulder when her kicks brought no response.

Apparently satisfied that he wasn't going to wake up, she started back toward the door to the room where Jolie was sleeping. Hannah knew she couldn't let Faye get near her daughter again. Even though the disadvantage was hers, she had no choice but to show herself. She moved out from behind the entertainment center, grabbing the only object in reach that might deter Faye, a pool cue that was lying on top of a dusty bumper pool table.

"Faye, you have my daughter," Hannah said. "Amanda

knows it and she's on the way to tell the police. It's over. Stay away from her.''

Faye whirled, and her eyes narrowed. "Look who else is here.''

A voice called from the kitchen. "Faye, who are you talking to?''

Hannah answered before Faye could, counting on the distance and door to distort her voice. "Mom, get the police. Right now. There's an intruder.''

There was something resembling a shriek from the first floor, then a scuffling noise, as if Mrs. Duncan was on her way out the door.

"Interesting,'' Faye said. "Imagine what they'll find when they get here.''

"I'm not going to let you take Jolie,'' Hannah said, brandishing the stick as she drew closer to Quinn and Faye. "It's over, Faye. The best thing you can do is walk away. I won't come after you. You'll have a head start.''

"No death by pool cue, huh? I can just walk out of here?''

Hannah knew a joke under these circumstances was a bad sign. "Please, Faye. Jolie's not your child. She's mine. She needs her real mother.''

"I know whose child she is, Hannah, but you don't deserve her. First you had Marsh's baby when I couldn't, then you chased him out of town.''

Hannah was confused. "What do you mean you couldn't have Marsh's baby?''

"Didn't know that, did you, Hannah girl? Marsh and I were lovers. I couldn't get pregnant with my own husband, but I could and did with Marsh. Not that he was happy about it, I suppose. But it did make him feel like a man for a little while. When I lost the baby I knew there'd be other chances, but before it could happen again, you chased him away. He was gone, just like that. And so was my chance for another child."

Hannah knew there would be time to think about this newest betrayal later, but not now, not when her daughter was in danger in the next room. "I don't care about any of that, Faye. Go find Marsh. Have a hundred babies with him. But this baby belongs to me."

"She's a beautiful little girl, isn't she? She looks a little like I did at that age."

"She's *my* daughter."

"Not for long…" Faye raised the wrench again, but she didn't aim it at Hannah, she held it over her head as if she were going to bring it down on Quinn's skull. With a cry of anguish Hannah leaped forward and used the pool cue like a bat to strike her hands.

The wrench went flying, and Faye, her eyes wide with disbelief screeched in pain. But before Hannah could leap at her and wrestle her to the floor, Faye fumbled inside her blazer and pulled out a gun.

"You bitch!" she screamed.

Hannah stopped just inches from Faye's outstretched arm. "If you kill me," she said, as calmly as she could, "it's a whole different ball game, Faye. They won't rest until they find you. Kidnapping's one thing, but murder's another."

"Like I care." Faye's hand was shaking, but she released the safety on the small handgun. "I'm going to kill you, then I'm going to take your daughter. She won't remember you, Hannah. She won't even remember you were alive. I'll be her mother."

"Mommy?"

Hannah stared at the doorway and saw the vision she had prayed for since the night Jolie was taken. Her daughter, her precious daughter, stood in the doorway in pink pajamas, rubbing sleep-reddened eyes. Jolie didn't move forward, as if getting up had taken all her limited energy. She stared blankly at Hannah. "Mommy?"

"Go back to bed," Faye ordered, without looking at the child. "Go right back to bed, Jolie."

"I want...my mommy." Jolie began to cry softly. "Mommy..."

"Faye, she's here, she knows. Let us go. There's still time for you to get away."

Faye's eyes were wild. "She belongs to me now."

"She never did." Hannah was paralyzed with fear. She was afraid Jolie would start toward her, and Faye would be required to take action.

Her worst fears were realized. Jolie frowned, then she stumbled toward Hannah. "Mommy..."

"Stay back," Faye ordered. "Do what I tell you, Jolie."

But Jolie had always had a mind of her own. She moved toward her mother as if she were walking in her sleep. "Mommy..."

Faye swung the gun toward the little girl. Hannah didn't think Faye intended to use it, but she couldn't take that chance. She leaped at Faye, but she was second in line.

Quinn rose to his knees and tackled Faye around hers, sending her crashing to the floor.

But not before she turned the gun on him.

Chapter 16

Jolie remembered very little about the days she had spent away from Hannah, and almost nothing about the shooting. In order to keep Jolie subdued, Faye had administered adult doses of antihistamines, and even when the little girl was awake, she had been too sluggish and disoriented to notice much of what was going on around her. Sometimes she talked about Mrs. Duncan, who she remembered fondly, and occasionally about the lady who had taken her for a boat ride late one night when she was sick.

She wanted to go for a boat ride again, but next time, with her mommy.

Tony Chandler had a new job. After Jake Whattley's scathing article about the abduction, a blistering reprimand from his superiors and a demotion from detective to traffic control, Tony quit his job and moved to Maple Ridge to change oil and tires in Walt Blackstone's service station. His wife and children had declined to make the move with him.

Tony's knock on the head was never mentioned by anyone. Clearly Tony had never reported that a woman got the better of him during an interrogation.

Faye was under lock and key *and* intense psychiatric evaluation in preparation for her trial, and a humiliated Mrs. Duncan had sold her Kelley's Island cottage and moved to Florida. Amanda and Daniel had bought it as a retreat for their own little family. The week after Hannah brought Jolie home they had been selected from a list of potential adoptive parents by a young woman in Southern Ohio who believed they would make the best mother and father for her unborn child. The baby would arrive in October.

On a sunny August afternoon when Lake Erie was bluer than a morning glory and the temperature was hot enough to wilt one, Hannah kicked off her sandals and collapsed in the grass with her daughter. Jolie wore a green ruffled playsuit lovingly made by her Arizona grandmother and frog barrettes holding back her golden curls. She had accompanied Hannah on her work rounds that morning, and now she needed a nap.

But Hannah found it hard to be away from her daughter these days. Each time she put Jolie to bed she wondered if she would see her again. The old Ohio farmhouse had a new, elaborate security system, and Jolie hadn't been back to the drop-in day care center at the Episcopal church. Hannah was agonizing over whether to send Jolie to the Montessori preschool she was registered to attend in the fall.

Jolie climbed in Hannah's lap, and Hannah circled her with her arms. "Are you tired, honey? Want to go inside? You can sleep in my bed. I'll lie down with you."

"No, I wanna sleep in *my* bed."

Hannah's arms tightened. Wisdom told her she had to start letting go of Jolie again. A child needed room to grow, and Hannah was in danger of smothering her. In the weeks since Jolie's return she had shut out everyone and everything to concentrate on the little girl.

She had even shut out Quinn, the man who had nearly given his life for her daughter.

She forced herself to release Jolie, who promptly scrambled to her feet. "Can I have a Popsicle?"

Hannah stood, too. "Just the thing. Then a nap."

Jolie didn't argue. Hannah had been told to expect behavioral changes, temper tantrums, an entire list of undesirable consequences from the kidnapping. But Jolie was the same sweet little girl she had been before her midnight encounter with Faye. "Can Ol'ver sleep in my room?"

"I bet he'd like that."

They started toward the house. Hannah knew she had things she ought to be doing for Lakeside Landscapes, but nowadays she delegated more authority, and her crews continued to perform well anyway. She had gotten a painful lesson on priorities, and she was an A student.

They were almost at the front door when she realized a man was sitting on her front porch, trying to soothe Fagan, whose teeth were bared in something just short of a snarl. Hannah shouted at the dog, who settled himself suspiciously at the other end of the porch. Quinn got slowly to his feet, a trick that was not as easy as it once had been. Faye had shot Quinn at close range, and the first bullet had shattered the bone in his thigh. The second had lodged below his shoulder, perilously close to his lungs and heart.

There hadn't been a third. Hannah had wrestled the gun from Faye and aimed it with a trembling hand until the Kelley's Island Police arrived. Quinn had been flown to the closest hospital by helicopter, and he had remained there, first in intensive care and later on the surgical wing, for two full weeks.

"Quinn." Hannah could feel color rising in her cheeks. "You look good. How are you feeling?"

"Terrific. I'm getting my energy back. My physical therapist cut my sessions to twice a week."

Hannah imagined that reducing the sessions had pained the young therapist greatly. Darcy Sayers was pretty and recently divorced, and the talk in Port Franklin was that Darcy had set her cap for Quinn. At least that was the talk from the half of the town who didn't believe Hannah had set hers first.

"So..." Hannah realized she didn't know what else to say.

Quinn took the conversation out of her hands. "How's my girl?" he asked Jolie.

Jolie let go of Hannah's hand and ran to him. He gave her a big hug, then set her away so he could see her better. "You look like summer, Jolie."

The little girl grinned. She had gone to Quinn's house with her mother every time Hannah took casseroles or cookies while he recovered at home, and Quinn had rapidly become her dearest friend. She knew that "the boat lady" had hurt Quinn, but probably due to the drugs, the memory of the shooting was vague.

"We're having Popsicles!"

"That sounds great," he said.

"Want one?" Jolie offered.

Quinn glanced up, and Hannah realized he was silently asking permission. "What kind would you like? Grape, orange or strawberry?" she said.

"Grape."

She left them alone on the porch, although it made her uneasy to turn her back on Jolie, even with Quinn in attendance. By the time she returned, Jolie was cuddled on the wicker seat next to him, telling Quinn about her day.

"Then we buried the flowers in a hole!" she finished up.

"I bet it's a very pretty garden." Quinn looked up at

Hannah and smiled. Something expanded inside her, something in real danger of bursting her carefully set boundaries.

He didn't stop there. "As a matter of fact, that's why I'm here today. I've decided to go ahead and put in that perennial garden you recommended the first time you did a consultation for me, and everything else, besides. Maybe Jolie could help. It sounds like she's a real gardener already."

Hannah could feel the blood rushing to her cheeks as she handed Jolie and Quinn their Popsicles. She knew what Quinn wanted, and it was more than day lilies and peonies. But she wasn't ready. She might never be ready, no matter how badly she wanted to be.

"Quinn, I'm not sure that's a good idea." She looked at the wrapper in her hand, peeling it back slowly and carefully, as if she were doing delicate surgery. "Perennials take a lot of care. I didn't know you very well back then."

"And now you've decided I'm not a perennial kind of guy?"

Her head snapped up, and she gazed at him, wondering if he realized what he'd said.

A perennial kind of guy.

"I guess I don't," she said, even though she had no idea if it was true. "Perennials take a lot of care. You have to be around to weed and water and thin. Even with easy-care plants. They're for homebodies, more or less, people who intend to hang around and fuss with them. Not big-shot authors who'll be running off at a moment's notice to discuss their latest bestsellers."

"Hannah, a book contract isn't the same thing as a bestseller."

On one of her quick stops by his house with food—which she had felt duty bound to provide, since he had saved Jolie's life—Quinn had told her that a major publisher had given him a healthy advance on his book about the Whithurst kidnapping.

"We both know this book will be big," she said.

He rested his Popsicle against his bottom lip, a lip she knew intimately. "I've never been a homebody because I never had a home. Now I do, and I intend to stay. Even a big-shot author has to have a place to come back to."

"Maybe you ought to give this more time. Try a January here on the lake first. See if you can tough it out."

"Funny thing, I was asking for your help with my yard, and now I'm getting advice on the climate."

"I just don't see the point of doing all that work for you if you're going to head off in the near future."

They finished their Popsicles in silence, although Jolie chattered away like a small Amanda. Quinn stood as soon as his was finished.

"Well, interesting conversation, Hannah. But I've got to make a stop by the library this afternoon before it closes." He ruffled Jolie's curls. "Have a great nap, kiddo."

"Are you doing research?" Hannah said, walking him to the steps. All other avenues of conversation seemed closed, and she had grasped that one just to hold off the silence.

"No, I'm going to get a book on perennial gardens." He stopped and turned to her. "You know, I know what you've been through, and by nature I'm patient. But you can't push me around or away, Hannah. I love you, and I'm here for the long haul. If you ever get your fear under control, give me a call."

He loved her? She couldn't even touch that. Instead she lowered her voice. "Fear? I have a right to be afraid. I nearly lost my daughter."

"And now between Marshall and Faye, you're scared to death to take a chance on the future. You're going to live hour to hour, minute to minute, and never let anyone into your life again, just in case you've been fooled.''

Anger flared inside her. ''You have no right!''

''Sure I do.''

She didn't ask why, because she was afraid he might tell her again. ''Look, I'm grateful to you for everything. I couldn't be more grateful....''

''But that's it? Is that what you're going to say?''

She clamped her lips together and forced herself to nod.

''You're a liar, sweetheart, but the trouble is, you may never *stop* lying to yourself. Take some advice from your daughter, why don't you, and get on with your life?''

''What a rotten thing to say!''

He kept his voice low so that Jolie wouldn't hear. ''There's a lot we can learn from kids. Jolie still trusts people to take care of her. She still loves you. She's still looking forward to every moment of her life. What about you? Can you say the same?''

''I think you'd better leave.''

''You think I'd better leave *town*, Hannah. The farther away the better. Only I'm not going to. Port Franklin has everything I want and need. And if you'll just look around, you'll find it has everything you want, too.''

He rested his fingertips on the banister and took the steps one at a time. She watched him go, her heart in her throat. ''Quinn...''

He didn't turn. ''Got a book you'd recommend?''

When she didn't answer, he started toward his car.

Hannah put Jolie's playsuit in the clothes hamper. She held out a bathtowel as her daughter stepped out of the tub, dried her sturdy little body, then slipped Jolie's new nightgown over her head. She'd thrown out the one Jolie had worn the night she was abducted, even though Mrs. Duncan had given it back. As a matter of fact she had thrown away everything Faye Wagner had ever touched except for Annie, who had a new button eye and lovely strands of orange yarn which nicely covered her bald spots. Annie was a heroine.

"You had such a long nap this afternoon," Hannah said. "Are you sure you're ready to go to sleep?"

Jolie considered, as if this newfound freedom to do as she pleased was tempting. But at last she nodded, and Hannah could see by her daughter's drooping eyelids that she really was sleepy.

"Mommy, why'd that lady take me in the boat?"

Hannah's breath caught. Jolie had hardly talked about the abduction, and she had never asked questions. Hannah had thought of many answers in case she ever did, but in the end, she had discarded all the lies. She knew it was important to be as honest as she could. "She wanted a little girl, Jolie. And she didn't have one of her own."

"Did you *let* her have me?"

"Oh, no, sweetie. You're my little girl, and I would never give you to anybody else. Never."

"Then she stole me?"

Hannah knew that Jolie's idea of stealing was very simple. A playmate took a toy and didn't give it back until a mommy made her. She used that analogy now. "Yes. She took you without permission, and I had to find her and make her give you back. But I did, and here you are."

"I cried."

Hannah's heart broke. "I know, sweetie. You must have been very scared."

"No, I was mad!"

"I bet you were." Hannah managed a trembling smile. "Very mad."

"Then I waited."

"Waited?"

"For you to come."

"And I did."

Jolie stepped up on the stool to get her toothbrush. "I knew, but I waited a long time."

Hannah couldn't help herself. "You knew?"

Jolie turned to look at her mother. She looked puzzled. "Uh-huh. You always come."

Hannah had been through a lifetime of emotion in a matter of days, but nothing had affected her more than this. Her daughter had survived the kidnapping nearly unscathed, and now she understood why.

Jolie had never even considered that her mommy wouldn't find her and bring her home. She had been angry that Faye had taken her, and despite her denials, she had probably been frightened at times, too. She had been ill and disoriented, but she had never doubted her mother's love.

Someday Jolie would grow up and her blind faith would turn into reasonable caution. She would learn to watch out for people who were not what they seemed, but she would also be capable of loving people who were. All because this one relationship, the love between mother and child, was strong and good.

Hannah, despite everything, was raising a happy, healthy little girl.

Just exactly the way her own parents had raised her. And now it was time to remember what she had learned. It was time to trust again.

She willed herself not to cry and upset Jolie. "Sweetie, I'm going out for a little while tonight. I'm going to call Mandy and see if she'll baby-sit. Will you mind?"

"Mandy'th coming?" Jolie paused midstroke with her toothbrush. "While I'm shleeping?"

Hannah knew from her tone that Jolie wasn't upset Hannah was leaving. She was upset that Amanda hadn't come *earlier* when they still might have had time to play.

"I promise next time she'll come while you're still awake," Hannah said.

Jolie removed the toothbrush. "I can show her Annie's eye."

"You bet you can."

Hannah was torn between dressing as a landscaper or a femme fatale, but in the end vanity won out. She'd had her hair trimmed by a professional after Jolie's return, and she took the time to curl the ends while she waited for Amanda to arrive. She wore a pale blue sundress which showed off her tan and long legs, and a beaded choker Amanda had given her for her last birthday.

She took one of Lakeside's pickup trucks to Quinn's house and discovered halfway down her driveway that the air conditioner wasn't working. By the time she turned into Quinn's driveway her skin was filmed with perspiration, and her hair was as straight as a board. She had taken the time to apply a little makeup, but she supposed that had melted away in the summer heat and humidity, as well.

Exit one femme fatale, enter one grubby landscaper.

Quinn wasn't home. It took her a moment to realize it, because she had counted on him being there. But his garage door was open and the Lexus—returned grudgingly by Jake Whattley once Quinn arrived home from the hospital—was gone.

There were other women in town—Darcy Sayers for one—who would be happy to provide him with an evening's entertainment. Hannah had as much as told him she didn't want him in her life. She had told him she didn't trust him to stay around or be the kind of man she needed.

She had looked at him, but who had she seen? The man who had stuck with her through the darkest moments of her life, the man who had taken two bullets for her daughter, the man who had taken her in his arms and given her comfort and, yes, pleasure when she would have sworn there was none to be found?

Or had she seen the man she married?

She thought about that man now. Marsh had come to visit Jolie as soon as Hannah brought her back to Port Franklin. He'd held his daughter for the first time in months, and Hannah had been stunned to see tears in his eyes. Later she'd asked him if Faye's story about the baby she'd lost was true. He had denied it emphatically, and Hannah had chosen to believe him.

She and Marsh would never be friends, and she would always wish she had chosen a better father for her child. But he was a tormented man who was trying to put his mistakes behind him. For Jolie's sake, Hannah could only wish him well.

Quinn was not Marshall. He wasn't like her ex-husband. From their first meeting she had experienced an attraction to him that was like nothing she'd felt before. And the power of that attraction had sent her running into the night. She had been so afraid she would make another mistake, so critical of her own judgment. She had believed that the only way to stay safe was to stay remote.

Now she realized that no matter how carefully a life was lived, no one was ever completely safe. Life was about laying foundations, then taking chances.

And she had a foundation to lay.

She walked around the back of the truck and unlatched the tailgate.

Quinn didn't remember leaving his outside lights on, but they were on when he pulled into the driveway. After his conversation with Hannah he had driven to Cleveland to see Jake. Along with another of Jake's buddies they had performed the supreme male bonding ritual, ordering pizza loaded with meat toppings and polishing off a six-pack over a televised Indians game. The Indians had beaten the Yankees, which hadn't helped his mood, because that meant he'd lost a bet with Jake.

He was driving Jake's van again and would be for the rest of the week. And he was driving it *home,* where an empty house waited for him.

On the way to Jake's he had mentally planned the things he would do to make his mother's house his. He would knock out walls, redesign the old-fashioned kitchen, trade geometric prints for the flowered valances. He would strip off wallpaper, panel the den, build a deck.

But he wouldn't put in that perennial bed, after all. Because every time he looked at it, he would think of Hannah. And putting Hannah out of his mind was going to be hard enough.

The garage door was closed, another surprise. He was almost sure he had left it open. Despite what had happened to Jolie he still regarded Port Franklin as a safe haven. He reached for his garage door opener only to remember that he had left it in the Lexus.

"The end of a perfect day." He parked in the driveway and entered through the side door, going through the laundry room to the garage to open the door.

A pickup was parked inside. A pickup with Lakeside Landscapes professionally painted on the door.

"Hannah?" He went back into the house and wandered through the first floor looking for her. It didn't occur to him to wonder how she had gotten inside. She could pick a lock faster than a child could pick dandelions. "Hannah!"

She didn't answer, but when he stopped and listened carefully he thought he heard water running.

He followed the sound up the stairs and into his bedroom. A blue sundress was thrown across his bed, and a woman's voice floated through the closed door to the ad-

joining bathroom. The woman was warbling an old Elvis
song.

"Are you lonesome tonight?" Quinn dropped to the bed,
grinning like an idiot. "Damned if I'm not," he said as the
song continued. Through a fog of excitement he realized
Hannah had a sweet voice, pure and high, not at all what
he would have expected.

She'd hardly had reason to sing on their desperate od-
yssey to find Jolie. Now there was a lot they still had to
discover about each other. He was going to savor every
minute of it.

He was waiting for her in his bed when she emerged
dressed only in a towel. He was bare-chested, the newly
healed scar a white slash against his tanned skin. In def-
erence to modesty, he had pulled the sheet over his naked,
newly scarred thigh.

"I decided the answer was yes," he said.

He'd startled her, he saw that. But this was Hannah, and
she recovered quickly. "What was the question, Quinn?"

"Am I lonesome tonight?"

She smiled. This, too, was sweet and very different. It
was the smile of a woman who was finding herself again.
He thought that in the years ahead he would probably cat-
alog a hundred different Hannah-smiles. He looked forward
to the experience.

"*Are* you lonesome?" She shook her hair back over her
shoulders.

"I am. But not just for sex, Hannah. I think I'm bone-
deep lonesome."

"I need more office space, and I've been considering
giving classes, maybe starting a teaching garden." She
shrugged. "My house would be so perfect. It's too bad
Jolie and I would need another place to live." She held the
towel against her breasts, but not with much enthusiasm.

He could feel himself responding to thoughts of what lay

under the towel, but he persisted, aware that if he didn't tell her his other thoughts, soon there would be no opportunity.

"I want that perennial bed," he said. "I'm a perennial kind of guy, whether you think so or not."

"Good thing, because I made a start on it while you were gone tonight. I've already laid out the borders and hauled in some plants for you to consider. Some of the things I chose take some experience to grow, unfortunately. You might need a little help."

"Not to worry. When I commit to something, I commit 100 percent."

She lifted a brow. "Commit?"

"Yeah. Commit to anything. Work, joy..."

"Could we work on that joy thing a little? I think we've sadly neglected it." She dropped the towel and stood in front of him, a long-legged vision wearing nothing but a beaded choker.

His breath caught. "I'd say we need to work on it a lot. It's important to get it exactly right."

She smiled seductively. "Oh, we'll get it right. You have my promise on that."

He groaned and opened his arms. She went into them without hesitation, the ultimate solution, the very last piece of the puzzle that had been Quinn McDermott's lonesome life.

"Just one more thing." She settled herself at his side and gently kissed the puckered scar on his chest. "You know I come with a daughter, but have you forgotten I come with a couple of dogs?"

His heart was pounding so fast he wondered that he could hear her over the roar. He slid his hands to her waist and beyond. "I'll corner the market in sausage biscuits."

"They'll learn to love you. Eventually." She kissed a

trail along his shoulder to the hollow of his throat. "After all, I did."

He circled her with his arms and pulled her on top of him. His heart was so full he didn't know what to say. But it didn't matter.

There was no more need for words.

* * * * *

INTIMATE MOMENTS®

™ *Silhouette*®

invites you to Go West, dear reader, to

Cameron, Utah

for the conclusion of Margaret Watson's exhilarating miniseries.

September 1999
The Marriage Protection Program...IM #951

Janie Murphy knew she was Deputy Ben Jackson's *only* hope for gaining custody of orphaned Rafael. But Janie thought Ben would understand her refusal when he learned about her past. Instead, he proposed an irresistible trade—her hand for his protection. And suddenly Janie's heart faced the greatest risk of all....

Available at your favorite retail outlet.

And if you want to uncover more of this small town's secrets, don't miss...

The Fugitive Bride (Intimate Moments #920) April 1999
Cowboy with a Badge (Intimate Moments #904) January 1999
For the Children (Intimate Moments #886) October 1998
Rodeo Man (Intimate Moments #873) August 1998

™ *Silhouette*®

THE
FORTUNES
OF TEXAS

*Membership in this family has its privileges
…and its price.
But what a fortune can't buy,
a true-bred Texas love is sure to bring!*

Coming in October 1999…

The Baby Pursuit
by
LAURIE PAIGE

When the newest Fortune heir was kidnapped, the
prominent family turned to Devin Kincaid to find the
missing baby. The dedicated FBI agent never expected
his investigation might lead him to the altar with
society princess Vanessa Fortune.…

THE FORTUNES OF TEXAS continues with
Expecting… In Texas by **Marie Ferrarella,**
available in November 1999 from
Silhouette Books.

Available at your favorite retail outlet.

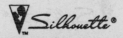

Silhouette®

Coming this September 1999
from SILHOUETTE BOOKS
and bestselling author

RACHEL LEE

CONARD COUNTY:
Boots & Badges

Alicia Dreyfus—a desperate woman on the run—
is about to discover that she *can* come home
again…to Conard County. Along the way she
meets the man of her dreams—and brings together
three other couples, whose love blossoms beneath
the bold Wyoming sky.

Enjoy four complete, **brand-new** stories in one
extraordinary volume.

Available at your favorite retail outlet.

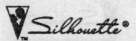

PSCCBB